The 2nd Faerie Tale Romance

THE GLASS GATE

a Retelling of Cinderella

by

HANNA SANDVIG

For Craig,

My very own Prince Charming.
Just kidding, you're my Fergus,
and I wouldn't want it any other way.

TÍR NA NÓG
N
W
E
S
the DWARVEN KINGDOM
the UNSEELIE COURT
KILINAIRE CASTLE
the ELDER FAE
INNER SEA
the ISLE OF MIST
PORT DELFARE
SOUTHERN GRASSLANDS
the SEELIE COURT

Pronunciation Guide

Tiernan - Tear (like crying) nin
Clíodhna - Clean-ah
Ella - Ell (rhymes with bell) ah
Saoirse - Sur-sha
Declan - Deck-lan
Leith - like Leaf, but a th instead of an f
Fiachra - Fee-ah-chra
Haru - Hah-roo
Fergus - Fur-ges
Orla - Or-luh
Rian - Ree-ahn
Calder - Call - dur
Jac - Jack
Imogen - Im-og-gin
Lynet - Lynn-ett
Neve - Nev
Ailish - Ay-lish

Faerie Glossary

Aos Sí - Also called the small fae or the small folk. Basically, anyone who is not one of the Tuatha Dé Danann or giants.

Brownies - Household keepers.

Cait Sìth - A powerful race of fae who can shift into the form of a black cat nine times. The ninth time they are trapped in cat form forever.

Cirein-cròin - Giant sea serpents, rumoured to eat whales or even large ships.

Cù Sìth - Giant green hounds with glowing red eyes. Their bark is an omen of death.

Danu - The ancestors of the Tuatha Dé Danann.

Dearg Due - Vampires. Drinkers of blood.

Draoi - Woodland fae with bark-like skin and hair that resembles leaves.

Faoladh - Fae cursed to shift into a wolf when the sun is down.

Leipreachán - Shoe makers and leather workers.

Glaistig - Horned fae whose bottom half is like a goats. Similar to a faun.

Grogach - A small hairy faerie with a messy appearance.

Peiste - Giant serpents that lurk in lakes, bogs, and moats.

Poukha - Shape shifters. Natural form is like a shaggy black cat crossed with a rabbit. They are prone to mischief.

Piskie - Tiny winged faeries

Sheerie - Also called will-o'-the-wisp. A tiny winged faerie that lives near swamps and often guides travellers to their doom.

Tuatha Dé Danann - High fae. Humanlike in appearance but tall and with pointed ears.

PROLOGUE

TIERNAN

I WAS EIGHT WHEN MY MOTHER DIED. Too young to realize how much she meant to me. Too naive to know I should be saying goodbye.

My father sat next to me, pale and sweating, while we waited for news of my new baby brother or sister.

The *Tuatha Dé Danann* don't have children easily. Even two children, eight years apart, was quite a feat. Every time my mother cried, he flinched. I fiddled with the dagger she had given me for my eighth birthday, even though I knew it annoyed my father. Weapons—he said—are not toys.

My mother cried out again. I had been told she would, so I wasn't concerned. But then there was a long silence that somehow seemed more worrisome than the cries had been. Soon, the large carved wooden doors creaked open, and the midwife bustled out. The brownie midwife held a little bundle wrapped in a blanket. I could just see a bit of black fuzz poking up at the top.

"A boy, Your Majesty." She gently settled the baby in my father's arms.

I peeked over. The baby looked red and squashy.

"Are they supposed to be that color?" I asked.

The midwife shushed me. My father didn't seem to hear. He just looked at the baby in wonder.

I glanced at the door the midwife had disappeared through, back into the realm of feminine mystery.

"I still remember the day you were born," my father said to me, and I rolled my eyes. This was the sort of thing adults always said.

The baby cried out and my father gently jostled him until his eyes closed again.

"What will you name him?" I asked my father.

His mouth opened to respond, but the sound of the door creaking open again cut him off. The midwife stood in the doorway. Blood stained her smock. Was that to be expected at a birth? I didn't know.

My father shot to his feet, keeping the baby carefully balanced. "How is she?"

"She's asking for you," was all she said.

My father blanched and walked toward the door.

"Both of you," said the midwife.

I stood as well and followed him in. My mother lay back on the pillows looking pale, her bright red hair, the same shade as mine, strewn about her. Her face was pale under her freckles. Clíodhna, the Elder Fae, sat next to her holding her hand. Clíodhna looked somber. The midwife carefully took the baby from my father, and he sat down on the bed next to my mother.

"Oh, my loves," said the queen. "How I will miss you."

I blinked, confused. She was right here. We didn't have anything planned. What was she talking about?

"I'm afraid it will be just the three of you," she said. "I'm sorry. I did so want to see this little one grow up tall and strong like his brother." She reached for me, and I crawled up onto the bed on the other side of her.

"Now, my darlings, I need you to promise me something."

My father was crying. I had never seen him cry before, and it unnerved me to see the tears running down his cheeks.

She squeezed his hand. "Now, I know you'll have a lot on your mind, what with running the country and raising the children. I know it will be hard for you, but I need you to promise me that you'll take care of the kingdom properly for Tiernan so when you retire, the Seelie Kingdom will still be strong, ready for him."

"I will," he whispered, his fist clenching.

"Now, Tiernan." She turned to me.

"Mother?" Worry began to bloom in me. Stories of women lost during childbirth ran through my mind. But she had already had the baby. Shouldn't she be safe now?

"Tiernan, ruling a kingdom is a hard thing. No one should have to do it alone. I want you to promise me that before the hour of your hundredth birthday, you will marry, so you'll have a partner to rule the Seelie Kingdom with you when it is time."

"What?" Marriage and ruling a country were the furthest things from my mind. "Three hundredth."

She gave me a small smile. "Is marriage so terrible?"

"I'm going to be the greatest *Rífhéinní* since Fionn mac Cumhail. I need time to train if I'm going to lead the Seelie warriors, not hang out with…girls."

"Girls can be warriors too, you know. I was. There's even been female *Rífhéinní* leading all the Fianna. Maybe you'll fall in love with a *banfhéinní.*"

I made a face. Girls—even warrior girls—were no fun.

"Two hundred, then. I'm serious, Tiernan." She squeezed my hand. "You must promise me this."

"Phrase it carefully." Clíodhna wiped my mother's brow with a damp cloth. "Any promises they make to you now will be binding. Be sure to say what you mean to say."

My mother nodded and looked me in the eye. "Tiernan, you must swear to me that you'll find your queen before your two hundredth birthday. That will give you plenty of time in the Fianna. But, you will be king someday, and I do not wish for you to carry this burden alone. If you don't find your queen by then, your father will find a bride for you."

I nodded.

She squeezed my hand. "Swear it."

"I swear it," I said. "I'll find my queen by my two hundredth birthday." Why worry about this now? Mothers.

She repeated her earlier request to my father, making him swear to find me a queen to help me rule if I didn't find one on my own.

A heavy hum of magic vibrated through the room. I'd been in the presence of vows and bargains but never felt anything as strong as this one.

My mind raced. What was causing the strength of this magic? What had I gotten myself into? My mother looked up at Clíodhna when she finished. The Elder Fae nodded reassuringly.

"It's done, Mari. You can rest now."

My mother smiled, closing her eyes. She squeezed my hand one last time and then her hand relaxed and fell from mine.

Clíodhna gently helped me up and led me out of the room as my father began to wail. "This will be a hard path for you, my dear," she said. "But there is strength in you; I know it."

Suddenly, I realized why the vow had had such strength, why the magic had hung so thickly in the room. It had been my mother's dying wish.

I hadn't said goodbye.

Even then, I knew there was no getting out of a deathbed vow. I would have to marry before my two hundredth birthday or be cursed by the magic released by the vow's breaking. But, I was just a kid after all, how hard could it be to find a bride in 192 years?

PART 1

CHAPTER 1

ELLA

ELLA, I'M TELLING YOU THIS BECAUSE WE'RE friends…"

"Are we though?" I shook out a mass of ivory lace and eyed the skirt critically. Too full?

"I think you might be a workaholic." Amber Watson perched on a stained velvet cushion that had been relegated to the back room of Bliss Bridal, Pilot Bay's most exclusive—by which I mean only—bridal boutique. The teenage intruder talked to me, but looked at her phone.

I should never have given her the Wi-Fi password for the bridal shop. My work had been so much more peaceful before she decided to 'keep me company' whenever she wanted to check her Instagram. "Who doesn't have time for one little coffee?"

I flicked a sewing clip at the younger girl's head. The bit of pink plastic bounced off her perfectly curled brown hair without making a dent in her concentration.

"Some of us have to work for a living, you know. When you're not in school, there are things that cost money. Like rent. And food." And bus tickets to New York for Portfolio Day at Parsons School of Design. But I wasn't ready to admit that dream to anyone. Not until the ceramic pumpkin under my bed was full.

It was slow going with my stepmother, Kimberly, subtracting room and board from my paychecks. According to Kimberly, now that I had graduated from high school, I had to pull my own weight when it came to the bills.

Who knew what the going rate for unfinished basement bedrooms was, but I was pretty sure they were not worth as much as I paid. But Kimberly knew everyone in Pilot Bay. If I left, she'd make sure I never found a place to rent or another job, so I just had to keep my head down and save what I could.

"Blah, blah, blah." Amber waved her hand to disperse my boring arguments. "Because we are such good friends…"

"We're *good* friends now? This is escalating quickly." I settled the lace skirt onto the dress form and began attaching it with straight pins.

"…I will buy you a latte from Pie in the Sky…"

"Chai Latte, please! Oat milk, not real milk." I wasn't about to turn down a free hot drink.

It was early April and sunny outside, but it was freezing in the workroom. My stepmother didn't believe in heating areas of the shop that weren't for customers. Or herself. Okay, really she didn't believe in heating my area. If I complained, she'd take the heating bill out of my paycheck too.

"...on the condition that you come out with me tonight." Amber tapped her phone once more with a flourish and looked at me triumphantly.

I froze, mid-pin. "Um, what?" Amber had been visiting me for over a year and occasionally brought me a latte to thank me for the free Wi-Fi, but we hadn't ever actually hung out.

"You know. Out. Where you leave the shop and do something fun with your very best friend." Amber stood and pocketed her phone.

"We're besties now?"

"Aren't we? Whatcha drawing?" She peeked over at my open sketchbook. "Is that a dress design?"

I flipped the book to a blank page and continued pinning. "Don't you have anyone else to harass?"

"No one that needs me as much as you do, Ella Daniels." She patted me on the head like a puppy and then sauntered out of the workroom.

I watched her go and then sighed. Surely, she'd forget about me once I was out of sight. Amber had the attention span of a goldfish. I spun my long, black hair into a high, messy bun and secured it with a pencil. I had a bodice to attach before the customer came for her fitting.

Two hours later, half my chai latte had been drunk, but the rest sat cold in a paper cup on my sewing table. Cissy was due any minute to try on her dress, and I was scrambling to finish. In my haste, I had stuck my fingertips so many times with pins that I sucked on one finger while I worked to keep from ruining the bodice with little dots of blood.

I heard the jingle over the front door and looked through the workroom door to see Kimberly and my dear not-so-sweet stepsisters, Madison and Hailey, sweep into the elegant showroom.

"Ella!" My stepmother shrugged out of her coat. "Do tell me you're ready for Cissy Gladstone's fitting. I just saw her with her mother in front of the hardware store. Girls, go check on Ella and grab the dress, if you please."

The hardware store was across the street. I hurriedly tied off the last basting thread and stepped back to admire the dress. It still needed some work, but it looked exactly like the dress from Cissy's wedding mood board.

"Oh, Ella, it's so pretty," gushed Hailey, slipping into the workroom. Her twin sister followed right behind her. "I'm always amazed someone who dresses like *that* can actually make something with so much style." She waved a hand at my thread-covered black leggings and worn gray t-shirt, a stark contrast to my stepsisters' perfect blonde hair and designer jeans.

"It's not all that great." Madison lifted the hem with a sniff. "I thought it was supposed to be beaded."

I sighed. "Beading comes after the fitting. It's the last step." I carefully lifted the gown off the dress form.

"Oh, let me help you!" Hailey reached across my cluttered sewing table.

"Please don't." I tried to pull the dress away but Hailey leaned over, and with a bump of her hip, sent my paper cup of chai flying, the cold drink splattering across my open sketch book, my gray hoodie, and the ivory silk of the dress.

"Oh no!" Madison winked at her sister. "Ella, you're such a klutz."

I stood in shock, my heart pounding as they whisked the dress out of my hands and out the door to the showroom.

"Mama, you won't believe what Ella did. I really don't think she should be allowed to have drinks back there with all that delicate fabric. Oh, hi, Cissy!"

The bell chimed again. I tried to breathe as my stepmother apologized to the bride and her mother about that clumsy girl who does the alterations. Alterations! I may have started with a gown off the rack, but by the time I had cut it all apart and reassembled it to make Cissy's dreams come true, it became a whole new dress.

I wiped a spot of tea from my cheek with a shaking hand. Deep breaths. There was no point in defending myself to Cissy or my stepmother. They wouldn't believe me anyway. I just needed to keep saving and get out of here as soon as I could.

The sky had darkened by the time I left the shop for the day. My sketchbook had dried out, the spots on the dress carefully blotted and washed, and all I could think about was getting home. Time to eat something—anything—and curl up in bed to watch Project Runway while I worked on my portfolio.

Maybe today would be the day when inspiration struck, and I figured out the theme for my designs. I sighed and pulled the pencil out of my hair, releasing the bun. It was taco night at Kimberly's house. I should know. I prepped it before work this morning. Maybe there would be some leftovers.

"This is what you look like for a night out?"

I shrieked before registering that the figure waiting by the door in the dark was Amber. Oh, right. I had forgotten, but obviously, she hadn't.

"I don't really do nights out." I tried to play it cool while my pounding heart and tight chest continued to act like I was being chased by an axe murderer.

"Obviously." She picked a stray thread off my hoodie. "But tonight you do. I mean, what else do you have planned? Leftovers and Netflix?"

"I could have plans!" I took a deep breath. Man, I was jumpy today. Had I taken my meds this morning?

Amber raised a carefully shaped eyebrow.

"Okay, so I don't have plans, but I could."

Amber linked her arm with mine and steered me down the street. "You need to live a little, Ella. You're only nineteen. This is pathetic."

"Hey!" The band around my chest eased as my nervous system finally listened to my brain and calmed down. Amber didn't seem to notice my small anxiety attack. I was well practiced at hiding them.

"I say it with love because you are my friend." She patted my arm and continued dragging me off course. "Just trust me for one evening. If it isn't the most fun you've had in years, I will never bother you again."

"Never?" On the surface, Amber sounded as bad as my stepsisters, but something had changed in her in the past year since she had started coming to me for alterations. She was still obsessed with clothes and her phone, but I was relatively certain that underneath her snark she had a good heart.

"Ever," she promised. "Probably."

"Oh, fine." Odds were good that Madison had eaten all the tacos anyway. There would still be dishes to do, but if I wasn't out too late...

"Yay!" Amber squealed. "You will not regret this."

"I already do."

CHAPTER 2

ELLA

WHERE ARE WE GOING? I do have nicer clothes than this if we're going to a party."

I followed Amber to the little cabin on the edge of town where she lived with her sisters. The towering trees of the forest behind dwarfed the cozy house nestled up against the mountains.

"I'd like to believe you." She glanced back at me with a wrinkled nose. "But I've seen no evidence of that."

"Hey!" I protested, although she wasn't wrong. "I at least have clothes with less tea on them."

"You were supposed to drink the latte, not wear it." Amber peeked through the little window in the red front door. "Perfect, they're gone already."

"Who?"

"Isobel and her fiancé. Come on upstairs." Amber led me inside, and we both kicked off our shoes by the door.

I followed Amber through the living room toward the stairs. The room was decorated in a mishmash of vintage furnishings with silky pillows and throws that wouldn't have been out of place in a fairytale castle. A striped gray cat opened one eye to observe us before settling back down to sleep on the couch.

"Don't you like him?" I hadn't met Isobel's mysterious fiancé, but I also didn't really know Amber's sisters very well, apart from the occasional alteration at the boutique.

"Oh, he's fine, they're just so disgustingly in love." We climbed the narrow wooden stairs and Amber opened the door to her room with a little shove. "Don't mind the mess."

Mess was an understatement.

"Is there a floor in here?" I tripped over clothes and textbooks as I attempted to find a place to sit.

"Who knows?" Amber pulled a dark red rose out of her purse and tossed it in a jar of makeup brushes on her vanity. Odd. Then she opened her closet, and all my objections were forgotten while I took in the explosion of dresses. Silks, velvets, lace, and twinkling crystals spilled out in a heap of rainbow pastels.

Amber kicked aside a couple of dresses that had fallen to the floor and swiped hangers along the closet rod.

"Blue for you, I think. And nothing too delicate." She pulled a dress out of the closet and tossed it to me.

Tripping over a pile of shoes, I sat on the bed and examined the dress. "Where did you get this?" I flipped it inside out and looked at the seams. "This is hand sewn! I've never seen such perfect tiny stitches. What kind of silk is this?" It felt smoother than raw silk but had a texture I'd never seen.

"I have no idea what it's made of. Spidersilk? Flower petals? The dew after a full moon?" Amber threw another dress at my head. "Try one on."

"Did you bring these from Vancouver?" I knew Amber's family had been rich before losing everything and moving to Pilot Bay, but these dresses would cost a fortune.

Amber tapped my head with a hanger. "Try. One. On."

"I could never wear a dress like this! Besides, there is no party in the Kootenays where *haute couture* princess is the dress code." I fingered the intricate lace edging one sleeve. Was it hand tatted? Who tatted lace in this day and age?

"Oh my goodness! Are you always this difficult?" Amber threw her hands up.

"I'm just curious." I looked back at the closet and tried to tally up how many dresses were in there and how much they must have cost.

"Okay, Ella, here's the deal. If you put on a dress, and come with me to the party tonight, I will tell you everything I know about where I got these and who made them."

"Fine." We both stripped down, and I changed into a pale blue silk dress with silver knotwork embroidery at the hems and neckline. It had sleeves that belled out before gathering into a cuff at the wrist. A silver sash nipped in the waist, and two underskirts swished with every step I took. Amber helped me tighten the back, the laces letting the bodice fit smoothly over my less generous curves.

"What size are your feet?" Amber dug through the heap of shoes in front of her closet. She had changed into a dark pink dress with three quarter sleeves and a full tea-length skirt in paler pink.

"Um, seven?" I glanced at my reflection in the mirror. I looked flushed, and my gray eyes sparkled. It was hard to deny that I was enjoying myself. I glanced at the rose on the vanity. "Wasn't that flower open before?"

Amber tossed a gray leather bootie at me and looked at the rose. "Aw, crap, we're going to be late. Try this on."

"I don't see what that has to do with the flower." I tried on the boot. If I laced it up tightly it fit pretty well.

"All will be revealed." She unearthed the other boot and then ran her fingers through her hair, smoothing the brown waves. "Let me do your hair quick and then we should run or we'll miss the dancing."

Amber swept one side of my hair up with a silver clip shaped like a spray of leaves, leaving the other side to tumble over my shoulder. She quickly painted on her own liquid eyeliner and then passed it to me before hunting through chaos in a drawer to find her lipstick.

"I've never seen you in a dress before. When's the last time you wore something other than leggings and a hoodie?" She pursed her lips and applied shimmery pink lipstick.

"Um…summer? I don't wear a hoodie in the summer." My eyeliner wasn't as neat as Amber's. I had a steady hand thanks to sketching, but I hardly ever wore make-up.

Amber looked at me in the mirror. "Ella. You can sew like nothing I've ever seen. You make women look fabulous every single day. Why don't you dress up a little? Sometimes?"

I sighed. It was hard to explain. "I'm busy, okay? I have a lot to take care of."

"Well, I think it's about time you let someone help you out for a change. Lucky for you, that someone is me." Amber tossed her lipstick back in the drawer and dabbed glittery powder on her cheekbones, and before I could protest, on mine as well.

"And what exactly are you helping me do? Crash a wedding? Join a Ren Faire? Steal a unicorn?"

"Have fun, of course!" Amber patted my shoulder. "Let's go!"

I grabbed my bag and followed her downstairs. We stopped at the front door and Amber pulled a couple shawls from a basket beside the door.

"No bag!" She plucked my bag out of my arms.

"Hey, I might need that!" I felt naked without my sketchbook along. What if I needed to draw something?

"You won't. Trust me." Amber hung the bag on a hook and handed me a shawl.

I had contemplated my gray hoodie again—just for walking to wherever we were going—but the soft cream shawl was probably a better fashion choice for the cool April evening. What was it knitted out of? And how were the stitches so tiny…

"Ella! Stop staring at the fabric, we have places to go. Boys to meet."

Boys. I hadn't dated anyone since high school. What was the point when all I wanted was to leave Pilot Bay behind? "I don't have time for boys."

"Just for staring at shawls. I totally understand." Amber clicked on her flashlight and strode around the side of the house. I trailed across the yard behind her as she marched to the forest, the thin beam of light bobbing along.

"Are you planning to murder me in the woods, or is this a bush party?" I ran to catch up.

"Um, sort of? Come on."

"Sort of a party or sort of a murder?"

I stuck close to her as we hiked along the path into the woods, dry leaves rustling underfoot. I tried not to think about the stories I'd heard about bears and wolves prowling the mountains surrounding Pilot Bay.

Honestly, I wasn't very outdoorsy. I had grown up in the Kootenays, surrounded by mountains and forests, but I preferred to spend time out of the elements and away from the bugs. And the bears.

Don't think about the bears.

Amber stopped once, shining the flashlight around before illuminating a neat stack of rocks. The top one had three interlocking swirls carved into it. What a pretty design. Maybe Celtic?

"This way, Ella." She left the wide track to follow what must be another trail, but who could tell in the dark?

"Are you sure you know where we're going?" I rubbed my arms as I trudged behind her, grateful for the shawl. "I don't see a fire."

"Almost there." Amber stopped and turned to me. "Now, this is going to be pretty strange. But you won't believe me if I try to explain, so we better just go for it."

"Go for wha—"

Amber grabbed my wrist and pulled me after her. Between one blink and the next, a meadow filled with swirling dancing figures appeared.

Fast-paced Celtic music pounded through the air. A giant bonfire in the middle of the clearing threw sparks up into a sky filled with more stars than I had ever seen.

I rubbed my eyes. Little twinkling lights danced in the trees surrounding the meadow, and long tables piled with food stood off to one side of the fire.

I blinked. Clearly, I had been working too hard. Had I fallen asleep at my sewing table again?

"How did we not see all this from the trail?"

Amber clicked off her flashlight. Even at the edge of the clearing I could still see her in the light of the stars and the fire.

"Because none of this was there. We're not in Pilot Bay anymore, Ella." Amber threw her arms out. "Welcome to Faerie!"

CHAPTER 3

ELLA

"W HAT?"

"The Seelie Kingdom in Tír na nÓg to be exact." Amber rummaged through her purse. "I can't be much more specific, I don't actually know which forest this is. I borrowed Isobel's invitation which had the location keyed into it."

"This is like…a role playing thing? Is everyone, what's it called…LARPing?"

"Nope, actual faeries. Like the ones who made the dress you're wearing." Amber fished out a pair of earrings and hooked one into her ear.

"Wha—" My jaw dropped as her ear transformed into a long pointed elf ear. She put the other one in and I watched it happen again.

"Cool, right? They're glamoured to make us look fae, and they have a translation charm that lets us speak and read the languages here." She dropped a pair of dangly gold earrings into my palm. "I'm not sure who all is here tonight, so it's best to blend in. If anyone asks, you're from the Isle of Mist, and you're here with a friend. The Mist Court fae are, like, the most hermity hermits you'll ever meet, so no one will know you're not really one of them. I wouldn't want you to get stolen away by some faerie princess in need of a seamstress. We don't all have a fae prince to keep us safe like Isobel."

I put the earrings in and gingerly felt the tips of my ears. They felt the same as always.

"The glamour is only visual. It doesn't actually change your ears. You make a very smexy fae, though. Let's party!"

My curiosity pulled me forward. What were they wearing? If the dresses in Amber's room were any indication of the skill that went into the clothing here, I needed to get a better look. Except...

"Wait!" I pulled Amber back.

"What now?" Amber looked longingly at the dancing fae.

"Can I eat the food?"

"Why would you not be able to eat the food?" Amber glanced back at me.

"In the stories, if you eat the food in Faerie you'll be trapped here forever!"

"I wish it were that easy." Amber tugged me forward. "But I've been eating here for a year and a half…more like years in Faerie time, and Isobel still makes me go to school every day."

"What about the other stuff? Glamours? Iron? Lying? Saying thank you?" My mind spun as I tried to remember other dangers from the book or two I had read when I was younger. Was I supposed to have some kind of necklace made from berries? Why had my mother only ever told me Japanese folk tales? I was *so* going to get turned into a toad.

Amber sighed. "I'm pretty sure they can lie. Not sure about iron. I haven't seen much around though, so that could be a thing. If I didn't say thank you, Lily would kill me. And…um, don't get glamoured?"

"That's not very reassuring."

"Oh, relax. If Isobel actually let me come to this party, it can't be too dangerous. She's obnoxiously over-protective. Let's dance already."

I let Amber pull me forward. The music of the fiddles and drums thrummed through my bones, making my toes itch with the urge to tap. Still, I edged toward the empty wooden benches near the edge of the clearing. Maybe I'd watch for a bit. Get my bearings.

"Oh, no you don't." Amber linked my arm in hers and marched me toward the dancers. "I promised we'd have fun. I know you like to hide—"

"I don't hide!" I protested.

"With your oversized hoodies and your wardrobe of black and gray."

"It's comfy."

"And your sewing dungeon."

"Well, I can't work in the showroom."

Amber stopped and grasped my shoulders. "Have you ever thought about what your life would be like—what you could do—if you actually let people see you?"

"It's not that simple." I wasn't hiding, not really. I was just busy.

"It's that simple tonight. No hiding. Let's party!"

I gave in to Amber and the music and let her pull me into the swirl of dancers. The fae almost looked human except for their pointed ears. Tall and beautiful, they whirled alone, in pairs, or in groups. Their clothing struck me as casual but beautiful, with skirts of silk cut like leaves and loose tunics with bits of embroidery that glowed in the twilight.

The music thrummed through my bones as Amber spun us laughing into the crowd. I wasn't what anyone would call a skilled dancer, but it didn't seem to matter.

Some of the fae danced with intricate steps and some swirled past with abandon. The effect was chaotic but beautiful and free. I soon forgot to examine the dresses as the music shifted from one song to the next. I spun on the trampled grass of the meadow until my feet ached and my throat was dry. I lost Amber in the mix, and when I turned to look for her, I collided with the dancer beside me.

"Apologies, my lady," panted the tall red-haired man. He wore a simple but perfectly cut linen tunic and dark trousers with tall leather boots. His green eyes sparkled, and his freckled face was flushed from dancing.

He gave me a courtly bow. I attempted a curtsy, almost tipping over as I realized how much I'd been twirling. The man laughed. His deep voice vibrated through me as he steadied me with a hand on my arm. I felt the heat of it through my silk sleeve.

He raised his voice to be heard over the music. "Let me get you a drink before we both fall over." He gestured a pale, elegant hand at the other side of the clearing where tables waited, covered with food and drinks.

"Well." I hesitated, looking around again for Amber. There she was, on the edge of the dancing green, arguing with her sister, Isobel.

By their hand gestures, it looked heated. Were they arguing about her bringing me along? Better to not find out.

I smiled up at the handsome fae in front of me. "A drink sounds perfect."

"Excellent." He offered me his arm, and I stifled a giggle as I accepted it. How was this happening? I had a sudden flashback to the one, awkward, high school dance

I attended and the gangly boys there. Apparently, they did everything better in Faerie.

"How do you know Saoirse?" He poured us each a goblet of some golden liquid. I sniffed it, but it didn't seem to be alcoholic.

"Who?" A sip revealed it to be a tart juice, colder than I expected after sitting out on a table.

"The birthday girl?" He raised an eyebrow, amusement glinting in his green eyes. "My foster sister?"

He jerked his thumb at a tall, brown-skinned woman with black hair twisted into multiple knots against her head. She narrowed her eyes at us.

I was crashing someone's birthday party? Thanks a bunch, Amber.

"I came with a friend." I waved my hand vaguely at the crowd. Better not to get Amber in trouble if she wasn't supposed to be here either. "I'm Ella."

I held out my hand, and to my shock, he bent over it and gently kissed my knuckles. Goosebumps traveled up my arm, but I covered my reaction with another sip of juice as he let my hand go, brushing his thumb over the back of it.

"Tiernan." He paused, obviously expecting a reaction. When I just smiled, he shrugged and continued. "It's not often I see a new face at a revel. I know all the noble Seelie ladies, and I would never forget one as lovely as you."

I laughed out loud. "So charming! Do those lines work on your noble Seelie ladies? Do they swoon for you?"

"Well, they don't usually laugh at me." Tiernan looked at me sheepishly, which was even more charming. He had probably been trouble since he was a toddler.

"But still, you must tell me where you've been hiding. Are you merely visiting Tír na nÓg?"

"I'm from the Mist Court." And that was my whole back story. Please let him not ask me any more questions. I turned to the table. "Do you suppose there's any chocolate on here?"

He plucked a small pastry from the tray beside him. "So it's to be like that, is it? Making me work for it?"

I stalled and grabbed a pastry too, taking a bite. Yes, chocolate. Perfection. I didn't like lying, but Amber had been clear. Don't trust the fae.

"You have the look of the Kami, but your accent is different. I can't place it, but I've heard it before. Do you have family from Takamagahara?"

I blinked in shock. My mother had told me stories of Takamagahara, back when she was still alive. She would tuck me into bed and tell me magical folktales of dragons, oni, and kitsune. Her stories made me feel more connected to a country I had never seen.

Takamagahara was real? Was it another world or part of this one? I had so many questions, but I couldn't ask any of them without revealing that I wasn't fae. "My mother." That was close enough to the truth.

He waited for me to say more. I took another bite of my pastry.

"Beautiful and mysterious." He gave a wounded sigh. "If you won't reveal your secrets to me, there's only one thing to be done."

"Oh?" Should I be worried? Was I going to have to come up with a better story?

"You'll have to dance with me, of course." He bowed and then held out an elegant long-fingered hand to me.

I hesitated. The wisest thing to do would be to try to disappear and find Amber. It was getting late, and my stepmother would be livid if I didn't get home soon. And was it smart to be drawing the attention of a fae?

Still, maybe Amber was right.

I reached out and took Tiernan's hand. He gave me a crooked smile.

Maybe it was about time I had a little fun.

CHAPTER 4

ELLA

THE MUSIC SLOWED BY THE TIME WE rejoined the dancers and quieted enough to allow for conversation. That was unfortunate because it allowed Tiernan to continue peppering me with questions.

"Come now, Ella of the Mist Court, you must tell me more about yourself."

"Oh, must I?" I raised my eyebrows, but I had trouble acting terribly offended with his hand hot against my back and all this attention on me. He was a shameless flirt, but it worked for him. There was something thrilling about having all his focus.

"We'll make it fair. If you answer me, I'll answer a question for you." He spun me around another pair of dancers, my silk skirts flaring out. "What about siblings, do you have any brothers or sisters? Or were your parents completely satisfied with your perfection?"

"Oh, please!" I laughed. "Dial it down a notch. I can't take the charm."

He laughed too, which made me like him better. At least he knew how to take a jab.

"No siblings, just two stepsisters. But since my dad died, they've made it clear I'm not actually part of their family. How about you? You said this party was for your foster sister?"

"Yes. I have a younger brother too, but he lives far away. My parents would have liked more, but my mother died giving birth to my brother." He said it casually but looked away from me.

"My mother passed away when I was little too."

"And then your father remarried?"

"Yeah, I guess he thought I needed a family again, but it all fell apart when I lost him too."

"I'm so sorry. For your parents, but also for bringing up such a depressing subject at a revel!"

I laughed, surprised out of my melancholy thoughts.

"What about food? What's your fav—"

"Tiernan! Stop flirting and come help me with this!" A fae man with shaggy dark hair staggered past under a pile of firewood.

"I'll be one minute." Tiernan held up a finger. "Don't go anywhere."

I nodded, and Tiernan dashed off to rescue his friend. I wandered to the edge of the crowd again and leaned against a tree. I watched the dancers, trying to memorize the details of a tea-length dress with a bodice made of glittering insect wings. If only I had brought my sketchbook along.

I should probably go home before the red-headed charmer came back with more questions, but I was reluctant to find Amber and leave.

I didn't want to go back to the real world just yet. I had never felt so inspired. If only I could come up with a way to spend more time in Faerie to work on my portfolio, I'd finally have designs that would stand out to the scholarship committee.

I needed to come back, and stay for more than just an evening. But how? Maybe Amber would have an idea.

A sparkle of light floated in the forest, a couple of paces away. Unlike the floating lights adorning the trees surrounding the clearing, this one glowed a pale blue and seemed to be moving closer.

When it stopped, hovering in front of my nose, I could make out a little person made entirely of glowing light. The person beckoned to me and floated back into the forest where they bobbed, clearly waiting for me to follow.

I leaned back against my tree. "You're very cute, but if you think I'm going to follow you into a dark forest, you're crazy."

"Ha!"

I jumped. I hadn't heard Amber sneak up on me.

"Ella's smarter than she looks." Amber put her hands on her hips.

"Hey!"

My friend shooed the little faerie off with a wave of her hand. "Get out of here, sheerie."

The sheerie flared once in annoyance and then floated carelessly away through the trees.

"Sheerie?" I asked, still mesmerized by the little glowing faerie as they faded from view.

"Tricksy little buggers. Sometimes they can help you find treasure or your way home, but wild sheerie are just as likely to lead you into a bog or off a cliff if you follow them. They have a strange idea of fun."

"Yikes." I rubbed my hands on my goosebumpy arms.

"Speaking of fun, you looked like you were actually having some. Well done! And with the crown prince no less."

"Who?" I turned back to the party and looked for the tall redhead in the crowd. He was laughing with a pretty blonde girl by the fire. I tried not to feel hurt. Apparently, his attention span wasn't that long.

"Tiernan, of course. He didn't tell you?"

I shook my head.

"Tiernan's the heir to the Seelie Kingdom. His father is the high king." Amber looked me over. "I take it he didn't mention that."

"It didn't come up," I said faintly. A prince? He had been so casual and friendly.

Amber snorted. "Turned on the charm, did he? Whatever he said to you, don't take it too seriously. He's been smiling that smile at girls for almost two centuries, and he's never settled down."

"Two centuries?! He doesn't look much older than me!"

"It's something about the magic of Faerie. When the fae reach adulthood, their aging slows way down. Humans too, if we hang out here. I've probably spent five years here in faerie time, and yet, I'm still in grade eleven." Amber rolled her eyes. "I like to tease Isobel about being engaged to an old man, but in Faerie, two hundred is the new twenty. Anyway, Tiernan is the world's biggest flirt. He leaves a trail of broken hearts wherever he goes."

"Are you speaking from experience?" I tried to suppress the flare of jealousy. It was silly of me to think there had been anything between us after one dance. He didn't even know who I was.

Amber sighed. "I wish. He is *fine*. But he's decided I'm like an honorary little sister or something. It's so annoying." She hooked her arm through mine, and we walked toward the tables.

I resisted the urge to glance back for the flirty prince. He'd clearly already forgotten me. I'd never see him again anyway.

"Should we be going home soon?" I plucked a stuffed mushroom from a tray. "If I'm home too late, Kimberly will make me work extra tomorrow."

"Oh, did I not explain the time thing to you?" Amber poured herself a goblet of juice.

"What time thing?" The mushroom was stuffed with herbs and some kind of nuts. Yes, please.

"Time goes faster in Faerie than it does at home." Amber picked up a small cake and poked the flowers on top. "We could be here for days and only a couple hours would pass in the human world. We will literally be back before she has time to miss you."

"That would have been nice to know when we got here." I snagged three more stuffed mushrooms. "Amber?" I turned to study her.

"Mm hmm?" Her mouth was full of cake.

"Do you promise this isn't a dream?"

"Only one way to find out!" She laughed and pinched my arm.

"Ouch!" I smacked her in return, giving my best glare.

"See! Totally real. You're welcome. Now come tell me all about your dance with Tiernan. He looks exceptionally delicious tonight."

We each grabbed a plate of snacks and found a mossy spot to sit with our backs against a tree. It had the perfect view of the dancing green.

There wasn't much to tell about my dance with Tiernan, so after we rehashed it, we sat and watched the revel.

Between the crackling fire and the haunting music, I soon found my long day catching up with me. My eyes closed.

CHAPTER 5

TIERNAN

I STRETCHED OUT MY LONG LEGS IN front of the popping embers of the bonfire. Most of the revelers had gone through the temporary gate back to their homes. A few slept on the soft meadow grass, leaving only the four of us awake.

"There are only four months left." Saoirse leaned back on her hands, watching the fire.

"And how was your birthday?" I asked her.

She rolled her eyes. "Very lovely. Much dancing. Don't change the subject. You have four months before your father is allowed to choose your bride. Choose the future Queen of the Seelie Fae."

"Oh, really?" I said. "Thanks for letting me know."

"Well, I'm sure it must have slipped your mind as you've been avoiding the subject for the past two hundred years," interjected Declan, pushing his shaggy black hair back from his face.

"I haven't forgotten, thank you very much." I glared at them both. "I'm aware of my responsibilities."

"Have you found the queen's crown, by the way?" Saoirse asked.

"I have not."

The crown, tied to the magic of Faerie, had disappeared when my mother had passed away. My father had never remarried, so it hadn't been needed, but it bothered me that I hadn't been able to find it anywhere in the palace. Had my father hidden it to strengthen the argument for his choice of my bride?

"Leith, they're ganging up on me. Back me up here." I turned to my oldest friend.

Leith looked thoughtful as he smoothed his fiancée's hair back from her sleeping face. Humans. They didn't have the stamina for revels.

"I know why you've stalled, Tiernan." He looked up at me, his good eye filled with compassion. An ever present eye-patch covered the other. "I was there, remember, when they found Brenna."

I winced at the memory and then pushed it firmly from my mind.

"What happened to Brenna was terrible." Saoirse threw a stick at the fire. "But that was decades ago. Are you just going to give up? Let your father pick some bigoted, tradition-bound girl to be co-ruler of the entire Seelie Kingdom with you? To block you at every turn and undo all our plans?"

I watched sparks fly up toward the darkness overhead.

"He won't," said Leith, mildly. "Tiernan knows what's at stake more than any of us."

I sighed and closed my eyes, feeling the heat of the dying bonfire on my face. One hundred and ninety-two years to find my queen. It once seemed like an infinite amount of time. But now, the last few grains were slipping through my fingers.

"What would you have me do, Sersh? Oh, master of romance."

She flicked a dark braid over her shoulder. "This isn't a matter of romance, Tiernan. It's a matter of politics."

"We could find you someone," said Declan. We all looked at him, and he shrugged. "I mean, surely we can do better than your father."

It was an idea worth considering. I had no interest in a love match. If I was going to be set up with someone, at least my friends would be able to find someone who would further our cause.

"Can you find someone in four months?" asked Leith.

"I can visit the courts we believe will support us." Declan shrugged. "You need to choose a bride before your birthday, right? Or your father will?"

"I need to *marry* by my birthday." I sighed. "That's what we promised my mother. So I need to find someone sooner, by the Samhain ball at the latest. I'll bet Fiachra has someone picked out already. He won't take kindly to interference. He already threatens any girl I've so much as danced with twice, if he doesn't think she'd be a good choice. If he knows what you're up to, he'll find a way to stop you."

Saoirse nodded.

Declan rubbed his chin as he stared into the fire. "What if we threw him off? Made him believe you had chosen a bride already? You could do that, right?"

I raised an eyebrow. "I suppose."

"What about Saoirse?" said Declan. "You two could pretend to be courting."

Saoirse dry-heaved, and I grimaced, feeling similar. Even if Saoirse had any interest in marriage—which she had made clear, she did not—we thought of each other more like siblings than anything else. The idea of having to hold her hand or kiss her to pull off the ruse was more than either of us could handle.

"I'm pretty sure we can't fake that," I said.

"It was just an idea," said Declan. "You have to admit, it would buy us the time we need."

"I can do it."

We all whirled around to see who had spoken.

Ella, the beautiful Kami girl I had danced with earlier, stepped out of the shadows. She tucked her black hair behind a softly pointed ear. Her gray eyes shone in the firelight.

"And you are?" Saoirse gave Ella a piercing look.

"This is Ella," I told my foster sister. "We met earlier. Ella, this is my sister, Saoirse. That's Declan, the youngest son of the Hawthorn Princess, and Leith, the Rose Prince, with his fiancée Isobel."

"Um, happy birthday?" The girl waved at my sister.

"What did you hear, little eavesdropper?" Saoirse glared at the girl as she nervously picked her way over to our group and sat down on the grass a safe distance away.

"I didn't hear everything you were saying, but you need someone to pretend to be Tiernan's girlfriend, right? So you have time to find him a better match than his dad will?"

"And why would you choose to do such a thing?"

Ella shrugged her shoulders. "Would I have to cook? Wash floors? Scrub pots?"

"Certainly not!" Declan looked vaguely horrified. Even as the youngest prince in a large family, washing floors wasn't something he worried about.

"Well, that's a good start," Ella said.

I recalled what she had said about her stepfamily.

"What do you think, Tiernan?" asked Leith.

My gaze flicked over to him and Isobel for a long moment. Of course I envied, on some level, what he had with Isobel. But love had always been off the table for me, which was, after all, the problem. I had danced and flirted with this girl tonight—and sure I'd enjoyed it—but I could resist her easily.

Liar, said a quiet voice in the back of my brain, which I firmly ignored. It had been a bit of fun at a party, nothing more. Besides, if she came from the Isle of Mist, as she said, she wouldn't be what I needed.

But that could make her a perfect choice to fool my father.

What about her? Was she only offering this to get away from her family? Or did she hope for something more out of me?

"And there's a ball? Would I be able to go to it?" Her expression turned dreamy.

"That could certainly be arranged." I relaxed. If this was about attending the Samhain ball—the most exclusive Seelie revel of the century—and not about me, it would make things less complicated.

Was this a good idea? On the one hand, it would be easy to pretend to be besotted with the slim pale girl looking at me with shining gray eyes. On the other hand, I would have to be very clear about this arrangement.

Four pairs of eyes watched me as I tapped my dagger against my leg.

"All right," I said to her. "We'll do it. You'll pose as my sweetheart until my engagement is announced on Samhain, and I'll make sure you attend the ball."

She smiled triumphantly, which made me wonder if there was more to her story than she had told me.

Saoirse must have seen it, too. "I don't like it," she said. "We don't know her. How do we know we can trust her? Where are you even from, girl?"

"The Isle of Mist," said Ella promptly.

"That's perfect," I told Saoirse. "The Isle of Mist is very traditional. Fiachra won't have any reason to dislike her."

"Exactly!" Saoirse pointed a finger at Ella. "Why would she help us? She could even be a spy for your father."

"Well, there's one way to know for sure. We'll go to *Croí Clioche*."

Saoirse's eyes widened, as did Declan's.

"You would go that far?" he asked.

"We won't do the ceremony, but it's the only way to be sure. Even you can't deny that. You can ask her anything you want."

I looked over at Leith, who gave me a small nod of agreement. Ella was peering at the stitching on the underside of her sleeve. So strange.

"If you're truly willing to do this—"

"I am." She looked up and I saw the resolve in her eyes.

"It could be dangerous," interjected Leith. "Even if Fiachra doesn't take issue with you, he will likely have his own choice for Tiernan made. The king is not forgiving to those who try to cross him."

Ella shrugged. "I'll stay out of his way."

"If you're willing to do this," I repeated, "meet me at *Croí Clíoche* on the first day of Lughnasadh. At sunrise."

"So early," grumbled Declan.

"Fiachra will doubtless use the festival as an opportunity to foist some princess on me. I'd rather not give him the chance." I turned back to Ella. "Leith is right. We would make sure you were guarded at all times, but it could still be dangerous for you. Give it some thought."

She opened her mouth to respond but I held up my hand. "Really think about it."

She closed her mouth and nodded.

"Well," said Leith, "it's time I took Isobel home." He gathered his fiancée up in his arms. She stirred but stayed asleep as he carried her to the gate.

"We should go too." Saoirse smacked Declan's shoulder.

"Yes, yes." Declan yawned. "Only you would plan an early training session for the day after your own birthday revel."

One would never guess it by looking at them, but they made an excellent team.

"I'll walk you to the gate, Ella." I turned back only to find the girl had gone already.

"I hope you two are as clever as you think you are."
Saoirse pinned Declan and then me with a look.

"Oh, so do I, Saoirse," I said. "So do I."

CHAPTER 6

ELLA

I SLIPPED INTO THE SHADOWS, WANTING TO get away before Isobel woke up and outed me. I had only met Amber's sister a handful of times, but she would definitely recognize me, pointy ears or no pointy ears.

"Ella, come on!" Amber whispered, breaking into my thoughts. Had I really just offered to be a fae prince's fake girlfriend?

"Way to snag yourself a royal hottie!" Amber tugged me back to the gate.

"It's not like that." I looked back at Tiernan and his friends, who were standing up and collecting their coats.

"Well, whatever it's like, you only have nine days in faerie time to get ready, so we better hustle."

What did one pack to be a fake faerie princess? Toothbrush? Underwear?

What had I gotten myself into?

We stepped through the gate, trading one dark forest for another. I looked up. The stars still shone overhead, but they felt dimmer than the stars in Faerie.

"So, you met Tiernan?" A voice spoke beside me in the dark.

"Wha-!" I almost knocked Amber over as I jumped away from the voice.

"Ouch! Miss Chloe, must you be so dramatic?" Amber grumbled.

"Oh, sorry my dears." The sound of hands clapping together rang out. "*Léas.*"

A light flared and revealed an older lady with curly gray hair—Miss Chloe, the town's head librarian. The light shone from a ring on her hand as she examined me through her gold-rimmed glasses.

"I...I don't understand," I said. What was the librarian doing lurking in the dark forest?

"My godson, Prince Tiernan, did you agree to help him?"

"She did, Miss Chloe. In fact, I think he liiiikes her!" Amber nudged me with her elbow.

"I think he likes everyone," I retorted.

Miss Chloe laughed.

"Wait, how do you have a faerie prince for a godson? What's going on here?"

"I have more than one, actually. I can't tell you much more than that, or it'll affect the outcome."

"What outcome?"

She ignored me and dug around in her purse. "Now, I only came to give you something. It should be helpful..."

I looked at Amber for help, but she just shrugged, obviously used to Miss Chloe.

She pulled out a set of keys with a chibi Captain America keychain. "Nope." Next came a paperback romance novel. "I'm sure it's in here somewhere...Aha!" She held what looked like an old-fashioned pocket watch. "This is for you, Ella."

I took the watch from her outstretched hand.

"Is this gold?" I turned it over in my hand. It was etched with an intricate Celtic knot and almost seemed to hum in my hand. Odd.

"Of course it is. Nothing holds magic like gold." Miss Chloe snapped her purse shut. "Now, open it, my dear, we don't have a lot of time."

The inside was a clock, as I'd guessed, with simple gold hands. It also showed the date in a small set of numbers near the bottom.

"Human time," explained Miss Chloe. "Now turn the knob."

I turned the knob on the side and instead of winding the hands of the watch, it flipped the entire clock face to a new date and gold filigree hands. I turned the watch over. The back remained the gold knot design.

"Faerie time," said Miss Chloe. "Our time is currently running much slower than theirs, so keep a close eye on it. You don't want to be late for your date with my godson."

"It's not a date," I mumbled, turning the knob to flip the watch back to human time and then over to faerie time again.

"Miss Chloe, you've been holding out on us," complained Amber. "Do you know how hard it is to tell time with an enchanted rose?" She turned to me. "Faerie time is always faster than human time, but sometimes it's twice as fast and sometimes it's twenty times as fast. It's super annoying. I have to set up my phone to take videos of it at night so I don't lose track of the days."

"Well, Amber, I don't have an endless supply of magical artifacts, you know. I can't make more until Moriath is defeated, and I can safely return to Faerie."

"I know." Amber gave a sigh of long suffering. "Other people always have the best luck."

"You seem to be managing just fine," said the librarian unsympathetically. "But you will need to hurry, Ella. Faerie time is running very fast right now. Keep an eye on the watch. Lughnasadh this year is the 26th day of Tinne, the 8th month. Sunrise is 6:30, and Amber knows where *Croí Clioche* is."

"I do?" asked Amber.

"It's on Isobel's map."

"I do," Amber told me.

"Now, off you two go, you've already lost five hours. Come see me when you're back, Amber. I need you to take care of something for me." Miss Chloe clapped her hands again, and the light blinked out. I could hear the crunching of leaves as she took off through the forest.

"That was...odd," I said.

Amber turned her flashlight on. "That's Miss Chloe for you. She's actually an ancient fae named Clíodhna, but I've been doing community service hours at the library for nine months now, and I still haven't learned much more about her. She enjoys her secrets. She's right though, we need to get you packed quickly, or we'll be late to meet Tiernan."

But as we followed the trail back to Amber's house at the edge of town, I started to question my rash decision. There was no way my stepmother would happily agree to let me leave for the weekend.

Never mind that I was nineteen and—as she constantly reminded me—not her child. She didn't like me being out from under her watchful eye, and I didn't want to risk angering her when I was so close to having enough money to be free of her forever.

But those dresses! I itched to start sketching what I had seen tonight. If I could spend longer in Faerie, see the fashions at a palace, go to an actual ball?! I would have all the inspiration I needed for my scholarship portfolio.

"Are you going to tell me why you decided to help Tiernan?" asked Amber once we were back at her house, changing out of our dresses. "Was it those pretty green eyes?"

I snorted. "Not exactly." I hesitated. I didn't usually show anyone my work, but I wanted to trust Amber, and I needed her help to pull this off. I pulled my sketchbook out of my bag and tossed it on the bed.

Amber, now dressed in joggers and a t-shirt, pounced on the sketchbook and flipped it open.

I winced and turned away. I hated watching people look at my drawings. It was like having someone crawl into my head.

"Ella! You've been holding out on me. I knew you were good at wedding dresses, but this is amazing!"

She didn't know anything about fashion. Nothing in that book was anything special.

"What does this have to do with Tiernan?" Amber pulled an elastic off her wrist and twisted her brown hair into a knot on top of her head.

"I'm entering a scholarship competition. For Parsons. It's a fashion design school in New York."

"Oooh, you want to be a designer? You would be totally amazing!"

"Hmm, maybe. But it's super expensive. The only shot I have at being able to go there is the scholarship. But it's very competitive. I need really unique designs, and I've been struggling to come up with a theme." I glanced down at the sketchbook, opened to a sketch I had done of a dress I found on Instagram, and one from *The Queen's Gambit*. The same inspirations as every other fashion nerd on earth.

"So going to Faerie would give you some new ideas?"

"Everything I saw tonight was so different." I sank onto the bed beside her. "The fabrics, the styles, the way the clothes are cut. I can't remember the last time I felt so inspired. It's just what I need to win the scholarship."

"And the hot fae prince? Just a side benefit?"

Or a distraction.

"He needs a fake girlfriend. I need inspiration. Not to mention having longer to work on my designs with the whole time-moving-slower thing. Win-win."

"Gotcha." Amber gave me a calculating look. "So are you going to tell him you're a human?"

"Should I?" I closed my sketchbook and put it back in my bag. "You said it wasn't safe to be a human in Faerie."

"It's not, especially at the Seelie Court. I mean, I've never been there, but Leith's told me some pretty scary stories. Tiernan's cool though. He's not going to kidnap you and make you sew faerie dresses until your fingers bleed or something." Amber got up and disappeared into her closet. "Do you need anything from your house?"

"A couple things." My travel watercolor set, maybe. And some pencil crayons.

"Here." Amber emerged with a leather shoulder bag. "Your current bag won't exactly blend in."

"Thank you!" I examined the chocolate brown bag made of butter-soft leather. Simple but beautiful.

"No problem, I've got three." Amber nodded at the door. "We should head over to your place and get you packed up and ready to go."

"What about Tiernan's friends?" I followed Amber down the stairs. "I know Leith's your sister's fiancé, but Saoirse seems terrifying."

"Saoirse *is* terrifying, but your main worry is the king. I've heard he's a real piece of work. Only thinks the High Fae count as people. Possibly has a dungeon full of the bones of faeries who've crossed him."

I shivered. "I think I'll keep pretending to be a fae. I doubt the prince will be impressed if he finds out I lied to him, and there's no way Saoirse will let me stay after that. She's already convinced I'm hiding something."

"Okay." Amber shrugged as we went outside into the night.

"You're not going to tell me that I shouldn't lie to him?" I adjusted my bag, and we walked back across town.

"Well, that would be bad if you were trying to have a relationship with him. But you're not. And you're probably right. The fewer people who know you're human, the safer you'll be. Isobel didn't see you tonight, did she?"

"I don't think so."

"Good, she's such a goody-two-shoes. We'll just not tell her. If she knows, she'll tell Leith, and Leith will tell Tiernan, and that's it for your story."

When we reached my house, the kitchen was a complete disaster, like every day. I had made enough tacos for two nights yesterday, so at least there weren't any pans to scrub, but I swear my stepsisters had a gift for getting every surface dirty.

My stepmother glided through, barely sparing Amber and me a glance.

"You're home awfully late, Ella. I can't promise to save you dinner when you show up at all times of the night, but maybe you'll find something while you tidy the kitchen." She turned back at the doorway. "And your little friend needs to leave before nine. You know the rules."

Amber stared at me as Kimberly left us, and I looked away in embarrassment. It was bad enough to admit to myself how my stepfamily treated me. I hated for anyone else to witness it.

"I'll load the dishwasher while you start packing." Amber started stacking plates. "Keep an eye on the time. You need to get away from that stepwitch, pronto."

I nodded, gratefully, but as I descended the stairs to the basement, my misgivings came back. Could I really pull this off? Was it worth annoying my stepmother?

I looked around my corner of the unfinished basement. It had a cement floor and no drywall. Beams overhead were crisscrossed with exposed wires and pipes. Instead of walls, sheets hung from thumbtacks stuck to the beams.

Only a month after Dad died, Hailey had cried about the unfairness of having to share a room with her twin sister. Instead of clearing out the spare room—Kimberly needed the space for her treadmill, after all—my stepmother moved my bedroom furniture down here. She had promised to get someone to finish the room, but that had been ten years ago.

I could sleep in a palace tonight. That was almost worth the risk on its own.

But first, I'd have to face Kimberly. My hands were shaking. I pulled out my suitcase and stared at it. Should I take a carry-on? To Faerie? How was I going to keep pretending to be fae? I didn't know anything about the fae!

I grabbed the bottle off my bedside table and shook out a pill. The last pill. My prescription was waiting at the pharmacy, but it would be closed now. Surely, I wouldn't need meds away from my stepfamily, living the faerie princess life?

I swallowed the pill dry and hid the bottle in my drawer. I didn't need confident Amber knowing what a basket case I was.

Deep breaths.

First, I found a sketchbook I had made in highschool art class. It was handbound and had always seemed too pretty to actually use, but hopefully it would pass for a faerie-made book. I slid it into my new bag with some pencils, charcoals, my travel watercolor set, and a pack of pencil crayons.

Then, I started pulling clothes out of my ancient dresser. Gray shirts, black shirts, leggings with holes, jeans with more holes. When Amber called down to me, I had all my clothes on my bed, and none in my suitcase. I looked at the watch. Three days had already passed in Faerie.

Amber's eyes flicked around my makeshift room, but she didn't say anything. She had a snarky comment for every situation, so I must have really looked pathetic if she was being nice. Then she looked at my bed.

"Okay, I see the problem." She picked up an ancient tank top and dropped it again. "We can tell them your luggage got eaten by trolls on the way over. They'll make you dresses out of flower petals or something."

I sighed. "I don't think I can do this."

"Sure you can. Don't you have anything nice, though? You're the most talented person I know. You make those small-town girls look like frickin' princesses every day. Why don't you have anything pretty?"

"I do have one thing." I desperately wanted Amber to know that I wasn't a total pity case. "Can you keep a secret?"

"Um, I've been traveling through a magical portal to Faerie for over a year, and you had no idea until tonight."

"True." I laughed, still feeling shaky but a bit steadier. My meds were starting to kick in. Or maybe it was just having someone to distract me that helped.

I knelt beside my bed. "I do have one cool dress. I didn't sew it, though. It was my mama's." I slid out the long wooden box, pushing aside my pumpkin-shaped cookie jar of saved money. Amber sat down beside me on the cold concrete, and I flipped back the lid, reverently folding back the tissue to reveal hand-painted red and pink silk.

"Whoa! Can I?" Amber touched the silk gingerly. When I nodded permission, she lifted the kimono and its pink, patterned, obi sash out of the box and spread it on the bed by my clothes. The kimono's deep red silk faded to pale pink at the hem with golden dragons peeking around blossoms and falling petals. I unfolded a sleeve to reveal the kanzashi comb with its pink silk sakura blossoms and lacquered prongs.

"My mother brought it when she moved to Canada from Japan to marry my dad." I traced a painted dragon on one wide sleeve. "She wore a white dress to her wedding and this one to the reception. It was passed down from my grandmother."

"Have you ever tried it on?"

"When I was little, my mom used to let me try it on and look in the mirror. She would tell me tales of the ryū, the Japanese dragons, and I would make up my own stories about the little dragons coming to life and playing with me. But when she died, and it became mine...I haven't been able to wear it. And besides—"

"Ella! I dropped a cup, and there's, like, glass everywhere. Can you come clean it up? I don't want to cut myself or something." Madison stood right at the door. Heart pounding, I threw my pile of clothes over the kimono.

"Whatcha doing?" Madison looked at us curiously. Had she seen the kimono? "Are you going somewhere?"

"I'm kidnapping her for the weekend," Amber told her with a hair flip. I remembered that they had been in the same friend group at school when Amber had first moved to Pilot Bay. She had changed a lot since then, but my stepsisters had only gotten more shallow and useless, if that was even possible.

"Um, good luck with that, Smella. As if Mom will let you go anywhere. Anyway, the broken glass? You'd better hurry up before someone steps on it." Madison gave the messy bed one more look and then let the sheet drop as she left.

"You don't need anything from here," Amber told me as we packed the kimono carefully away, and slid it back into its hiding place. I nodded, my mind made up.

"You're right. I don't." I looked around my pitiful excuse for a room and grabbed my new bag. Madison could clean up her own mess. I was ready. "Let's go to Faerie."

CHAPTER 7

ELLA

KIMBERLY WAS NOT IMPRESSED WITH ME, BUT with all the work done for the weekend, and Amber hanging around to witness the exchange, she had no choice but to let me spend the weekend away.

She did manage to make some sweetly veiled threats implying that if I didn't show up for work Monday morning, I would be out on the street. I didn't usually stand up to her about anything, but this would be worth it.

Amber and I trekked back under the streetlights to her house to grab another faerie dress. A few days would have passed in Tír na nÓg, so I certainly couldn't be seen in the same dress I wore to the revel. I held the watch in my hoodie pocket. It calmed my jangling nerves, reminding me that I should have no trouble being back by Monday. This would be great.

"What time is it?" asked Amber as we tromped into her entryway.

I checked the watch. "We have two days and one hour. We aren't worried about Isobel seeing me?"

"She and Leith are out of town for the long week-end." Amber dashed up the stairs to her room, and I ran after her.

"But I just saw her at the revel."

"Well, somebody might have done some Googling and discovered that her favorite author is doing a book signing in Florida tomorrow." Amber yanked open her closet.

"She's going to fly to Florida?" I pulled off my hoodie and tossed it onto her bed.

"Naw." Amber pulled out a cream dress and eyed it critically. "Too weddingy?"

"Too weddingy."

She slid it back into the closet. "She and Leith will go through the Rose Gate to one of the portals in Florida close to the book signing."

"There are portals all over?" I stripped out of my gray t-shirt.

"Yep." Amber pulled out a pale purple dress.

"That one." I reached out for it.

"So bossy, I love it." She handed me the dress. "Yeah, there are portals all through the human world. Any gate leads to any other gate, unless it's locked to you. So the Seelie fae don't use Unseelie gates, but there are tons of gates. Anywhere the fae decided they wanted to visit often."

"They wanted to visit Pilot Bay often?" I asked, through layers of purple chiffon as I wiggled into the dress.

"Not lately, but I guess there was a gold mine near here back in the 1600s. The fae love gold and silver. They can create magical objects with them or something. That does look good on you," she added approvingly. "Anyway, Isobel and Leith will be gone for like, a month in faerie time, and even then, they don't visit Rahivea very often, so they shouldn't be able to blow your cover."

"Rahivea?" I asked.

"The Seelie capital, where you'll be."

"And what *are* Seelie?" I flopped onto the bed in a puff of skirts. "I'm never going to pull this off."

"Sure you can. Just bat your pretty eyelashes at him and talk about how you've never left the Isle of Mist before."

I glared at Amber.

"Okay, okay! So, Tír na nÓg is a continent in Faerie. The southern half is Seelie territory and the northern half is Unseelie. Oh, and the dwarves live way up north in the mountains. Stand so I can lace you up."

I stood. "And I'm supposed to be from the Isle of Mist? Is that Seelie or Unseelie?"

Amber deftly tugged at the laces, tightening the back of the dress. "Technically, Seelie, but they kind of do their own thing. The Seelie Kingdom is split up into a whole bunch of courts, and the Mist Court is very isolated. Okay, it is kind of complicated, are you sure you don't want to tell Tiernan you're a human?"

"Would you?" I turned to face Amber.

She tilted her head. "Yeah, probably not. I mean, like I said, Tiernan's pretty cool. Although I don't know him super well. I have no idea about his friends, though. In general, the fae are as likely to steal and imprison a human as they are to befriend one."

I shivered. "I only have three days of human time to do this. I don't have time to be stolen and imprisoned."

"I mean, if you're going to be stolen and imprisoned, you could do worse than a hottie prince."

I raised an eyebrow at her.

"Not that sort of girl. Gotcha." Amber turned me back around and tied the back of the dress. "You'll need a backstory, then."

"Ugh." I slumped. "It's going to be hard enough pretending I'm not human. How am I going to keep a backstory straight?"

"We'll keep it simple." Amber chucked a hairbrush at me. "You live with your horrid stepfamily of trolls on the Isle of Mist."

"Trolls? Really?" I brushed out the tangles a night of dancing had put in my hair.

"You're right, that doesn't make you fake girlfriend material. It's close to the truth though." Amber tapped her chin. "Let's say the Mist Prince is your stepmom's uncle. That makes you a noble, but not so important that anyone should have heard of you."

"Great step-niece of the Mist Prince?" I committed it to memory.

"Perfect. And then, you'll have one more issue."

"What's that?" I handed her back the hairbrush.

"*Croí Clíoche.*"

"Bless you."

"*Croí Clíoche* is a sacred stone circle in the heart of the Seelie Kingdom," she said. "And there's only one reason Tiernan would choose to meet you there. Well, two reasons. You aren't getting engaged, are you?"

"What? No. This is all just pretend."

"Okay, so I haven't been there, but I know it has a *fáinne menhir*. It's this rock with a hole in it. I was at Isobel's engagement ceremony—it's a whole thing for the fae—and there's this part where you like, stick your hands through the rock and then you can't lie. I guess the point is to start your engagement off with truth or whatever."

"You've lost me, why does this matter if I'm not getting engaged?"

"He must want to make sure you're not a spy or a gold-digger or something. I bet you'll have to hold hands through the stone and answer questions."

"What?!"

"Still want to go through with it?"

I took a deep breath. "Yes."

I needed to be able to do this. I couldn't stay in Pilot Bay with my stepfamily forever.

"The first issue is your ears. I don't know if the earring glamour will work for this. We have to get there sooner to do something about them."

"A glamour counts as a lie?"

"Not sure, but let's not find out. We'll cover your ears. And for the rest… Well, if you want this bad enough, you're gonna have to be clever. Think you can handle it?"

I put the glamoured earrings back into my ears, and we looked at the reflection of the dark-haired fae girl staring back at me.

"Oh yeah," I said. "I can handle this."

We arrived in Faerie through the Rose Gate half an hour early, counting on Tiernan not being there yet. A little chickadee flew off, startled as we appeared through a gate made of three giant stones. We arrived in a meadow bathed in silvery pre-dawn light. Amber had explained that all the Seelie gates in Tír na nÓg and the human realm could lead to any other Seelie gate. Instant travel. After spending so long saving for a bus ride to New York, it was the most incredible magic I could imagine.

I felt a strange hum in the air, almost a tingling. "Do you feel that?"

"Feel what?" Amber walked past me, into the clearing.

The hum faded into the background. Had I imagined it?

"Never mind."

Amber and I wandered through the long dew-covered grass to find flowers to weave into a crown for my hair. Towering evergreens edged a circle of standing stones surrounded by dewy grass and little white wildflowers. In the center stood what Amber told me was the *fáinne menhir*, a tall standing stone carved with runes and symbols I didn't understand. A hole was bored through the middle of it.

"So." I picked a little white flower. "If Leith and Tiernan are both princes, does that make them brothers?"

"More like brothers-in-arms." Amber gathered some little ferns. "When they were young, they fought together in the Fianna."

"What's the Fianna?" I should have been taking notes.

"It's like a war-band thing. It actually took me a while to figure it out, but they call all the Seelie warriors the Fianna." She picked a handful of flowers. "But then they have groups of nine who train together, which are also called a fianna. They seem pretty tight. They even have matching tattoos. It's very hot. Anyway, Leith retired or whatever when his parents were killed and he had to become the Rose Prince."

"Leith is the prince of…Roses? Is he gonna be a king someday like Tiernan? Will your sister be a queen?"

"Leith is the prince of the Rose Court." Amber scrutinized our collection of flowers and foliage. "We should have looked up wreath-making on Pinterest first. Anyway, it works like this. The Seelie Kingdom is ruled by the possibly evil king, Fiachra. But it's split into a bunch of courts and all the courts have, like, plant and flower names. They each have a prince or princess taking care of them, but they all answer to the Seelie king. He rules from the Seelie Court at Rahivea. And Isobel will be the Rose Princess. All the Seelie nobles co-rule with their spouses. She'll be even more bossy than she is now."

"Have you ever been to the Seelie Court?" I attempted to braid the stems of my flowers together. I should have picked longer stems.

"Nope." Amber was having better luck with her attempt, so I passed her my flowers to add to it. "Isobel says it's not the safest place for humans to go wandering about. We mostly stick to Kilinaire Castle and the countryside. It's so lame. I've always wanted to go to Rahivea. The palace is supposed to be so cool. And you get to go during Lughnasadh, which is, like, giant party time. Please take notes. I want to hear all about it."

"Okay." I smiled. "Deal."

We finished the wreath just as the sun started peeking through the trees.

Amber took the circle of flowers in both hands and muttered, "Hold!" A hum like the one I had felt entering the clearing flared briefly and disappeared.

"Okay, I enchanted it to not fall apart." She handed me the flower crown. "I'm still learning how to use magic, but it should make up for our less than awesome wreath-making skills."

"Humans can use magic? Am I supposed to be able to use magic?" I gripped the wreath more tightly than was wise. "I'll never pull this off. Are you sure you can't stay?" I asked her, desperately.

"I wish." Amber took the wreath from me and carefully set it on my head so that even if my pointed ears disappeared, the tips would still be covered. "Tiernan knows me, and he would be very curious about what I was doing with some girl from the Isle of Mist. I'll figure out a way to be in touch soon."

I gave her a sudden, tight hug.

"So affectionate," she gasped.

"I am your best friend, after all. You said so."

"I knew I'd win you over. You'll be fine." Amber winked and disappeared through the stone arch.

I stared at the ring of standing stones and took a deep breath. Maybe I should have stopped by the pharmacy for more meds after all. No, Amber was right. I was going to be fine.

"There she is," an Irish-accented voice called from behind me.

I spun around. Tiernan, flanked by Saoirse—who eyed me suspiciously—and Declan strode toward me. The crown prince's copper hair was neatly slicked back, and he was impeccably dressed in slim, dark green trousers tucked into tall black boots. A perfectly tailored emerald green jacket with leaves embroidered in lighter green at the cuffs and collar and shining brass buttons matched the pale green vest underneath.

He caught me staring and winked. "As radiant as an early morning—"

"Please." I waved my hands at him. "I already agreed to do this, you don't have to keep laying on the charm."

Declan laughed at Tiernan's wounded expression, and Saoirse smacked the crown prince on the back of the head as she walked to the center of the ring of stones.

"There's no poetry in your souls," Tiernan called after them. "Milady." He gestured for me to go ahead.

"My lord," I matched his tone. He didn't seem to catch my snark so I double-checked my wreath and lifted my skirts to keep up with his long-legged strides. Saoirse and Declan waited for us by the standing stone. The pair were dressed much more casually in leather pants and linen tunics. Saoirse didn't strike me as someone who'd be into dresses.

"You didn't bring any belongings from the Mist Court?" asked Saoirse. "No one packed you any clothes or supplies? Who did you say your family was, again?"

"My stepmother is the Mist Prince's niece." I patted my shoulder bag self-consciously. "Was I supposed to bring more?"

"Of course not." Tiernan glared at his sister. "It would be an insult to Rahivea's hospitality." He turned back to me. "Shall we begin?"

CHAPTER 8

ELLA

TIERNAN WALKED AROUND TO THE FAR SIDE of the stone, and stuck his hand into the hole. I reached into the opening and felt his warm hand clasp mine.His hand felt more callused than I expected from a prince. A tingle ran through my hand and up my arm. Apparently, it had been too long since I had held hands with a boy.

Wait, that wasn't a normal tingle. It grew to a vibration, and I gasped as all the runes on the stone lit up, glowing from within.

"All right, Sersh." Tiernan adjusted his hand in mine. "Ask your questions."

"Why are you willing to help Tiernan?" Saoirse pinned me with a glare.

Okay, no lying. But did the Fae even understand fashion design? If I told them about my portfolio project, would they make me show them my work? I shuddered. I hated having people flip through my sketchbook. Honestly, my life plans were none of their business.

"I've never been to the Seelie Court," I said. "I'm curious about what it's like." True enough. I was especially curious about the tiny embroidery and strange fabrics.

"And your guardians, will they not miss you?" asked Tiernan.

"I live with my stepmother and her two daughters." I looked down at my feet. "They will only miss having me there to wash the dishes."

"They make you wash their dishes?" Declan frowned.

"Wash the dishes, cook the food, clean the house, and work in the shop all day while they do nothing." Well that was a bit more than I had meant to say! Stupid glowing rock. I swallowed.

"They treat you as a servant?" gasped Declan.

"You can see why it might be nice for me to get away for a little while."

Declan nodded. "Good enough for me."

"You're easily won over," said Saoirse. "Are you a spy?" she asked me. The girl didn't beat around the bush.

"No."

"Did you swear allegiance to the Seelie king or any of the princes or rulers in Tír na nÓg?"

"No. Seriously, I'm just a girl." I glanced at Tiernan, who nodded. He believed me.

"How old are you?" asked Declan. "You don't look older than a hundred or so."

"I'm nineteen." I winced as they all stared at me in shock.

"We're not doing this." Tiernan tried to release my hand, but I grabbed his tightly back. No way was I letting this chance slip away.

"Why not?" I fixed him with a look.

"I can't put you in danger like this. You're barely an adult."

"I'm not a child." I squeezed his hand. "This is my choice." I said more quietly.

He gave me a measuring look and then nodded. "All right then. Any more questions?"

Declan shrugged but Saoirse stepped toward me.

"If I find out that you have somehow been untrue, in any of this, you will be back home with your wicked stepmother before you can blink. Understand?" She patted the sheathed dagger at her side. "That is, if I let you live."

I gulped. "I understand." I understood that I definitely couldn't tell any of them at this point that I was actually human. They would not take it well.

I started to release Tiernan's hand but he grasped mine again.

"Before we go forward with this, you must promise me something." He grimaced. "Well, there's not really an easy way to say this."

"I guess you're going to have to say it the hard way then." I narrowed my eyes.

"It's only...you can't fall in love with me. Okay?"

"What?" I sputtered.

"This is a business arrangement. No love. It's temporary. You know that, right? It's just temporary."

I gaped at him. "Yes! I'm aware it's temporary! It's just a holiday, right? All I'm here for is some pretty dresses, an invitation to the ball, and a couple of months without having to scrub anybody's dishes."

"Okay," he said. "But be really sure."

I yanked my hand out of his. The runes flared brighter before the light faded away.

"Yeah, well, maybe you should be careful not to fall in love with me! Did you ever think about that?" I shook my hand until the tingling feeling went away.

He snorted. "Oh, that will never happen."

"What?!" I straightened. "What's wrong with me? I mean, I know I'm not whatever your usual princess type is."

"No, no, no, you're fine."

"Gee. Thanks."

"It's only—it's not a problem. Just be careful. Girls say they're not going to fall in love with me, and then it ends up happening. Be on your guard, okay?"

I rolled my eyes. Apparently, once the charm wore off, this was what I was left with. "Well, fine. That's very clear. Rule number one." I held up one finger. "No falling in love. Strictly business." I stuck a second finger up. "Rule number two—"

"I don't know if we need rules, exactly." He crossed his arms.

"Obviously, we do. Rule number two. No bedroom business."

Declan choked on a laugh.

"Bedroom business?" Tiernan raised an eyebrow.

"That's right. You know what I mean."

"I do know what you mean. But I don't know why you seem to have taken me for some sort of rake. You think I'm just going to tumble any vaguely pretty maid in my path?"

Well, at least I was vaguely pretty. "I don't know what kind of person you are. I hear that girls are falling in love with you left, right, and center. I wanted to be clear."

He leaned forward. "I will have you know, I'm faithful to my future queen."

"Declan?" I asked.

The tousled fae shrugged. "As far as I know he just kisses them at parties. So many parties…"

Tiernan glared at his friend.

"Saoirse?" I looked at the warrior fae.

She sighed. "I really choose not to ask about that sort of thing."

The prince's green eyes bore into mine. "So, what's your third rule?"

"Third rule?"

"Well, if you have two rules, I assume you have a third."

"You came up with the first rule!"

"Rule number three!" barked Saoirse. "No betraying the crown prince."

"Agreed." I rolled my eyes.

"Doesn't hurt to be safe," she muttered.

"Are you supposed to kiss now?" asked Declan.

Tiernan and I stopped glaring at each other to glare at his friend.

"It's not actually a hand-fasting!" Saoirse punched the dark haired prince's shoulder.

Tiernan sighed and turned to Declan. "Do you have any candidates in mind for the queen?"

Declan pushed his messy hair back from his face. "I have a couple. It's too bad Princess Tuala married last year. She would have been a good choice."

"She has her own court to inherit. A half-human princess would have been a tough sell to the court anyway." Tiernan tapped a finger against his leg.

"Isn't it your choice, though?" I asked.

"It is and it isn't." Tiernan turned, and we followed him back to the gate. "The Seelie monarchs need the support of the people and the land. Without that connection, we can't rule, and the crown will pass to someone else."

"I have some other ideas," said Declan.

"Okay, be discreet, and send me regular reports. I'll send Morna with you." Tiernan whistled, and a blue jay with a dark head flew down from a treetop and landed on Declan's shoulder.

I stared at the bird open mouthed as Declan and the jay disappeared through the stone arch.

"I know. Only monarchs have avian familiars." Tiernan winked at me. "The king's control over the land is starting to slip. You can only be cruel for so long and maintain the will of Faerie."

"Oh sure, let's tell her everything," grumbled Saoirse.

"She's bound to notice, Sersh. Why don't you check in with our fianna and set up a schedule for guard duty? We need to keep Ella safe."

Saoirse saluted the prince and disappeared through the stone arch.

"They argue with you about everything, and then they still do what you tell them to?" I asked.

"Of course. They're my seconds-in-command, but I am still their *Rífhéinní.*"

I tried to untangle that sentence. What was a *Rífhéinní?* This was clearly something different than just being the crown prince. It sounded military?

"You don't have a Fianna on the Isle of Mist?"

"I'm not sure." Should I be sure? I should have asked Amber more questions.

"I suppose your isolation keeps you safe, even being so close to the Unseelie lands." He held out his hand. "So, are you ready?"

"Ready for what?" I eyed the hand suspiciously.

"Ready to meet my father and his court?"

I took a deep breath. Was I? If I wanted to back out, I could still say no. I could go through this gate alone and head back to Pilot Bay.

I weighed my options of a potentially deadly, evil fae king versus my stepsisters, who had probably gotten every dish in the house dirty by now, even if hardly any time had passed in the human realm. They were just that skilled at creating messes for me.

If I returned, I might never leave Kimberly's house and end up working in her shop forever. The best way to escape was to pull together a brilliant portfolio and win that scholarship.

"You know what? I am ready." I put my hand in his.

"Don't worry, Ella." He winked. "It'll be fun, I promise."

At least that would make Amber proud.

PART 2

CHAPTER 9

W E LEFT THE HILL, AND A BREATH later, stepped into a beautiful high-walled court-yard. The midday sun filtered down through the branches of flowering trees, and a fountain tinkled nearby.

As I turned full circle to take it all in, I gaped at the gate we had stepped through. Unlike the gates of roses, branches, and rough-hewn stone I had seen thus far, this gate was crafted entirely of glass.

Sculpted to look like two arching trees with inter-twined branches overhead, the gate sparkled in the light. Its thin glass leaves threw rainbows at the walls of the courtyard. The trunks were anchored into the stone floor with spiraling golden symbols circling the base.

"I've never seen anything so beautiful!" I gingerly touched the trunk of one glass tree.

"This is the Glass Gate." Tiernan squinted up at the sparkling branches overhead. "Clíodhna herself crafted it for my grandfather. Only the royal family can pass through it, to the heart of Rahivea."

Miss Chloe? How old was she?

"Tiernan! You're back! And who is this?" I spun to see a man striding toward us. He looked as pretty as a J-pop star—bonus points for the pointed ears—with long black hair pulled back from his face in a partial ponytail. A large sword was strapped to his back. A fae from Takamaga-hara?

"Haru!" Tiernan punched the man's shoulder in greet-ing. "Did Saoirse put you on first guard duty, or did you just miss me?"

"Oh, you know I pine for you whenever you're gone, but the king wanted to know the moment you returned. He has some girl for you to meet." Haru glanced at me and shifted his feet. "Which will make this a bit awkward. Not the best day to bring a girl on a castle tour."

Tiernan caught my hand, twining his fingers through mine. I smiled up at him, as if we held hands all the time. As if I wasn't vibrating from the feel of his palm against mine.

"Haru, this is Ella, my future queen. We met at Saoirse's birthday revel."

"Your..." Haru looked dumbfounded. "What?!"

"She'll be staying at the palace until the Samhain ball when we'll announce our engagement."

Haru closed his gaping mouth. "With your father here? What are you thinking? No offense, Lady Ella."

"None taken," I said with what I hoped was a relaxed smile.

"Does Saoirse know about this? We have patrol in a fortnight."

"Sersh likes her."

I bit back a snort at the blatant lie.

"It's love, Haru. Be happy for me." Tiernan smiled down at me with besotted devotion. He really was exceptionally good at this. It was unsettling. I smiled back.

Tiernan clapped his hand on Haru's shoulder. "Well, run off and tell Fiachra. But maybe take the long way around? I want to get Ella settled."

"Another member of your fianna?" I asked Tiernan as we walked between the stone pillars leading into the palace.

Tiernan nodded absently. "I wonder who Fiachra is planning to ambush me with. I'm extremely grateful to you for saving me from whoever it is. Maid!" He waved at a small woman, about as high as my knee. Her dark brown hair was tucked under a white kerchief that contrasted with her mottled brown skin, and she wore a neat blue linen dress with an apron.

"Your Highness." The maid curtsied, then looked at me curiously.

"This is Lady Ella. Do we have a suite of rooms available for her in the family wing?"

The maid's eyes widened in shock. "Of course, Your Highness," she answered. "I dusted the west suite this morning."

"Perfect." Tiernan gestured for the small woman to lead us.

The palace was graceful and bright with tall arching ceilings and chandeliers glittering overhead. At first glance, it reminded me of a grand mediterranean-style castle, but what I had initially thought to be a green rug running down the polished marble floor was actually soft moss under my shoes.

Vines climbed along the pale plaster walls. Falling water tinkled as gleaming rivulets poured down the walls of alcoves into marble pools at the bottom. I caught a flash of gold darting under a pond lily in one.

"Here are your rooms, my lady." The maid reached for the lower of two doorknobs on the polished, pale wood door. The door was split in two, presumably so that taller fae could go through like a normal door but smaller folk like her could go through the bottom half. The doors were latched together so that they swung open for us all to enter.

We stepped into a sitting room. Two couches and a low polished table faced a marble fireplace. The outlines of golden flowers crawled up the white plaster walls. Instead of a back wall, gauzy curtains drifted between stone pillars.

I walked across the tiled marble floors—with moss between the slabs instead of grout—running my hand along the burnished gold edges of one of the couches and stepped through the curtains onto the balcony.

As I stepped outside, I felt a tingle and then the air warmed. There must be some sort of magical air conditioning going on inside.

On the balcony sat a table with two chairs and plants everywhere. Some were potted in the corners, some spilled down from somewhere higher up. Vines wrapped around the edges of the railing and continued down. But what took my breath away was the view.

The curtain swished, and I turned to see Tiernan leaning up against the railing next to me. Close, but not touching my arm with his.

"Welcome to Rahivea."

I looked down. The palace continued on further than I had expected. The courtyard we had entered through must not have been the bottom floor. Other balconies dotted the palace walls.

Below sprawled a city unlike any city I'd ever seen in the human world. Instead of the gray of cement and steel, Rahivea was lush and green with buildings of pale wood or white stone wrapped around enormous trees. Nearly all the rooftops were green, some with neat gardens and some with sprawling vines or wildflowers.

"A far cry from the Isle of Mist?" Tiernan bumped his elbow into mine.

"I've never seen anything like it." I smiled at him.

"Well, you'll soon see it all up close. If you like, we can go down and enjoy the Lughnasadh festivities. We could get some lunch at the fair."

Reaching into my bag, I felt for my pencils. A festival meant costumes and probably people from all over. Inspiration galore.

"I would love that."

Tiernan tapped both his hands against the railing and straightened. "Unfortunately, I must speak with the king first."

"Is he going to be very angry?"

"Probably. But don't you worry about it. I'll be back in no more than an hour and then we'll go have some fun."

I smiled, trying not to worry. After all, this was his plan. He knew what he was doing.

The prince and I walked back inside as the maid set a bouquet of flowers on the table.

"You there! Brownie! What is your name?" he asked the small woman.

Honestly, I almost expected him to snap his fingers at her. Was he only nice to me because he thought I was a noble?

"Imogen, Your Highness." The maid curtsied.

"Imogen, you'll be reassigned to take care of Lady Ella while she's here. I'll stop in and clear it with the housekeeper this afternoon."

Imogen nodded, her eyes wide. "I would be more than happy to. Thank you, Your Highness!"

"Perfect. I'll leave her in your capable hands then." Tiernan turned back to me, and my stomach growled loudly. I sighed in embarrassment, but he just laughed. "Lunch soon, I promise. I'm sorry, but I must take my leave." He kissed my cheek casually.

I caught my breath and let it out. It was only an act for Imogen's benefit.

"I'll count the moments until I see you again," I told him, solemnly. His eyes twinkled with amusement to see me playing along. Then, with a bow, he left me with Imogen.

The small maid and I stared at one another. She was a brownie? I assumed that referred to the type of faerie, not her job, but I had seen other small people with mottled brown skin in similar outfits around the castle.

"I'm sorry, miss." She shook her head. "I'll show you the rest of the rooms."

The rest of the rooms included a bedroom with a fireplace in the corner and a tall, four-poster bed draped with white gauze curtains. I ran my hand across the bedspread. Silk. A carved wooden wardrobe stood against one wall.

It was much smaller than I had hoped, containing only a couple of pairs of silk pajamas and a few empty hangers.

"We will of course bring you up a selection of day dresses. I'm sorry we weren't expecting you."

"Yes, Tiernan likes surprises, doesn't he?"

"I suppose?" She clucked nervously, then showed me where the extra blankets were kept. I couldn't imagine needing any in this perfectly temperature-controlled bedroom.

Next she showed me the bathroom—white marble again—with vines surrounding the large open window. Steps led down to what Imogen called a tub but looked to me more like a pond. It was large with clear blue water and floating lily pads and lilies. I dipped in my hand and found it to be the perfect temperature for bathing. A small current stirred the water, keeping the pool fresh.

And, happily, faerie castles appeared to have indoor plumbing. There was a small room with a toilet and a sink with a large mirror.

"Does your ladyship require anything else?" asked Imogen.

I looked all around at the suite of rooms, easily as big as the entire main floor of Kimberly's house.

"It's perfect," I told her.

"If you need anything, of course, just ring for it." She waved her hand at a golden bell by the door.

"Thank you!" I waved goodbye to Imogen and sat down on the nearest sofa. Pulling out my sketchbook, I started a list of things I hoped to see today.

CHAPTER 10

TIERNAN

I PAUSED OUTSIDE THE DOOR TO MY father's office, taking a moment to push down all my distaste for him, all my fear for the safety of the people I loved, and all my worry that I wouldn't be able to pull this off.

Ella teased me about my charm, but with Fiachra for a father, wearing a mask was a survival trait. Vulnerability was not a luxury I had.

Not if I wanted to pull this off.

I knocked.

"Come in."

The heavy door creaked as I entered. As always, I carefully didn't glance at the sheerie lanterns while I approached The King sitting behind his desk. His raven, Cethin, perched on a roost beside him.

Fiachra's icy glare was pinned on a leipreachán cowering in front of his desk.

"Tiernan, I'll speak with you shortly." Fiachra didn't look up at me. "Once I've dealt with *this*."

The small faerie quaked under the joint glares of the king and his raven, the bird a visible reminder of my father's powerful connection to the land.

Cethin ruffled his feathers as the pressure of Fiachra's power increased in the room. Even though the land itself was beginning to rebel by giving me one jay, I couldn't hope to usurp Fiachra on my own. I needed a bride who would side with me against him, and then I needed to pray the magic of Faerie would accept her and that together we might have the strength to take him down.

"Who is responsible for this?" growled the king, poking a finger at one of the three pairs of expertly crafted leather shoes lined up on his desk.

I winced as I examined the offending shoe. Its intricate tooled leather was stamped with a design of oak leaves and acorns. This cobbler must be new. Someone should have warned him to never use symbols of my mother's birth court.

"It was me, Your Majesty," the small cobbler whimpered.

Fiachra leaned forward. The leipreachán grew even paler as a rustling of wings whispered in the dark corners of the room.

This was getting out of hand. My father had a connection to every bird in the corvid family—except my Morna—throughout the realm, but ravens were his favorite. He only manifested shadow ravens when he felt especially wrathful.

I stepped in front of the poor shoemaker, my back to the king.

"You are dismissed," I told the leipreachán, coldly. "Gather your family and be gone immediately."

With my back still facing the angry king, I gave what I hoped was a look of reassurance. I had no intention of having him and his family thrown out into the woods without provisions.

I'd have to talk to the leatherworkers later and have him reassigned somewhere he wouldn't run into the king again. My life at Rahivea was a delicate balance of convincing my father that I was the son he wanted, so I could continue my work outside of the capital without his constant attention, while trying to do what I could for the small folk—the *Aos Sí*—here. I needed to work at it harder than ever if I also had Ella to fool, but it would be worth it.

"Begone." I waved my hand, and the cobbler gathered the shoes and ran.

As the door closed behind him, I felt my father's power ramp back down. The dark shadows in the corners grew still until only Cethin and a stray feather or two floating down from the bookcases remained.

"You're too soft." Fiachra waved at the chair across from his desk.

I sat with all the casual grace I could muster.

"We can't be executing perfectly competent master cobblers." I leaned back and crossed my ankles. "The leipreacháns would revolt and then I'd never get decent shoes. Some of us have appearances to maintain with the ladies."

Fiachra snorted. "Speaking of ladies, I hear you've brought a guest." He said the words casually, and I fought the urge to shiver. Ella had only been in the castle for half an hour, but of course he knew.

"Yes," I kept my tone light. "The Lady Ella. I think you'll like her."

"Oh, will I?"

"You know how you're always saying—" *demanding, threatening* "—that I should find a nice…traditionally minded girl to marry."

"You intend to marry this girl? Where is she from? The servants say she looks like a foreigner." Fiachra looked curious, which was an improvement over wrathful.

"Ella is the step-niece of the Mist Prince. She's lived her whole life in Tír na nÓg."

"Hmmm…"

I could tell Fiachra was considering this. The Isle of Mist was technically part of the Seelie Kingdom, but we rarely had contact with the secretive Mist fae. Even so, they were known to be cruel to the *Aos Sí* and sent their tithes regularly. My father had never felt the need to flex his power there.

But would that be enough to make him approve of Ella and keep her safe while we distracted him from Declan's attempts to find me a bride?

"Well, I hope you aren't too fixated on this Etta…" he began.

"Ella."

"…to consider other options." Fiachra stroked Cethin's inky head. "I have someone for you to meet at dinner. And there are many other lovely princesses in the kingdom. I know it's difficult for you to consider settling down, but your birthday is approaching. This is a serious business after all, Tiernan. The future of the kingdom is no light matter. We must choose wisely."

Didn't I know it? And while I was tempted to announce a formal engagement to Ella, if only to keep from having to talk to any more *lovely princesses*, I couldn't make it official and then appear to change my mind later. I already had a reputation as a ladies' man. I couldn't be seen as fickle. My kingdom needed to be able to trust my word.

For now, what I needed was time.

"How about this? I'll introduce you to Ella—I'm sure you'll love her as much as I do—and you can introduce me to…whoever you have lined up."

"And?" Fiachra regarded me closely.

"And I'll announce my decision at the Samhain ball." Hopefully that would give Declan enough time to find me a better option.

"You'll present your bride to the court at Samhain," Fiachra clarified, no doubt considering how to keep anyone he didn't approve of away from the ball. "That will suffice."

"Perfect." I rose, adjusting my jacket. "Now, if you'll excuse me, I promised Ella I'd take her to the Lughnasasdh celebration. I'll see you at dinner."

Now all I had to do was ensure that Ella wasn't someone he wanted to keep away from the ball. Or worse, eliminate completely. It should be easy enough. All she had to do was be herself, a Mist Court noble.

When Ella and I reached the Glass Gate, Haru was waiting for us in the courtyard. I could tell by his expression that he wasn't buying any of the stories I had told him, but I wasn't about to talk to him about it now, especially here where the walls had ears.

"Haru." I grinned. Hiding my unease under charm had always worked for me. "We are about to go down to enjoy the festivities."

"Great," said Haru. "I'll accompany you."

"Haven't you already been?" I asked.

"Yes, but I ran into Saoirse, and she insisted I be on guard duty today for Ella."

I rolled my eyes. "When I'm not with her. I'm perfectly capable of taking care of her on my own."

"Saoirse suggested that you might be distracted. I'll come along." Haru crossed his arms.

"Distracted? I think I can handle it. I'll remind you that I can best you sparring two times out of three."

Ella muttered something about macho nonsense under her breath and looked up to the sky. Haru didn't budge.

"Well, then," I said to him. "I hope you're excited for more bilberries." I knew for a fact that Haru hated bilberries.

"I look forward to it." He gestured toward the gate. "After you."

I sighed. There was clearly no getting out of it. I held up my elbow to Ella, who smiled up at me winsomely. The girl was a disturbingly good actress.

"My lady," I said. She put her hand on the crook of my elbow, and we stepped through the Glass Gate. We weren't going far, just down into the city square where the festival was being held.

A riot of sounds and smells assaulted us on the other side. There was nothing quite like the Lughnasadh festival. Ella looked all around, her eyes wide, taking in the stalls of bellowing merchants, smells of fried food, and the roar of the crowd from over where the competitions were being held. Doubtless the Isle of Mist couldn't compete with Rahivea for holidays.

"What first?" I asked her.

She looked up at me with a twinkle in her eyes. "Well, I was promised lunch."

"Ah, yes, and Haru is dying for more bilberries. Let's go."

We wound our way between the crowds of people, many of whom called out to me in passing or patted my shoulder as they went by. The Seelie fae were a touchy-feely bunch, but I was used to it. Ella, on the other hand, looked a little taken aback by the familiar ways of the crowd.

I stopped for a moment. Closed my eyes. Sniffed. "This way." I grabbed her hand in mine and pulled her along. Haru would have to keep up.

"Here we go." I pulled her up to one of my favorite stalls.

"Three orders," I called to the glaistig. The woman's goat hooves clacked on the cobblestones as she bustled about collecting three skewers of fried potatoes and three golden bilberry hand pies. I thanked her, and she nodded a horned head, pocketing the gold coin worth more than she'd make all weekend at the fair.

I passed out the food. Haru grumbled something about noxious fruits while chewing on his skewer and glaring at me.

Ella ate a bite of potato, and her eyes closed in happiness.

"No matter where you go," she said, "nothing beats fried potatoes at the fair."

"Agreed." I polished mine off in seconds and started on my pie.

We wandered as we ate, perusing the vendors. Fae from all over the Seelie Kingdom flocked to the capital for Lughnasadh, setting up temporary stalls to sell anything you could imagine. We browsed jewelry, fine dresses, fabrics, birds—some of whom could talk—and weapons the sellers claimed to be enchanted, even if there was only a ten percent chance of it being true. Ella licked the last of the bilberry pie off her purple-tipped fingers.

"Good?" I handed her a handkerchief. "Or are you a hater like Haru?"

"Amazing." She wiped her fingers clean and handed it back to me. "They taste just like huckleberries…which grow on the Isle of Mist."

I tucked the handkerchief away before taking her hand back in mine to make sure she didn't get lost in the crowd. Nothing to do with the feel of her slender fingers sliding between mine.

"So, are you going to buy her a gift?" asked Haru.

I had almost forgotten he stood behind me, but alas, he remained. I turned back and gave him a look.

"A token of your true love?" Haru held up a garish necklace studded with paste jewels. I noticed his hand pie had vanished but his fingers were unstained. I would wager he'd given it to a hungry-looking child while my back was turned.

"Could you go fetch us something cold to drink?" I narrowed my eyes at my friend. He huffed and set off.

"He's right," I said quietly to Ella. "I should buy you something to show off later."

The girl looked longingly at a stall crammed with dresses and scarves.

"Not jewels?" I asked. "You can keep it when you leave. Pick out anything."

"I just want to take a closer look…" She trailed off, tugging her hand from mine to run her hand softly along a drape of blue silk.

I tried not to mind. I was the Seelie crown prince. I wasn't about to be jealous of a scarf.

I was still glaring at the scarf rack when Ella nudged my shoulder and pointed at the table.

"Is that…?" she started.

"A dragonette egg," confirmed the red-cloaked vendor with a nod, running her hand over the deep turquoise orb. It sparkled with flecks of gold in the sunlight. "It's due to hatch any day now."

"Oooh," Ella exhaled, delight shining in her dark eyes. "Oh, no, no, no!"

Of course, it was Haru back again. He hadn't even gotten the drinks before returning to be the ruiner of all things fun.

I spun to face him. "You have feelings about dragonette eggs?"

Haru pointed at the offending object. "That is not a dragonette egg. It's a ryū egg."

"Same same." The vendor laughed. "Small pet dragon."

"No, not the same!" Haru threw up his hands. "ryū make terrible pets! What are you thinking, selling one at the fair?"

"It's a ryū egg?" Ella gasped.

I hadn't thought it possible, but her smile grew even bigger.

"We'll take it," I said abruptly, wishing for nothing more than to see that expression continue.

"Tiernan." Ella glanced at Haru and then whispered to me. "I'm not staying. You can't buy me a ryū egg."

But while she protested, she turned back to the egg and touched it gently.

Honestly, what was I thinking? She was right. She wasn't going to stay. Somehow, in the enjoyment of the day and the play-acting, I had forgotten one important fact. She was leaving in three months.

The smart thing would be to listen to Haru and leave. Ella ran her hand over the turquoise egg again, reverently, and I knew with regret that I was not going to do the smart thing today.

Hopefully, her stepmother wouldn't mind a small dragon around. And, if it came to it, I was willing to adopt a new pet if it meant making Ella happy for the time she was here. She was risking her life to help me deceive the king. Surely, a baby dragon wasn't too much to give in return.

"If you want it, we'll figure something out," I said under my breath. "And you can't tell me you don't want it."

"My mama always told me stories about ryū." Ella looked wistful. "I never thought I'd ever see one."

"How much?" I asked the vendor.

"Forty gold pieces," said the cloaked fae.

Ella ran her hand over the egg, and I was tempted to just toss the money at the vendor, but that wasn't how things were done.

"Surely it's not worth more than twenty-five."

"You know the going rate for dragonette eggs, do you? Thirty-five."

I almost laughed at her sass, but I had a reputation to maintain, at least for a bit longer. "Is that how you speak to the crown prince?" I raised an eyebrow.

"Thirty-three." She paused. "Your *Royal* Highness."

"Thirty." I pointed to the rack that had caught Ella's eye. "And the blue scarf."

"Done." The cloaked woman wrapped the egg carefully in the silk scarf while I counted out the money.

The vendor slid the egg into a linen bag and handed it to Ella, who cradled it against her chest.

Haru made a noise of exasperation.

"I'm sure it will be fine," I said to Haru. I repeated it to myself.

"Oh yeah, fine," said Haru. "It will only run feral in the castle, steal everything shiny it lays its eyes on, build nests in the gardens, and that's merely the havoc it will cause before it's old enough to create portals. And that's for as long as it stays around. It will hatch and be gone within a week."

"Are you saying you think I will be a terrible dragon mother?" Ella glared at Haru. "I'll have you know, I'm very good with animals."

"No one makes a good ryū mother," said Haru. "It doesn't matter how lovely you are with small dogs. The ryū will leave you as soon as it's able, steal everything from the castle, and make its way back to Takamagahara."

I sighed. Well, at least if what he said was true, I wouldn't have to worry about what to do with it after Ella left. It sounded like these little dragons were very handy at taking care of themselves.

"Oh, it'll stay." Ella narrowed her eyes. "You wait and see."

"If you feel so strongly about it," I told Haru, "you can always take it back to the empress. I'm sure she'd be happy to see you."

It was a low blow, bringing up his mother, and I knew it.

Haru blanched and then pointed at me. "I'm not the one who should have to return this egg. This vendor is obviously—" He turned around as I did, only to find the cloaked woman gone. In her place sat a tiny man with green moss growing out of his ears.

"Where's the woman who was here a moment ago?" I asked.

"Oh, she was only watching the shop for a moment while I went to get some lunch," said the old man. "Lovely girl. Lovely. I don't know where she came from."

I looked at him in disbelief.

"Where did you get the ryū egg?" Haru demanded, his finger pointing at the little man.

"Ryū egg?" asked the man. "Why on earth would anyone want a ryū egg? They make terrible pets, you know."

Haru threw up his arms in exasperation.

I laughed. I knew I should be worried, but I couldn't help it. Clearly, we had been played. But I've always had excellent instincts about people, and something in me knew the woman in the red cloak may have been a trickster, but no real harm would come of it.

"We should probably go back to the palace." I smiled down at Ella. "And find a warm spot to stash that."

Ella nodded, carefully hugging the egg to her chest. "You know," she said. "I think you're right. Lughnasadh might be my favorite holiday too."

CHAPTER 11

ELLA

I SPUN SLOWLY, WATCHING MY EMERALD DRESS shimmer in the gilded full-length mirror. There was something about this fabric. I'd never felt anything like it before. I desperately wanted to ask Imogen and the little winged faerie who had helped me dress what it was made out of, but I was afraid that I was already supposed to know.

It had the structure of satin but none of the heaviness. Tiny little specks of something glistening like crystals were woven into the strands. I glanced at my bed where my sketchbook was shoved under the mattress and resolved to write down as many notes about the dress as I could when I got back from the dinner.

I swallowed.

The dinner.

I was trying not to think about it. I was going to have to meet Tiernan's father and the nobles of the Seelie Court. My chest tightened. I took a deep breath. Four in, hold it, four out. Just the way my doctor had told me to.

I patted the note in my pocket. I wasn't alone in this. When the merchant at the fair had handed me the egg, she had also slipped me a folded scrap of paper.

Hey, bestie, it's me! I know, I know, I probably look like some old fae lady. It's a magic cloak, pretty sweet, hey?

Miss Chloe accosted me right after I got back and sent me to meet an old friend who gave me this egg for you. She says this dragon can portal between worlds, so once it hatches, we should be able to pass messages. Hopefully. Apparently if you tie a note to its leg and picture my gorgeous face, it should deliver it to me. If it wants to. It's not a perfect solution, but either way, you get a baby dragon, so that's awesome! Fingers crossed!

XOXO

Amber

I really hoped their crazy plan would work because I needed all the help I could get to pull this off.

A sharp knock came from the door. All the little faeries who had helped me get ready jumped with a shriek.

"Is my lady ready for dinner?" Tiernan's most charming voice rang through the door to my suite of rooms. The faeries turned to me with wide eyes. They must not be used to dealing with the prince directly.

"Open the door. I'm sure he doesn't bite." I knelt beside the fireplace and uncovered the turquoise egg, resting my hand on the smooth shell. It felt warm but not too warm in its little nest of silk in a basket.

"The egg looks cozy." Tiernan squatted beside me. He had changed for dinner into a suit with a jacket made of dark blue velvet and gold embroidery. "That's good?"

"I suppose?" I said. "I don't know anything about ryū eggs."

He cleared his throat. "Um, clearly, neither do I, but Haru begrudgingly informed me that it should be kept warm and safe. And we should have some fish ready for when it hatches."

"Like…in the room?" I wasn't excited about sleeping with the smell of fish in here, but if that's what it took to make a baby dragon happy, then I could handle a little fishy smell.

"I'm sure we'll have time to get some from the kitchen. Haru says it should take a little while from the first crack, and I don't see any lines yet."

I nodded.

"Ella."

"Yes?"

"We can't sit and stare at the egg all night."

"Can't we?" I sighed. He was right. After all, this was what I had come for. To help Tiernan. To convince his father and the Seelie Court that he had found his bride.

I ran my hand over the hard shell one more time and covered it back up before standing. "Okay. Let's do this thing."

"Yes." Tiernan rose too, looking as reluctant as I felt. "Best to get it over with."

He held out his arm to me again, which I was almost used to by this point.

Down we went, through hallways and down a large staircase, toward the smell of food. We stopped at the entrance to a great hall with many long tables draped in white linen. Twinkling lanterns danced overhead, not held up by anything as far as I could see.

The walls were draped with garlands of wheat and flowers. The hall buzzed with chatter from the tall, stately fae milling around. Judging by their fine clothes, I assumed they were nobles. Smaller faeries, many with wings, horns, or tails, darted around with trays of food and pitchers of drink.

It occurred to me that I had yet to see any servants over waist-high or any nobles shorter than me. When we stepped into the hall, the entire crowd stilled. In the silence, a crash rang out. A wine glass dropped in shock.

The little brownie beside the door cleared his throat and proclaimed, "His Royal Highness Prince Tiernan and Lady Ella."

The whole crowd stared at us with wide eyes. Maybe if I held perfectly still, the floor would be a friend and swallow me up. Because it obviously wasn't the arrival of the prince that made the room come to a complete standstill.

They just hadn't expected him to bring a guest.

We entered the room, and the chatter picked up again at a higher volume than before.

Tiernan led me across the hall. The courtiers drifted to their seats, some shooting me curious looks and others sending icy glares. Everyone wondered, doubtless, who I was and why I was with the crown prince.

I, on the other hand, wondered who created all the fae fashion. The ladies wore full skirts and fitted bodices that wouldn't be out of place in a BBC drama, but they also had flowers in their hair that bloomed while I watched, skirts that changed color when they spun, or star-spangled bodices with lazily swirling nebulas.

The men, most of whom had long, flowing hair, were dressed just as elegantly, with vests embroidered in moving thread and jeweled buttons carved in the shape of little creatures.

In the corner, a string quartet played hauntingly beautiful music. I glanced their way and then did a double take.

"Are those humans?" Maybe Amber had been overre-acting. These were the first humans I'd seen and they didn't look like slaves or anything. The woman and the three men were all dressed in dark blue satin with perfectly styled hair.

"The musicians? Yes, but don't worry, they're glam-oured," said Tiernan.

"Glamoured?" Why would I be worried?

"They're only here to play. They likely don't even know we're in the room."

I looked at the musicians more carefully and felt a chill as I noticed their glazed eyes, staring dreamily into space as they played. One of the men had a bleeding finger but continued playing anyway.

I stumbled but made myself keep walking so that I didn't give myself away.

Tiernan sensed my distress and said in my ear, "Fi-achra's idea of entertainment, I'm afraid."

Did the prince have some compassion for the glam-oured musicians, or did he just not like having humans around? I couldn't be sure enough to trust him with my secret.

We stopped in front of the head table. Seated on a large, carved wooden chair in the center was a tall man with long black hair and a full beard, shot through with silver. He was crowned with twining gold branches and leaves.

His icy green eyes, the same shade as Tiernan's but with none of the warmth, narrowed. He also didn't look impressed. On the back of his chair perched an inky black raven who eyed me with as much affection as the king.

"Father." Tiernan gave a small, stiff bow. "May I present the Lady Ella. Ella, this is King Fiachra."

The king's eyes bored into me. I curtsied in a way that I hoped didn't look completely awkward.

"Your Majesty." I looked up.

As I straightened, I felt the weight of his gaze.

"Welcome to Rahivea, Ella of the Mist Court." King Fiachra leaned back, steepling his fingers. "So lovely of you to join us for Lughnasadh."

A shiver ran down my spine. I had brushed off Leith's warning, but this man seemed very capable of having me taken care of in a back alley if he decided I was a threat.

Tiernan looked unconcerned as he led me around the table, but his grip on my hand tightened. He sat two seats down from his father with me next to him.

"I've invited guests as well." The king gestured to the seats between us. "Tiernan, you remember the Aster Princess and her daughter Lynet."

I hadn't even noticed the other guests at the table. The younger fae seated beside Tiernan was slim and blonde and looked about my age, although I wasn't sure what that meant for faeries. Maybe she was three hundred and fifty. Her mother looked barely older, but her eyes had a calculating look to them. They both glared at me.

So great.

Hopefully we would get food soon so that I would have something to do with my hands. I hoped Tiernan appreciated this because it felt like the worst idea I'd had in a very long time. No amount of pretty dresses could be worth this truly terrible dinner.

The mother turned to me. "I thought I knew all the Seelie nobles. Where did you say you were from?" Her eyes flicked from my eyes to my hair. "I don't recognize your accent."

Where are you from? You don't look like you belong. Different realm but the same old questions. The story of my life as a mixed-race kid.

I took a steadying breath. "The Isle of Mist. My stepmother is the niece of the Mist Prince." Please don't ask more questions.

The Aster Princess sniffed. Her daughter leaned forward.

"Will you be here long?" she asked, pointedly. A group of small, winged faeries flew over, balancing a tray of soup bowls between them. Everyone took a bowl.

"Ella will be staying until the Samhain ball when we'll formally announce our betrothal." Tiernan reached for my hand and smiled at me. I batted my eyelashes at him.

Lynet glared daggers at us.

"And will you be here long?" My annoyance started to overwhelm my anxiety. I took a sip of the golden squash soup. "I do hope you'll stay for the wedding. Only three short months, after all."

"The Aster princesses are our guests until Samhain as well," stated Fiachra, feeding a morsel of bread to his raven. "When my son will make a choice that is best for the Seelie Kingdom."

Ouch. I'd be more offended if I wasn't a human orphan. He was right. I wasn't Seelie queen material. But Tiernan stiffened all the same.

"It's fine," I whispered to him, raising my eyebrows to remind him that it was just a game.

He nodded but didn't relax. This was about more than my honor, after all.

Lynet and her mother continued to glare daggers at me for the rest of the meal in between simpering at King Fiachra, who ignored me completely. I pretended to enjoy my meal. But in reality, I ate very little. My stomach was in knots.

I told myself that this must be the worst of it. For how could anything be more awkward than this dinner?

CHAPTER 12

ELLA

LATER THAT NIGHT, I LOUNGED ON ONE of the sofas in my suite of rooms. I had changed out of the shimmering green gown and into a soft blue set of pajamas with wide loose pants and a slip-style camisole top made of what felt like voile. I twisted my hair up on top of my head with a spare pencil stuck through it.

I calmed down from the evening's tension the way I always did. By sketching.

I had already gone through five pages. I had never seen anything like the clothes the faeries wore, and I didn't want to forget anything.

So I sketched neckline after neckline. I tried to remember the drape and flow of the skirts, the intricate embroidery at the hems. This would be my inspiration for my Parsons entrance portfolio. I could feel it.

I'd never be able to create a bodice out of rose petals, which was the only explanation for one of the dresses I had seen, but I'd never felt more full of inspiration.

My fingers were starting to cramp, and I had smudges of charcoal all over my hands, but I couldn't stop.

I had started with notes and sketches of remembered details, but now I was in my own world. I tried to imagine what sort of gowns I could create, sketching fashion models dressed in faerie-inspired clothing.

A knock at my door jolted me out of my fashion design trance.

"Come in," I called, wondering if it was another little faerie back to check on me. They had helped me out of my gown and into a perfumed bath in the plant-filled marble bathroom, but I had shooed them away when they tried to scrub my back for me.

But it wasn't the lower half of the door that opened. My visitor was much taller.

"Tiernan said you didn't eat much tonight." Saoirse set a tray with a metal dome on the coffee table.

I flipped the sketchbook shut and slid it under a throw pillow.

"What are you working on?" Saoirse asked. "Artist, are you?"

"Oh, it's nothing." I flexed my cramped fingers. Saoirse was the last person I'd show my sketchbook to. I could just see her jeering at the frilly designs. "What did you bring?"

She gave me a skeptical look but took the lid off the tray. It held fruit, some thinly sliced, chilled meat and cheeses, and some round flaky pastries that reminded me of croissants.

My stomach growled.

Saoirse laughed. "Sounds like Tiernan was right."

"I couldn't eat," I confessed. "It was too tense in that hall. Where were you, by the way? If you're a princess, aren't you supposed to be present for awkward royal dinners?"

Although, dressed as she was in worn leather leggings and a well-made but simple linen tunic, I looked more like a princess than she did.

She snorted. "That's not exactly how it works. I'm invited to all the royal events, sure, but I also find it easy to get out of them. I make people uncomfortable."

"That's hard to believe." I made myself a little sandwich from the tray, leaving the cheese. "You're so…sweet."

She picked up a slice of meat. "No one ever kept a fianna in line with sweetness."

"I suppose not."

We munched in awkward silence.

"Thanks for the food," I finally said.

"I suppose we can't have you starving." Saoirse took a vicious bite out of an apple.

"Look," I said. "I know you don't trust me, but I promise, I'm not a spy, and I won't get in the way of whatever you guys are plotting here." I sighed. "I just needed to get away, you know?"

"Your stepfamily is that bad?"

"When Kimberly married my dad, I thought it would be fun, having sisters and a new mom." I fiddled with a pink pear. "It had just been us for so long."

"I've never had a sister," said Saoirse. "How was it?"

"I never really found out. They were only ever nice to me when my dad was in the room. And then when he died…"

"They no longer needed to be nice?" guessed Saoirse.

"Let's just say that I certainly wasn't family." I sighed. "More like an unpaid servant."

"I'm surprised they let you come here for three months," said Saoirse.

"Hmmm."

"They do know you're here, right?" She tilted her head.

I was saved from having to decide on a response by the faintest crackling noise from the direction of the hearth.

"The egg!" I sprang up, my hair tumbling out of its messy knot. I ran across the room to the fireplace and uncovered the egg. Sure enough, a bit of the shell had cracked and pushed outward.

"That's the ryū egg Tiernan gave you?" Saoirse peered over my shoulder.

"It's hatching!" I said. "I don't know what to do!"

"Don't ask me," said Saoirse. "It's your egg."

I looked at her, wide-eyed.

"I'll go get Tiernan." She stood.

"Hurry!"

As another crack appeared on the pearlescent teal surface, I heard the door open and close as she ran out. Setting the basket on the coffee table, I climbed back onto the couch with the silk-wrapped egg. I unwrapped it and examined the shell. No more cracks appeared in it, but I could swear I felt something shift inside. Cradling the egg in my arms, I continued to stare at it.

Nothing.

How long did Haru say it would take? I just hoped it waited long enough for Tiernan to get here with the fish. It probably only took moments, but it felt like hours before he burst through the door, barefoot in loose pants and an untucked pale tunic.

He looked so unlike the perfectly groomed, charming prince I had come to expect that I stared at him in shock.

"I brought the fish!" He brandished a wooden bowl.

Oh right, the fish. I waved him over to the table, and he set the bowl down beside my tray of food before sitting next to me on the couch. "How close do you think it is?" he asked.

"I have no idea," I responded.

The egg gave a little wiggle and another small crack appeared.

"It can take up to an hour or two from when the first cracks appear." Tiernan ran his hand through his hair. "Oh good, Sersh brought you some food." He poked around at the tray.

"Help yourself," I said.

He grinned and loaded up meat and cheese onto a roll, which he polished off in a matter of seconds. I hadn't really paid attention at the dinner, but maybe he hadn't eaten much either. Or maybe he was just one of those boys who could never eat enough.

Tiernan wiped his hands clean on a napkin and leaned forward, looking at me intently. He reached for my cheek and paused for a moment.

I may have stopped breathing.

Then he rocked back again. "You have some smudges on your cheek."

I self-consciously remembered my charcoal-covered fingers and made myself not glance at my hidden sketch-book.

"Must be from the fireplace," he said.

I handed Tiernan the egg and rubbed the mark off with the back of my hand.

The egg wobbled, and he handed it back to me. It cracked again while in his hands, and we looked at each other wide-eyed.

It was happening.

CHAPTER 13

TIERNAN

THE RYŪ SHELL BROKE APART ON ELLA'S lap as the little dragon pushed the walls of its former home away. The baby ryū was about as long as my outstretched hand. It didn't have wings like a dragonette would, but rather a long, lithe, scaled body with a little tuft of dark fur at the end of its tail and hints of a little feathery mane around its ears and down the center of its back. Tiny golden horns sprouted in front of its ears.

The little dragon sat up, tilted its head, and chirped.

Ella looked at the baby ryū in wonder, her eyes wide as she gently ran her finger down its green, scaled back. It gave a little wiggle, and we both laughed.

I had a sudden sensation of hunger, even though I had just finished a sandwich.

Ella looked at me. "Did you feel that?"

I nodded and grabbed the bowl of fish, and Ella held out a small bite to the ryū. Immediately, the dragon snatched it from her fingers with tiny sharp teeth and then chirped again. I got an unmistakable image of more fish.

I pulled out a little bit, and the ryū scampered across Ella's knee and up my leg to snatch the morsel from my fingers.

"Did you know they could do that?" she asked.

I shook my head. "I've always heard the ryū are very intelligent, or at least that their larger cousins are wise and can communicate with the fae, but I didn't know this was how they did it."

The little dragon chirped again, and I fed it a piece of fish as it sat on my hands.

"What will you name it?" I asked.

"It's female, I think," she said. "Do you think so?"

"I do." Even though I didn't know how to tell the gender of baby dragons, the mental impression seemed, undeniably, feminine.

"I think I'll name her Kiyohime." Ella held out her hand, touching the tips of her fingers to mine. The little ryū scampered across our outstretched hands and up her arm.

"Hime is 'Princess' right?"

"You speak…Kami?" Ella looked up at me.

"I speak fifteen languages, but I'm only fluent in six of them."

Her eyes grew round, and I remembered how very young she was.

The little ryū turned around in her hand and then tucked itself in a little ball with its tail covering its nose.

"Well, I only know a handful of Kami words," she said. "Mama wanted me to fit in…here, so she never taught me. Mostly, she told me stories."

"Like the one about Kiyohime?"

"Right. Kiyohime." She yawned. "Mama used to tell me a story about a princess."

"Not a dragon?"

"Well, you see the princess had a sweetheart, a priest. He came to visit her often, and they had decided to marry. But then her suitor changed his mind. Kiyohime flew into such a rage at his changeable nature that she turned into a massive dragon. As one does."

"And then what? Did she eat him?"

"The priest took cover under a bell, and she let out a mighty spout of flame that melted the bell, killing him. It's a bit gruesome."

"Well, that's love for you," I said.

"I'm not sure that's the moral of the story." Ella ran a finger down the sleeping ryū's back and Kiyohime shivered.

"People always speak of love as if it's the most magical thing you can experience. But it does seem, just as often, to turn someone into a monster." Like my father.

Ella looked like she wanted to argue further—when you're young, it's easy to be a firm believer in the power of love—but a giant yawn interrupted whatever she was about to say.

It had been a long day, even for me, but Ella looked about to fall asleep sitting up. I gently picked the egg shards out of her lap and set them on the table. Then I slipped the little ryū out of her hands and tucked her back into the bed of silk scarves in the basket.

"I'm sorry." Ella yawned again. "I'm just so sleepy."

"Into bed with you." I helped her up, and she leaned on me as we found her bed. I pulled back the covers, and she slid under the blanket.

"Here you are." I tucked the basket with the sleeping ryū into the crook of her arm.

She smiled sleepily. "Thank you," she murmured as she closed her eyes.

I looked down at her, reaching to brush a strand of hair off her face, but I stopped myself and clenched my fist at my side instead. Gathering up the fish and eggshells, I left quietly so as not to disturb the sleeping princesses.

Saoirse leaned against the wall in the corridor, facing the doorway.

"Are you on guard duty now?" I asked her with a quirk of my eyebrow.

"It was supposed to be Fergus, but I lured him off with a tale of a rare bird. I wanted to know how the little dragon hatched."

I glanced back at the closed door. "It's a girl," I said with a laugh.

"Oh, boy." Saoirse studied my face. "You've got it bad."

"I've got what bad?" I handed her the bowl and started walking.

She wiggled her eyebrows back at me.

"She's only helping me out for a bit. That's all," I said.

"If you say so." Saoirse handed the bowl back to me. "But I take back my objections. She's a sweet girl. I still think she might be hiding something, but her heart seems to be in the right place."

"It doesn't matter if she's sweet," I said. "She's going home in three months."

"If she didn't, would it really be the worst thing to let yourself love someone?"

The story of Kiyohime might be just a tale, but my father was very real. The light had never reached his eyes since the death of my mother. Only cruelty.

The Seelie Kingdom wouldn't survive another tyrant.

"It might be," I said, finally. "It might just be the worst thing in the world."

CHAPTER 14

ELLA

I WOKE WITH A START.

Small golden eyes were staring into mine. A small nose pressed against the bridge of mine, and I got the distinct and strong impression of hungry.

I blinked.

The golden eyes blinked.

Hungry.

"Okay, little Kiyo. Let's see what we can find for you to eat."

I sat up with a yawn. Early morning light filtered through the sheer curtains and my balcony. Morning birds chirped outside my window. I still felt tired from yester-day's adventures. Hopefully, the fae knew about caffeine.

I found a lightweight robe of floral voile in the wardrobe and tied it on over my pajamas, tucking the little dragon into a pocket as I walked to the suite's living room. Kiyo poked her little head out of the top and chirped.

"I know," I said. "Hungry."

I eyed the bell by the door.

"So if I ring this, what do you think will happen?"

Kiyo looked at me expectantly.

"Right, I guess we'll find out together."

I rang the bell, and moments later, a knock sounded at the door. I opened it to find Imogen waiting next to a low cart with a metal dome and a teapot on it.

"Breakfast, miss?" She pushed the cart into the room, and I looked at her in wonder. She must have been waiting with the tray ready to go.

"Thank you," I told the little brownie. "That was fast!"

Kiyo scampered down my arm and leapt lightly onto the cart, causing the maid to shriek, which then caused Kiyo to jump backward and tumble off the back of the cart.

I smothered a laugh and picked up the little dragon.

"This is Kiyohime." I held Kiyo out to the brownie, who had a hand over her heart.

"Of course, miss," she said.

"I don't suppose there's any fish in this morning's breakfast?" I asked.

Thankfully, Tiernan had taken the bowl of fish with him last night. Because even if Kiyo might have been happy to smell it before breakfast, I was grateful not to wake up to it.

"Smoked trout, miss," said the brownie. "Will you be having your breakfast at the table or out on the balcony? It's a beautiful morning."

What would I be doing at home right now? Doubtless, making multiple egg white omelets for my stepsisters and stepmother, which they would eat half of with some lemon water, complaining the whole time. And then I'd have dishes.

"The balcony would be lovely," I said.

The brownie set up the meal outside at the little table amongst the millions of plants on the balcony. The morning sun touched the green city below with gold.

"If that's everything, miss, I'll be off to fetch your dress for the day." Imogen curtsied.

"This is perfect, thank you, Imogen!"

Imogen blushed and pushed the cart out. Kiyo scampered down my arm onto the table. I lifted the dome covering the tray and the little dragon pounced.

"Whoa, whoa!" I picked her up. "Let's see what's in here."

Hungry, said Kiyo.

"I know, I know. Okay, so…" I looked at the spread. Definitely more than one human could eat. We'd have to see how much the dragon would polish off. There was a little dish of smoked fish as Imogen had said, rolls sprinkled with seeds, butter and soft cheese, two small blue-spotted eggs, sliced fruit that looked like an orange, but the slices were shaped like stars, and a golden pastry smelling of cinnamon and chocolate. The steaming tea pot looked promising.

Kiyo wriggled free of my grip and pounced on the chocolate pastry.

"Excuse me," I said. "I have it on good authority that you're a carnivore."

The little dragon didn't listen. She ripped off a piece of pastry and ate it in a blink, little tail swishing in something between a wag and a cat flick. A wave of satisfaction rolled off her.

"Yes, I'm sure it is delicious." I picked her off the treat and set it on the far side of the table. "But you can't start with dessert, you know."

Kiyo chirped at me.

"You need some protein." I made a little pile of fish and added some orange before setting the dragon down in front of it.

She began devouring the pile. I laughed and set to work on my own breakfast.

The smoked fish was salty and delicious, and the star-shaped oranges tasted like normal oranges but better. I poured myself a cup from the teapot, happy to find that it smelled like black tea. Chai was my poison of choice, but I happily accepted liquid caffeine in any form.

When we had both eaten a good amount, I tore off the section of the pastry that Kiyo had already chewed on and set in front of her while I finished the rest of it.

"You're right," I told her. "It is good." I licked my fingers clean. "So, little friend, what are we going to do today?"

Kiyo sat up on her haunches and blinked. I got an impression of red hair and freckles. A little glimmer of childlike love. Did she think Tiernan was her daddy? What did that make me? She blinked at me.

"I don't know where he is. Off doing prince stuff, I guess. I don't have any claim on his time, after all. Not really." I tried to keep my voice light, but it occurred to me that I really didn't know when I would see him next. I shook my head. It didn't matter. I had a mission, after all.

A little rap sounded at the door. Imogen was back again with my dress for the day.

"We," I told the little dragon, "are going to do some stalking."

The formal gardens behind the palace were the perfect place to people watch.

I spent the morning lurking in bushes with my small green accomplice and sketching noble fae ladies and gentlemen. My unwitting subjects strolled the paths and sat by the pond, and while their style was very interesting—and entirely different from both the festival and the formal dinner—I also sketched the many, many kinds of smaller faeries who trimmed hedges and fed fish.

Once again, I noticed that none of the servants were my height. The *Tuatha Dé Danann,* evidently, did not weed flower beds.

"Ella!" Tiernan strode along the path, looking as princely as ever in a crisp suit of pale blue silk. "My love!"

I stashed my sketchbook and charcoals into my bag and stepped out to meet my fake fae boyfriend on the path.

"There you are, my golden sunbeam." The prince held out his hands to me as he approached. A male brownie carrying a large wicker basket followed a few paces behind.

I restrained myself from rolling my eyes at his ridiculous compliment. Apparently, the Tiernan from last night was gone, and I was stuck with Prince Charming. I settled for a sweet smile. "Good morning."

"My darling dewdrop, what were you doing in the shrubbery?" Tiernan grasped my hands in his.

"Oh, you know…" I tried to think of a good reason to be skulking around behind a bush. "Just admiring the…snails? What's in the basket?"

"I thought you might be hungry."

"How thoughtful." And I was, honestly, touched for a moment before he continued in a low voice.

"You can't hide all morning if we're supposed to be courting," he said under his breath, tucking my hand into the crook of his arm and escorting me along the path.

Ah, yes, must keep up appearances. "Well, my sweet sticky bun," I said.

He narrowed his eyes at me for a moment before his charming smile returned.

"I was out enjoying the fresh air. A picnic sounds lovely. Oh, I'm sorry." I had gotten charcoal smudges on his pale blue jacket.

"How are you always covered in soot?" he murmured, examining my fingertips. "I'll have to start calling you Cinder Ella at this rate." He ran his thumb along my finger, and I realized we had both stopped walking.

He cleared his throat. "Shall we sit by the pond?"

I nodded, giving myself a little shake.

We strolled down the flower-lined path, the little brownie trailing behind. It looked like a big basket for someone knee high, but Tiernan didn't so much as glance back.

When we reached the pond, we admired the silvery fish with their long, graceful fins. Meanwhile, the brownie spread out a picnic blanket and opened the basket.

"That will be all," said Tiernan, and the brownie bowed and left.

"Thank you!" I called after him. Both the brownie and the prince looked at me in shock. "Didn't your parents teach you to say *thank you*?" I glared at Tiernan, arranging my skirts as I sat on the blanket.

"No, Fiachra did not teach me to thank the help for doing their jobs." Tiernan poked through the basket, lounging on the blanket like the spoiled prince he obviously was. "Now, what have we got in here? Ooh, smoked pheasant sandwiches, I believe."

He handed me a little bundle wrapped in waxed linen and tied with a golden ribbon. "Iced raspberry tea and lavender honey cookies."

At the word cookie, I felt a stirring in my shoulder bag as Kiyo squirmed her way out, scampered across the blanket and disappeared into the picnic basket in the blink of an eye.

"Good morning to you," laughed Tiernan. I caught a glimpse of that half smile again, the real one.

I realized I was staring and focused on unwrapping my sandwich. It had some sort of soft cheese on it. I debated whether it would be more rude to pick apart my sandwich or spend the afternoon having gas.

No cheese.

"You don't like camembert?" asked Tiernan, halfway through his own sandwich.

"I don't eat dairy." I didn't elaborate. I was not discussing lactose intolerance with a fae prince.

He shrugged and polished off his sandwich before pouring us each a glass of iced tea. I fed my cheese to Kiyo, and we ate the cookies Kiyo had left us while watching fish and enjoying the late summer sun.

I was starting to relax when the last people I wanted to see appeared in the garden. Lynet and her mother were headed our way, shaded by a silk canopy held by tiny winged faeries overhead.

"Maybe they won't notice us," I said under my breath.

"Who?" Tiernan turned to look. "Ah. I'm afraid we won't be so lucky."

Sure enough, the ladies made a beeline for our picnic blanket.

"Your Highness." The Aster Princess and her daughter curtsied deeply.

Tiernan nodded at them but didn't get up, so I didn't bother to either.

"So fortunate we ran into you," continued the princess.

I snorted. She ignored me.

"I was hoping you might show Lynet the gardens. She was only a little thing last time we were here." The princess deigned to glance at me. "I'm close friends with the king, you know."

Apparently not that close, if they hadn't been here in years, but what did I know?

"Alas, we are busy." Tiernan held up his glass of tea. "Aren't we, sugar plum?"

I choked on my tea in an unladylike fashion.

"She would, of course, be welcome to join us," said the older princess while Lynet bared her teeth at me.

Didn't fae princesses practice smiling? Hers needed some work.

"Another time," said Tiernan, smoothly.

"Of course, Your Highness." The Aster Princess smiled stiffly and dragged her glaring daughter back down the path, the little faeries flying fast to keep up with them.

"You know, I don't think she likes me," I said, sadly.

"Very true," Tiernan fed his last bite of cookie to Kiyo. "I, on the other hand, will be your devoted servant—"

"You aren't already? I thought this was true love."

"Naturally, but even more devoted, if you'll help me dodge them for the rest of the afternoon."

"I do need to do something, actually."

"Yes, my pearl?"

"Please stop that," I finished my drink and handed him the glass to put away. "I need to make a call."

CHAPTER 15

ELLA

WE PACKED THE DISHES AND SCRAPS OF food back into the picnic basket, which Tiernan handed off to another blue-dressed brownie in the hall. I still marveled at a world in which there were no dishes to do.

Kiyo was back in my bag making satisfied noises as she munched on a leftover scone. I was going to have to start cleaning out my bag every day at this rate.

Tiernan led me to the same wing as my rooms were in, but we took a different staircase. A tall fae man stood guard at the doorway, a spear in his hand. He nodded to Tiernan as we passed.

The corridor was lush with moss underfoot, like my area, but darker with a jungle of plants arching overhead. Flickering lanterns of gold and glass added to the light from occasional windows.

I stopped and looked at a lantern more carefully. Inside was a tiny person made of light, like the one I had seen at the revel. This one lay on their side, curled up in a ball. Tiernan waited beside me, saying nothing, just watching me.

I ran to the next lantern. It too had a tiny imprisoned faerie, this one raging against the glass. Whatever cries they could have made were muffled by the glass.

I whirled on Tiernan. "Why are they trapped like this?"

"They're sheerie," he said, as if that explained it.

"I know what they are!"

"Tricksters. You never know when one might lead a traveler off to their doom."

"And have any of these sheerie led travelers to their dooms?" I asked.

"Who can say?" said Tiernan. "They are captured around marshes by the order of the king. To keep the way safe."

"What?" I said. "He catches tiny people and puts them in lanterns?"

We passed yet another lantern. This sheerie sat with a listless stillness.

"Your uncle doesn't keep sheerie lights?" Tiernan cocked his head. "Many of the more traditional princes do. Come on. We have to get moving if we're going to make your date with your stepmother."

He opened the door to a suite of rooms, similar in size to mine but furnished in rich wood and green velvet.

Spears, swords, and daggers hung on display over a fireplace. A suit of chainmail and one of leather armor hung on stands in one corner.

"These are your rooms?" I hesitated at the door.

"Did you want to ask the king to use his mirror? In here." Tiernan opened a door.

I took a step in while looking overhead at lanterns which glowed with a steady, yellow light.

"No imprisoned sheerie for you?" I didn't bother to keep the bitterness out of my tone.

"Not on Tuesdays."

I looked back one more time at the lantern prisons in the hallway. Maybe I could find a way to accidentally let them out later.

"Ella?"

"Coming!" I shut the door behind me and followed Tiernan across the sitting room to his study. A large desk took up much of the room. Two extra chairs stood in front of it. For Saoirse and Declan, I guessed.

The wall behind the desk was covered with built-in bookcases, although most of what was on it appeared to be tightly wound scrolls and notebooks with handwritten spines.

The wall across from the window had a map of a large island. I went up to examine it closer. It was hand drawn and beautifully done. This must be Tír na nÓg.

There were golden stars dotted across it, like shining constellations. I touched one.

"The gates of course," murmured Tiernan by my ear.

I shivered. I hadn't heard him behind me.

Near the bottom of the map, the cartographer had drawn a crown. Probably Rahivea. Far north, about halfway up the continent on the east, sat an island surrounded by swirling lines. The note below it read: The Isle of Mist.

"Homesick?" Tiernan touched the island.

"Nope." I shook my head. "There's so much to see here."

He gave me a crooked smile. Right answer.

"Here's the mirror." Tiernan gestured to a shallow golden bowl held up by the branches of a tree, also made of gold. It reminded me of the Glass Gate, and I wondered if Miss Chloe had made this one as well.

Tiernan hovered his hand over the surface of the water, not quite touching it. "Have you used a mirror before?"

I shook my head, and he didn't seem surprised. This was a precious enchanted object. It made sense that a girl kept around for doing drudge work wouldn't have spent a lot of time with one. After all, I only got a new phone if my stepsisters gave me a used one.

"All you have to do is picture the person you intend to talk to firmly in your mind. If their mirror is also active, it will show them. So, if your stepmother has activated her mirror, you should be ready to go."

"Thank you," I said. "Do you mind if I have a little privacy?"

"Of course not." Tiernan gathered up a pen and a few papers from the desk. "I'll just be outside. Don't worry, my study is spelled to keep eavesdroppers from listening in."

I would have to trust him on that one, but it would make sense if this was where he ran his army from.

When the door shut, I closed my eyes and thought of Amber's face. Hopefully this would work. I needed some answers.

The water rippled even though I hadn't touched it. When the ripples cleared, Amber peered through the re-flection, still in the clothes she had been wearing when she left me, eating a cookie. She squealed.

"Ella! How's castle life? How long has it been for you?"

"About a day and a half."

"And things are going okay so far?" She took a bite of her cookie.

"I think so," I said.

Amber leaned closer to the water's surface. "Is the castle huge? Have you kissed Prince McHottie yet?"

"I don't think you understand what fake dating means. We're not kissing."

"How are you going to convince anybody it's true love without even so much as a peck?"

"Moving on! Yes, the castle is pretty amazing. I never do any dishes. Magical dresses appear every evening. But they also keep tiny glowing faeries locked in lanterns, so not all of it is cool."

"That's terrible! Isobel says a lot of the more traditional Seelie nobles don't view the small folk as people, really."

"Speaking of which, there are like a million kinds of fae here, and I don't know what most of them are called. I've been trying to figure it out, but maybe you can help."

I reached for my sketchbook, disturbing a sleeping Kiyo in the process. She popped out and crawled up onto my shoulder, peering down into the water. She chirped happily upon seeing Amber and leapt off my shoulder toward the water.

I flinched, expecting a splash. Instead, she disappeared with a pop before reappearing on Amber's shoulder. Amber yelped. The little dragon peered down at me and chirped in delight but didn't reenact her Olympic diving trick. Instead, she scampered down my friend's arm and took a bite out of her cookie.

"Amber, this is Kiyo."

Amber stroked the back of the dragon and giggled as Kiyo squirmed happily.

"It's nice to meet you, Kiyo. Out of the shell, I mean."

"Okay." I held the sketchbook up to Amber, showing her the sketch of Imogen. "I think I figured out that all the knee-high ones with the patchy brown complexions are brownies."

"That's right," Amber said. "They're usually, like, household servants and things."

"Okay. And this one?" I pointed out a sketch of a tiny winged faerie.

"Piskie," said Amber.

"Like pixies?"

"Yeah, pretty much. Although, I don't know what they'd do with Tinkerbell."

I flipped to the page where I had drawn the street-food vendor with her goat's feet.

"That one I don't know." Amber turned her head. "Miss Chloe?"

Amber sidestepped, and the face of the curly-haired librarian appeared.

Miss Chloe peered through her gold-framed glasses at the sketchbook. "She's a glaistig."

"Nice," I said. "And this one?" I held up a sketch of a man with whorled bark-like skin and leaves for hair.

"A draoi," said the librarian.

"Okay, thank you. That helps. Although, I'm sure there are a whole bunch more that I haven't had a chance to draw."

"Well, you can always send Kiyo with a little drawing," said Miss Chloe. "We'll do our best to decipher it."

"I hope I can remember them all." I slipped my sketchbook back into my bag.

"Any other questions?" asked Miss Chloe.

"I don't think so," I said. "You're kind of a big deal over here, you know. Do you miss it?"

Miss Chloe tapped her chin. "Kind of a big deal. I suppose that's one way to put it. I do miss my cottage. I hope my roses have managed in my absence. Of course, I'd love to take a more active role in caring for my god-children, but the human world does have its advantages."

"Can't go back to Faerie until you finish watching *Loki*, is that it?" teased Amber.

"Impudent child."

"So if Moriath suddenly fell off a cliff and you had two more episodes of *Loki* to go, you would up and return to Faerie without knowing how the season ended?"

"Well." Miss Chloe looked thoughtful. "I mean, I'd probably finish the season. But that's neither here nor there. Moriath is very sure-footed."

"I should go." I looked at the door. "Tiernan thinks I'm talking to my stepmother, and really, there's only so much I would have to say to her."

I fished out a bit of chocolate I had hidden in my pocket and waved it in front of the mirror. "Come on, Kiyo."

The ryū disappeared off Amber's shoulder and reappeared on my arm with astonishing speed. Bye bye, chocolate.

"So, that's why she loves you so much." Amber laughed.

"Feed her treats and she'll be yours forever."

Kiyo climbed back into my satchel looking for crumbs.

"If you need to talk to us again," said Miss Chloe, "send a note with Kiyo, and we'll be here for you, night or day."

"Thank you." I felt stronger knowing I had friends at my back. "I'll talk to you later. Wait, how do I turn this thing off anyway?"

Miss Chloe told me the words to say. Once I repeated them, the water reflected my own face back at me again. I poked my head out the door.

"How was your talk?" Tiernan glanced up from his notebook.

"Good, thank you. For letting me use your mirror, I mean, and intruding on your space like this."

"Well, after all." Tiernan winked. "You're my true love."

CHAPTER 16

ELLA

I MANAGED TO GO A FULL WEEK without seeing King Fiachra. I spent my days sketching and exploring the castle grounds, and I took my meals with Tiernan or in my room.

But it seemed my good luck had run out. I'd been informed that we were dining with the king tonight, and my anxiety was on overdrive.

Imogen braided my hair into an elaborate crown. Every now and then, she muttered something under her breath, causing the back of my neck to tingle.

Was she working magic on me? Whatever she was doing, my silky slippery strands of black hair were actually staying where she wanted them, without any pins or goop that I could see. I was curious but afraid that asking would reveal too much. Probably all noble fae ladies had magic hairdressers.

"Where is that dress?" she muttered, leaning over and pulling the bell one more time.

Imogen brushed a poof of powder across my cheeks. That gave my face not only a healthy glow but also a bit of shimmer. Amber would approve.

"Would you like earrings to match the necklace?" She fastened a chain of dainty golden leaves around my neck.

"No, thank you!" I resisted the urge to touch the tips of my glamoured ears.

I was saved from further explanation when the lower half of the door burst open. A knee-high faerie with pale blue skin scurried into the room, arms full of pink chiffon.

"About time," sniffed the brownie. "Quickly now!"

I slipped out my robe, and the two of them helped me into the dress. It was less grand than the dress I had worn to the Lughnasadh feast, with a fitted bodice and flowing skirt in an airy blush silk. A belt of golden leaves matching my necklace nipped in the waist, and tiny gold beads were scattered down the skirt. I ran my hands down the tiny pleats of the bodice, marveling at the perfect fit. How had these faeries measured me?

The blue faerie that had brought the dress turned to go.

"Wait," I said. "Would it be possible for me to meet the faerie who made this dress?"

"I'm so sorry it was late," she stammered. "We don't have a selection to fit your measurements yet. It's no excuse, I know, but we did have to make this dress today."

They had made it in a day? A dress like this would take me at least two weeks. With a sewing machine.

"I'm not upset at all. I wanted to thank her, and I'm just…I'm interested. I enjoy clothes," I finished lamely.

The blue faerie looked at me incredulously. "I would have to…your ladyship really wants to go downstairs to the seamstress quarters?"

"Yes," I said, firmly.

"Downstairs," repeated the faerie.

Downstairs where all the servants were waist high. Was I going to end up crawling? I fingered the tiny perfect stitches. It would be worth it even if I had to crawl.

"I'll have to ask Grainne's permission. It's very unorthodox."

"I understand," I said. "Let me know."

With another puzzled look, she scampered out.

I took one last glance in the mirror. I smiled. I would wear this dress like armor. The Seelie King would not catch me unprepared. Not tonight.

King Fiachra seemed to have decided to ignore me rather than interrogate me tonight. Instead, he spent the entire dinner drilling Tiernan about the Fianna.

I tuned them out. It was a lot of talk about who was on patrol, where, and with whom, and who had trouble with their subordinates.

As far as I could tell, nobody was at war with anybody or anything like that. So, I spent the dinner sneaking tidbits of food to Kiyo, who was curled up on my lap. We had finally gotten to the dessert course, and she pleaded into my thoughts to give her all my chocolate trifle. I couldn't imagine the mess she would make if I did.

I feared she had already stained my skirt with the berries that had topped the salad. Hopefully, no one would notice.

Tiernan explained to his father his plans for going on patrol next week.

I fingered the skirt of today's dress and tried to commit the beading to memory. It seemed that when I finished wearing a dress, it got whisked away never to be seen again. Really, I would have liked a good hour with each one. I definitely needed that trip to the seamstress.

"And Ella will stay here, I assume," said the king.

"She's coming with us." Tiernan settled his arm across the back of my chair.

"What?" I jerked my head up, making Kiyo squawk and hide in my bag.

"Naturally, you'll want to accompany me on patrol." Tiernan tapped his fingers on the table. "We don't want to be separated for an entire month of patrol and then another month while the fianna is stationed at Port Delfare."

I swallowed. "Are you patrolling on horses?" Not that I knew how to ride a horse, but it sounded nicer than hiking.

"No horses for this patrol. We'll be on foot."

"And sleeping at inns?" Please tell me there are inns.

"Tents, I'm afraid."

I looked from Tiernan to his father, wondering if they were joking with me. I had signed up for a princess-in-a-castle holiday, not camping, or even worse, backpacking.

"I'm good," I said. "I'll wait here."

"You won't miss me?" Tiernan raised an eyebrow.

"Well. Of course." I wished I could follow my little dragon into my bag to hide. "I'm just not, you know, very outdoorsy. I'll be fine here! Getting to know the castle-…and…planning the wedding. I'll meet you at Port Delfare." I paused. "There are real beds at Port Delfare…right?"

"How exceedingly well-matched you are," drawled the king.

Tiernan looked at me intently. I knew I should agree to make this look convincing, but honestly. Camping. For a month. Not only were there sure to be some sort of monstrous faerie mosquitoes out there, that was four weeks I wouldn't be able to spend working on my portfolio.

I batted my eyelashes at him. He glared back and then forced his face back into what I liked to call his Prince Charming smile.

"I would truly love to have you come," he said. "You could meet the rest of the fianna, and I'd like to keep you close." He looked at me meaningfully.

He must be worried about leaving me behind. Huh. Well, Fiachra obviously didn't like me, but he also hadn't done anything to make me afraid of him.

I smiled back at Tiernan. "I couldn't possibly. I have things to work on for the wedding, after all." Time to make my exit. "Thank you so much for dinner. It was delicious. As always, I mean. Thank the cooks?" I rose from my chair. "I'll see you all in the morning…so tired." I yawned broadly.

"My son, surely you won't let this minor disagreement come between you two."

"Of course not," Tiernan ground out.

"At least kiss your sweetheart goodnight before she goes. I would hate to see you part in anger."

"I'll walk you back to your room," offered Tiernan, rising from the table.

"No, you can say goodnight to her here." Fiachra took a sip of his wine. "I have more to discuss with you tonight."

Tiernan walked over, and I plastered what I hoped was a loving smile on my face. There was clearly no getting out of this. My chest squeezed, and I felt my breath coming in rather short. Honestly, my reaction seemed a bit excessive for a pretend kiss, but it's not like I had any experience with faking a romance. I had always made the costumes for school plays. I was never a Juliet.

"Good night, Ella." Tiernan carefully placed his hands on my waist. I felt the heat of them through my dress.

My breath snagged.

The prince pressed his lips against mine. Just for a moment. Only long enough for a lover's good night. But the warmth of it, the pressure of his lips on mine, remained as I turned to leave.

I fled back to my rooms. The tightness in my chest, the pounding of my heart only increased, making me hope, desperately, that this game was one I could win.

Rule number one. Don't fall in love. I had thought it would be easy.

CHAPTER 17

ELLA

THREE DAYS LATER, I WOKE TO SOMETHING wriggling next to my head.

Kiyohime.

"Just a minute. I'll ring for some breakfast," I said, groggily. The little dragon gave a satisfied chirp. She didn't sound hungry like the morning before. I opened my eyes. The ryū sat proudly on top of a pile of shiny objects.

A necklace, a belt, a fork, a couple of coins. Oh dear. In her forelegs, she held what appeared to be the remains of a raspberry tart. What? I sat up. Raspberry jam was smeared across the crisp white pillowcase. I felt my hair. Sticky. Ugh.

"You're not gonna make any friends with the staff this way," I told the dragon. She tilted her head and took another bite of raspberry tart. "I think that's enough sweets before breakfast," I scolded her, reaching for the tart.

Before I could grab it, the dragon jumped into the air and disappeared in front of my nose. With a popping noise, she reappeared on the bedside table, eating the raspberry tart. So that explained how the little magpie had acquired her stash.

"You've really mastered those portals, haven't you?"

I had been hoping that Haru was exaggerating about how mischievous ryū were. Apparently not. Kiyo chirped smugly and polished off the rest of the tart before proceeding to lick her little claws clean.

"Well, at least that should tide you over long enough for me to have a bath. I think you got jam in my hair."

First, I hid the stash of treasures in my bag. I'd have to ask Tiernan how to return them. After all, he was the ryū daddy.

I bathed quickly, worried Kiyo would get into more trouble. She just lounged happily on the edge of the tub, her little belly round with the raspberry tart.

I changed into one of the simple day dresses that had been added to my wardrobe. The pale green skirt swished around my ankles.

"Well." I looked at the little dragon. "You might have scavenged breakfast, but I'm hungry."

I rang the bell by the door, and Imogen appeared shortly with the breakfast cart.

"You little scamp." The brownie waggled a finger at Kiyo. "Scared the kitchen staff half to death this morning, popping about." She said it almost fondly. Perhaps she'd gotten over her own fright of the little dragon.

"Kiyo!" I scolded the dragon, who looked utterly unrepentant.

"The sewing mistress has agreed to let you visit." Imogen took the dome off the food cart. "Whenever you're done with your breakfast, that is."

I ran to my bed, pulled out my sketchbook, threw it in my shoulder bag, and then smeared some jam on a roll and tucked a piece of fruit into my bag. "Ready!"

"You really are serious about this."

"I wouldn't have asked if I wasn't." I scooped up Kiyo, who had already polished off the smoked fish. I was going to have to start ordering more fish if I wanted to eat any. I tucked her into my bag. "Don't eat my orange."

She sent me a feeling of satisfaction. She was quite full, thank you. She was not going to be stealing my orange. She proceeded to investigate my bag and chirped happily when she found her stash of treasures.

I peeked out the door. A young fae named Jac had been on guard duty, but he must have run off to the bathroom or something. Perfect. Maybe it was silly, but I didn't want anyone reporting back to Tiernan, or even worse, Saoirse, about my obsession with fashion.

Imogen led me down the hall and past the tall, grand staircase I usually used. She pressed her hand on a lever and a section of the wall slid out to reveal another set of stairs. This explained why I had seen so few servants in the hallways. I ducked my head through the door. I had to bend over a bit as we went down the stairs but, happily, did not need to crawl.

After a couple of twists and turns, I realized I was not going to escape the network of passageways within the palace walls without help. Unless I learned Kiyo's trick of portal jumping. At last, Imogen opened another door. I ducked through after her into a vast open room.

"Grainne!" called the brownie from the doorway. "Lady Ella is here." She turned to me. "I beg your pardon, miss, but I have to leave you here. I have much to do this morning. Like every morning."

"Of course." I waved her off, but I barely heard her, I was so entranced by the sight before me.

One wall was entirely windows, letting in the morning light through diamond-paned glass. Another held floor-to-ceiling shelves stacked with bolts of fabric, rolls of trim, and glittering jewels.

I tucked the little dragon further down into my bag in hopes that I wouldn't find my room full of jeweled trim when I returned.

Fae of all kinds worked at tables the perfect heights for them, and scattered throughout the workroom were dress forms of more sizes and shapes than I had imagined possible.

"You wanted to see me?" said a voice by my ear.

I turned, expecting to see someone my height, but a piskie hovered beside me. She was about the height of my hand, with wings that reminded me of a butterfly's in blue, purple, and black. Her greenish-blonde hair was pulled back in a severe bun and large round glasses perched on her nose.

"Was there something the matter with your last dress? Our time-frame was rather rushed. We can't be expected to work miracles, you know."

"The dress was amazing," I told the little piskie. "It was, in fact, just what I needed."

Grainne's brow remained furrowed, but her eyes softened a little. "Well, of course. That's our job. If you don't mind, I do have to get back to work."

But I was not ready to leave. I had just stepped into the most intriguing place I had found yet in my adventures, and I was not about to be dismissed.

"Do you mind if I look around?" I pleaded.

"What could possibly interest a *Tuatha Dé Danann* in the sewing room?"

"Please?" I wished I had thought more about my back story. I couldn't tell her I made bridal dresses in Pilot Bay and was trying to get into Parsons.

Grainne examined me, hovering in front of my face with her hands on her hips. Then she nodded.

"Well, I suppose we can take a few moments to show you around." She turned and bellowed to the room in a voice that seemed much too loud for such a small creature. More magic? "I expect to see everyone working at full speed. No gawking. Don't make me look bad in front of the nobility."

There was a flurry of motion as everyone in the room suddenly busied themselves with their tasks.

"What would you like to see?" She turned back to me.

"Everything," I breathed.

She gave me a sharp look.

"The fabric?"

Grainne flew off. Was that the right choice? Wrong choice? I scampered after her.

CHAPTER 18

ELLA

AS YOU CAN SEE," SHE GESTURED WITH her arm, "this is where we store the fabric. The most common fabrics start here, and they progressively get more precious as you go down the aisle."

I looked at all the neatly stacked bolts of material. It was like a fabric warehouse on steroids. Ladders of various sizes leaned up against the shelves. On the top were the large bolts, and they got smaller as I went down. I would guess they saved the scraps from larger garments to make smaller garments. Very efficient.

I examined what felt like lightweight wool. Each bolt had a tag hanging off the end and, of course, they were arranged not only by fabric type but by color within the sections. The left section was mostly browns, greens, and blues. I recognized the gardener's uniform fabric amongst the linen.

I ran my hand lightly over the bolts as we walked. Some fabrics I recognized. Cotton, linen, wool. As we got into the finer fabrics there was silk, both fine and raw, like I would expect, but there were also other things. *Spider silk*, read one tag attached to a fine gauze spun through with threads with the tiniest bit of stretch to them. *Jackalope Angora* read another tag.

Kiyo popped her head out of my bag and crawled down my arm to examine fabric with what looked like glints of gold or silver or even little crystals, like the dress I had worn the first night.

"Can you smell the sparkles somehow?" I asked the dragon.

These fabrics had an extra notation on their tags. 'Charmed against stains,' said one. Handy. 'Charmed against the cold,' said another. Now, that would be useful for all those winter brides who insisted on outdoor photos. 'Charmed against deception,' read another, and I wondered if the wearers of this fabric knew what they were wearing.

"While you're down here," said Grainne briskly. "You might as well tell me what you like. So we can have more dresses made up for you."

"I love this one." I ran my hand down a bolt of blue chirimen. The floral gold pattern on the textured silk reminded me of a kimono design.

"An import from Takamagahara." Grainne tapped the bolt. "Lovely choice. Would you like it done up in Kami style or Seelie?"

"Seelie," I decided, curious to see what they'd come up with. "But what happened to the dresses I've already worn? How many more do I need?"

Grainne barked in laughter. "You really are from a backwater kingdom, aren't you? The *Tuatha Dé Danann* do not re-wear clothes."

"But you spent an entire day making me a dress!"

"Fifteen seamstresses spent an entire day making you a dress," corrected Grainne.

"What's going to happen to it then?" I asked. "I would happily wear it for another night."

Grainne gave me a look as if trying to figure me out. "We couldn't allow you to. The amount of gossip that would incur against you would be heinous! And you, an honored guest of the prince! We simply couldn't allow it. It would make all of us look bad."

"Will someone else get to wear it?"

"Come, I'll show you."

I followed the piskie as she flew across the room to a work table where my pink dress lay spread out. Or, I should say, the remains of the dress.

One brownie with a pair of wickedly sharp scissors efficiently chopped the dress down into pieces. The bodice was removed and the boning stacked in a neat pile. The ribbons that had laced up the back had been wound around a wooden spool. Kiyo scampered across the table to where a pile of crystal beads lay. The brownie carefully sliced the seams of the skirt.

"So, you make new clothes out of the dresses?"

"Sometimes we sell them," said Grainne. "Depending on how it held up to its first wearing."

I winced as I saw the brownie cut around the berry stain where I had spilled my dessert. "Sorry about that."

Grainne shrugged. She must be used to careless nobles. "If it's a particularly distinctive fabric, we naturally wait a while before making something else. So yes, some clothing is cut down for smaller garments, and some are sold at the market in town."

"I'm glad you don't throw it out." This was nothing like the wasteful fashion industry back in the human realm.

"Throw it out?! Are you aware of how much enchanted rose charmeuse costs? Of course you don't." She shook her head. "Nobles! Throw it out?"

Another piskie flew up beside us.

"It's Isla, Grainne. She's crying again."

Grainne clucked in annoyance. "You'll have to excuse me. Feel free to look around but don't let that dragon touch anything." She flew off.

Kiyo dropped the crystal she held and gave an injured chirp.

I scooped her up and wandered to the next table over where a small horned faerie embroidered ferns with golden thread onto green velvet.

"What are you working on?" I asked the little man. He jumped nervously.

"This is a vest for the king to wear tonight to dinner," he said.

I glanced over at the notes beside the scrap pieces of dark green velvet. There was a list of the king's measurements, a couple of notes and swatches of fabric to show the rest of the king's outfit for the night, and some extra notes. *Absolutely no orange*, said one of the notes. *Take the back in by a quarter inch from the last measurements. Charm against sneezing.*

"Is that what you're doing now? Charming it against sneezing?" If gold was used to make enchanted objects, it would make sense to use golden thread to enchant clothing.

The faerie blushed. "His Majesty has a bit of a cold," he said. "It wouldn't do for him to sneeze at dinner."

Where had Grainne gotten to? I didn't want to interrupt Isla, whoever she was, but I did want to know if it was okay for me to do some drawings while I was there. Would that be stealing someone else's creative work? Were these traditional designs or their own?

I scanned around the room in the direction she had left and saw a row of shelves filled with rolls of paper, probably for drafting patterns. Cautiously, I walked over and peeked around the shelves.

Grainne was tucked back into the corner with a small girl who looked about five or six years old, but if she stood up, she'd probably just reach my knee. Her skin was a rich brown and whorled like bark. Bits of twigs and leaves sprouted from her green hair.

The girl sniffled. "I want my mama."

"I know, my love." Grainne used a softer tone than I had heard from her but still firm. "And you'll see her on Sunday."

"But I want her now." The girl, Isla, broke into hiccupping sobs and hid her face behind her knees.

Grainne looked up and saw me. "I'm sorry, Lady Ella, for this display. It's only her first week as an apprentice."

"Where's her mother?" I asked.

"Her mother works in the kitchens, but Isla showed a greater aptitude for fabrics, so here she is."

"And she can't see her mother until Sunday?"

Grainne gave me an incredulous look, and I wondered how much I was slipping in my disguise as a noble woman.

"Junior apprentices get one day a week off to spend with their family. For the rest of the week, she works here, of course, and sleeps in the dormitory with the other apprentices."

"How old is she?" I knelt down beside the little girl.

"Six, as is customary for junior apprentices. It's always a hard transition for the first couple of weeks."

"Six?!" I gathered the child up into my arms. She stiffened and then snuffled against my shoulder. "She's just little!"

"Well, that's the way it is with the small folk," said Grainne. "I don't know how things are done on the Isle of Mist, but maybe you just didn't pay attention. The *Aos Sí* must work for their keep, lest they be thrown out into the forest. That's the way it has always been."

Clearly, I wasn't going to change an entire culture of faeries in my short time here, but I wasn't about to leave this child here to cry. I stood, settling Isla on my hip. She was all twiggy angles, but clung to me like a human child.

"Her mother works in the kitchens? Alright, let's go."

"It isn't her mother's fault," said Grainne nervously.

"Oh, no, I know," I said. "It's obviously a bigger issue. But I think this little one needs a hug from her mama. I don't know the way, though."

Isla sniffled and looked up at me hopefully. I probably wasn't behaving like a proper fake fae noble, but I didn't care.

"Go on, then." Grainne whistled, and the faerie she had been talking to earlier flew back over. "Show Lady Ella to the kitchens."

"Thank you for the tour," I said. "It was amazing."

Grainne's face softened. "You're welcome to stop by anytime you like."

"Thank you!"

I followed the faerie out of the magical workshop. The piskie flew ahead of me, fluttering nervously, as we wound through the short and narrow passages of the castle's downstairs.

Soon, we opened up into a clattering and noisy kitchen. Like the seamstress workshop, it was set up with stations at various heights for the various workers.

My guide led me past spits of roasting meat and tiny faeries with large knives slicing vegetables to a table that came up to about mid-thigh on me. A waist-high faerie, who looked like a draoi, like Isla, arranged slices of ruby-red strawberries onto golden tarts.

"Mama!" squealed the little girl, wiggling until I set her down. She raced over to the pastry chef who scooped her up with a cry.

"Isla! It's only your first day!"

"I know." The little girl snuggled into her mother's shoulder. "But I missed you."

"I'm so sorry for the trouble, my lady," said the pastry chef. "Isla's been nervous."

"It was no trouble." I ran my hand over the leafy hair of the little girl. "Can she stay here with you for a little while? Or will you get into trouble?"

I glanced around for anyone who looked like they were in charge.

"Do you promise to be helpful?" The faerie set her daughter on a stool next to the table.

"Oh yes, Mama!"

"And no stealing strawberries this time," her mother teased. "Well, maybe just one."

Kiyo popped her head out of my bag in interest.

"And for you, too?" The pastry chef laughed. "So this sweet-toothed little one belongs to you?"

"Sorry." This must be who my dragon was terrorizing in the early mornings.

Kiyo made a show of finding the best strawberry out of the bowl to eat.

I turned to the piskie who had let us in here. "Could you let whoever's in charge of the junior apprentices know that Isla will not be going back to the seamstress workshop today? And then she'll be sleeping with her mother tonight." She nodded and flew off.

"And every night until I say otherwise," I added to Isla and her mama. After all, what was the point of being a princess if you couldn't make a little twig child's day a bit better?

Chapter 19

Tiernan

"AGAIN!" Saoirse bellowed.

I braced myself and parried Fergus' sword thrust, ducking to the side as I did so to avoid the full brunt of the larger man's attack. The burly, bearded fae grinned at me as he lunged again. I smirked back.

All around me, I could see the rest of the fianna doing the same as we got in one last training session before leaving Rahivea on patrol. Saoirse stopped and adjusted Jac's stance before continuing to spar with him. At barely sixteen, Jac was the only one among us who had never seen combat in his short time with the fianna. The rest had fought in our share of border skirmishes with Moriath's wolves, but thankfully, only Declan and Saoirse had fought beside me in the *Aos Sí* uprising a century before.

Saoirse barked out another order, and this time I lunged. Practice was always important, but after nineteen decades of training, it was all muscle memory. My gaze wandered to the sidelines where Ella sat under a tree with the baby dragon sleeping beside her.

With the entire fianna training today, I'd wanted her close by. I didn't trust my father's men to guard her. The Kami girl rubbed her nose, leaving a swipe of black across her face. Sooty fingers again? What was she doing?

I attempted to disarm Fergus and failed. It was hard to see what Ella was up to with her knees up and her skirts billowing about her, but it looked as if…yes, she was drawing. Or possibly writing, but the charcoal suggested art. So that was why she was smudgy all the time. She wasn't playing in the fireplace; she was drawing with charcoal.

"Tiernan!"

I winced as Saoirse smacked my arm with the flat of her blade.

"Focus!"

"You're not even my opponent," I complained.

"I know, but Fergus is too nice to smack you when you're staring at pretty girls during training." My sister narrowed her eyes at me.

"Well…" I protested but realized she was right, so I smiled sweetly and shrugged.

Saoirse rolled her eyes. "Water break!"

Fergus and I saluted each other and sheathed our swords.

Saoirse handed me a canteen. "Your little sweetheart is stirring up trouble."

"Ella?" I glanced over at the girl. Still drawing. She didn't look like trouble.

"Hmm, I hear that she removed a junior apprentice from the seamstress's workroom and gave orders that she should stay with her mother." Saoirse took a drink from her own canteen.

"What was she doing down there?" I didn't question how Saoirse knew this. She made it her business to know everything.

"Who knows? But if I heard, then the king heard. And if the king heard…"

We both knew the risks of Fiachra thinking my choice of a bride was anything less than traditional.

"She was supposed to be able to fool him." Saoirse screwed the cap back on her canteen. "I thought the Mist Court was as traditional as they came."

"That's what I thought too. Maybe the Mist Prince has had a change of heart. I'll make sure Declan adds it to his list. Keep an eye on Ella."

"I already am."

"Good." I squeezed her shoulder and strode over to where Ella was sitting. The girl was so engrossed in what she was doing that she didn't notice me until I was right beside her. She swiftly slammed her sketchbook shut, startling Kiyo awake, and sat on it.

Hungry? Kiyo sent me an image of lavender cookies.

"No treats today, I'm afraid," I told the little dragon as I sat on the grass beside Ella.

Kiyo yawned and tucked her nose back under her tail and went back to sleep. Evidently, my company was less interesting without cookies.

"It's too late for that," I told Ella. "I figured out your secret."

Ella looked at me in horror. "Um, I—"

"Although I don't know why you're hiding it." I took a swig of my water before continuing. "It's not as though drawing is an unladylike pastime."

I glanced over at the twins. Rian said something that made Orla snort water out of her nose. "Not that we're terribly concerned with ladylike behavior."

Ella relaxed a little. "I just don't like to show anyone my sketches."

"Why not?" I asked, intrigued. "Wait. Are you drawing us?"

Her cheeks flushed pink.

"Are you drawing *me*?"

"I was not," she snapped, but her blush went deeper.

"It's fine. Don't be embarrassed," I teased. She was too cute. Could I make her blush pinker? "I'm sure it's hard to resist such a perfect model as myself. As an artist, I mean," I added.

Oh look, I could.

"It's not like that," she said with a huff, crossing her arms. "Not everything is about you, you know."

"If you say so." I winked. Even her nose was pink by this point. Adorable. But not what I had come over to talk to her about.

"I hear you're stealing junior apprentices from the seamstresses," I said.

"How did you hear about that?" She looked horrified. "Did I get anyone into trouble?"

"Oh, it's fine." I made a mental note to make sure it was actually fine. Saoirse had probably sorted it out and paid whoever was involved to keep it quiet. "But it does make one wonder why you were downstairs in the first place and why you interfered once you were there."

"I was thanking the seamstresses."

"Always thanking the help." I laughed. "And?"

"And Isla was crying. Six is far too young to be separated from your parents." Ella examined her sooty fingers.

Ah, that was it.

"How old were you when you lost your mother?"

"Five," she whispered.

"I was eight."

We sat in silence for a moment.

"Ella, I…" I trailed off, cocking my head to the side. I could sense Morna approaching.

"What is it?" she asked.

"A message, I think. I better go and see." I stood. "I'll let you get back to not drawing me."

Ella rolled her eyes and I walked away, chuckling.

When I reached the edge of the clearing, the jay squawked and flew down from a tree, landing on my outstretched hand. Morna tilted her head, and I could swear she cocked her sassy white eyebrow at me. I fed the blue bird a little handful of dried berries I kept in my belt and untied the scrap of paper fastened to her leg.

Morna hopped up onto my shoulder, and I got the sense that Declan had been frustrated when he tied the note on.

Juniper and Poppy Courts unhelpful. I suspect your father threatened them already.
Heading to Yew Court next.
- D

I crumpled the paper in my fist. Did Fiachra suspect my ruse with Ella, or was he merely threatening the princesses he didn't approve of as insurance? Ella wasn't acting like the traditional princess I had expected. And while I liked that in her, it wasn't helping convince my father.

Should I risk it and tell her everything?

I coaxed Morna back onto my hand and gently pressed her crested head to my forehead.

"Go back to Declan." I sent her an impression of my friend and the Yew castle.

The jay squawked and took flight.

"Break's over!" Saoirse called. "Tiernan, you're with Haru."

She split up the rest of the group, and I faced Haru, who had removed his shirt in the late morning heat. I glanced over at Ella, who had pulled out her sketchbook again.

Might as well give her something fun to draw.

I pulled my tunic over my head and threw it to the sidelines. I glanced over, and sure enough, she blushed even pinker than before with her mouth slightly open. I winked and drew my sword, purposefully flexing in a way I knew drew attention to the knotwork tattoos across my shoulder and back that I shared with the rest of my fianna. Girls loved tattoos.

Ella looked pointedly away while continuing to sketch, but she glanced back when she thought I wasn't looking.

I grinned and began to spar with Haru. Having a pretend sweetheart was far more fun than I had anticipated.

CHAPTER 20

ELLA

I OPENED MY DOOR A CRACK AND peeked through. Haru was on guard duty today. Perfect. If it had been Saoirse, I never would have gotten past her, and I felt bad getting Jac into trouble again.

But Haru deserved it for being such a snob.

"Okay, Kiyo. Here's the plan.ö I sent the ryū a mental picture of what I wanted her to do, and she cocked her head to the side.

Unlike me, Kiyo liked Haru. The grumpy Kami fae still refused to admit that keeping the ryū egg had been a good idea, but I saw him slipping her treats whenever he saw her.

"It's fine," I told her and sent her another mental image with Haru smiling at her. The dragon chirped and disappeared.

A second later, I heard Haru yell and then he opened my door. Kiyo had done a fantastic job. Raspberry chocolate tart dribbled from his head down through his long silky hair.

Kiyo chirped apologetically.

"Haru! I'm so sorry! She wanted to give you a treat. She must have misjudged the jump."

Haru smiled weakly at Kiyo while picking pieces of raspberry out of his hair.

"It's alright, Kiyo," he said. "It's a very nice thought, but next time in my hand maybe."

"Come on, come on." I waved him inside. "You can wash up in here."

Haru followed me through my suite of rooms to the bathroom. "Next time, maybe convince her to fetch me something less sticky."

He closed the door behind him. I waited until I heard the water running.

"Come on Kiyo!" I grabbed my bag and dashed out the door and across the hall into the labyrinth of the servants' passageways.

"Don't worry,ö I reassured the ryū. "Haru still loves you.ö

On the other hand, did he still like me? Probably not.

It was a perfect morning. Two hours later, Haru still hadn't found me. Perhaps he was too embarrassed to admit to anyone that he had lost me in the first place.

I'd happily spent my free time exploring and sketching in the sewing room. I flitted from watching lace being tatted by a group of piskies at one station to a brownie drafting the pattern of a dress for a fae with two tails and then to a small horned fae Grainne introduced as a spell crafter who was busy enchanting golden thread to ward off carriage sickness.

I was currently perched in a corner sketching the details of the nearly finished dress that Grainne had told me I was to wear to dinner tonight. The gown was made of the blue and gold silk chirimen I had picked out the day before. The contrast of the kimono fabric done up as a Seelie fae-styled strapless gown was gorgeous and sparked all sorts of ideas.

"Ella, there you are."

I closed my sketchbook as Grainne approached. My designs seemed childish compared to the skill of the fae seamstresses.

"I've never met a *Tuatha Dé Danann* as interested in dresses as you." The piskie settled on a brownie-sized dress form, folding in her wings. "And the questions you ask! How do you know so much?"

"My mother died when I was five." I tucked my sketchbook into my bag, startling a napping baby dragon who disappeared with a pop.

"My father remarried," I continued. "And my new stepmother owned a dress shop. The first time I walked in and saw all the beautiful gowns, it was like walking into—" A fairy realm. "A dream. I had always drawn dresses a lot, and I was fascinated by how these dresses were made. Then my father passed away as well, two years later, and my stepmother put me to work in the dress shop. I think she meant it as a punishment, and in some ways, it was. I worked every day after school. I didn't have time for friends or parties like the other kids. But I never got tired of the dresses. I always wanted to learn more. As I grew older, she did less and less work, and I took over the sewing room."

"She still took all the credit, I'll wager," sniffed Grainne.

"She did. I'm curious how they're managing without me."

"Well, my dear, if that spark in you survived all the years of your stepmother's cruelty, you're clearly a modiste at heart. And you're welcome down here anytime you'd like."

A small shriek rang out from across the room, and Kiyo appeared in front of me, wrapped in a strand of sparkling crystal beads.

"This one, on the other hand…" Grainne glared up at Kiyo.

I sighed and untangled the little dragon, returning the crystals to the horned spellcrafter.

"No more stealing, dragon." Grainne flew up and smacked Kiyo on the nose. The dragon looked at Grainne sorrowfully, but the piskie raised an eyebrow, uncowed by a dragon whose head nearly came up to her waist.

"All right, troublemaker." I tucked Kiyo back into my bag. "Let's go find you some lunch. Goodbye, Grainne, thank you!"

I ducked my head and concentrated on counting turns as I went. The staircase grew darker, and I wished I remembered the command Imogen had used to turn the lights on. If the magic would even work for a human girl.

I reached the landing and fumbled for the doorknob—somewhere near my knees?—when a hand clamped around my mouth, muffling my scream. I felt something sharp against my neck. My heart hammered against my ribs. My breath came in sharp gasps.

"You should go back to where you came from," my captor whispered in my ear. I recognized the voice. Lynet. I knew she didn't like me, but I hadn't expected an actual dagger from her.

"My mother has been training me to be the queen all my life," she said. "I'm not giving it all up for some little nobody from the Mist Court. Go home before you ruin everything."

I took a deep breath and threw my head backward, causing a sharp cry from my captor as we both tumbled through the door into the corridor.

"Ella!" yelled Tiernan, racing toward me.

The princess scrambled back, clutching her bloody nose.

"Haru! Grab her! We need to find out who planned this."

The princess raced down the corridor, still trying to stop her bleeding nose. Haru ran after her, but Lynet had a decent head start.

Tiernan dropped to his knees in front of me and grabbed my shoulders.

"What were you thinking, slipping your guard like that? I told you it wasn't safe!"

I touched my neck gingerly, and my fingers came away bloody. I stared at them in shock. Tiernan pulled me onto his lap and pressed his handkerchief to the cut.

"It's not deep, don't worry. Fiachra will pay for this," he ground out.

"But it wasn't him," I gasped, gulping for air. "It was that girl from the Aster Court."

"My father never does things directly. It wouldn't inspire confidence in the nobles to have a murderer for a king. He will have convinced her it was her idea."

I gave another gasp for air. Tiernan adjusted me so my back rested against his chest.

"Breathe when I breathe," he said. "You've had quite a shock."

He counted slowly, and I could feel the slow rise and fall of his chest against my back. Eventually, I was able to breathe again, matching my breaths to his.

"I was just curious about how the dresses were made," I whispered.

"And that required escaping Haru?" His voice rumbled next to my ear.

"He doesn't like me. I thought he'd tease me."

Tiernan laughed. "Would being teased be better than a knife to the throat?"

I leaned back against him. "Fine, you're right."

"And how were the dresses? Worth all this fuss?"

I relaxed a bit more. "Wait until you see the one I'm wearing tonight to dinner."

"Dinner with the king? That's not happening. You'll eat in your rooms tonight with Saoirse. I'll make an excuse for you."

"And tomorrow? I can't stay in my rooms all day."

"You won't have to." Tiernan drummed his fingers on his knee. "We're leaving in the morning."

I scrambled off his lap and turned to face him. "I promise I won't slip my guards anymore! I've learned my lesson."

Tiernan helped me up on my shaky legs. "I'm not leaving you here. Not after this. Let Imogen know that you need to get packed. You're coming on patrol."

"Oh. Yay," I said weakly.

"Tenting is preferable to assassination, I would think." Tiernan held my elbow as we walked down the hall toward my rooms.

"I suppose." I sighed. "But only barely."

PART
3

CHAPTER 21

ELLA

O W!" I stepped back and glared at a tiny branch dangling from overhead that had somehow hooked itself into my left nostril. "How is that even possible?" I batted the branch away.

Next to me, Fergus grunted. The burly bearded man was my assigned hiking partner for the hour. Tiernan's fianna consisted of nine members, including himself. Eight of them were taking turns keeping pace with the slow, out-of-shape seamstress. The obnoxious redheaded ninth one kept his distance. Because I was, as he put it, in a snit.

He wasn't wrong.

Not even my amazing new cloak of green felt with gold stitching, my slim pants that looked like twill but somehow felt and stretched like joggers, or my gorgeous knee-high leather boots could cheer me up.

"I've already swallowed two bugs, had one fly up my nose, and had something bite my ear earlier. It was not a mosquito."

Fergus scanned the trees around us as we walked. "And you tripped over that root and fell on your face," he pointed out.

"Well, I wasn't going to bring that up. Thank you very much for reminding me." I touched my sore nose gingerly. "Why are you guys into this? Like, I know it's your honorable duty to keep tabs on Seelie villages or some such."

Haru had explained it to me earlier. While staring at Kiyo as if he couldn't believe she was still around. I had felt awfully smug about it, and that's when I had tripped and fallen on my face. Kiyo had portaled away with a squeak but now scampered through the forest beside the path, chasing butterflies. At least I hoped they were butterflies.

"You don't like the woods?" Fergus looked at me, perplexed.

"I mean, they're all right to look at." I waved my hands at the towering moss-covered cedar trees. The red soil made the path springy, and mushrooms of all sizes dotted the forest floor amidst tiny white starred flowers.

"Fine," I admitted. "Nature is beautiful. But why does it keep attacking me?"

Fergus shrugged. He didn't seem to be the chatty type.

He froze. I stopped too, in alarm.

"Bear? Skunk? Griffin?" I had no idea what roamed these woods. Did I even want to know?

Fergus peered into the distance and cocked his head. Then he nodded and pulled a tiny notebook out of his pocket, jotting down something.

I peered over his shoulder. Rows of tiny notes with numbers beside them.

"Aegnus' warbler," murmured Fergus.

"So it's not gonna eat us?" I asked, my heart still pounding.

"First one this season." Fergus was as cheerful as I had ever heard him, tucking the notebook back into his pocket before striding forward again.

I adjusted my heavy pack and ran to catch up. "So you, like, keep track of all the stuff you see?" I said.

"Not stuff," said Fergus. "Birds."

"Huh." I had always pictured birdwatchers as elderly couples sitting on their porch watching a hummingbird feeder. But judging by the notebook, this giant of a fae man, with a silver axe strapped to his back—who looked like he could snap me in half without breaking a sweat— was a birder.

"How many birds have you seen today?"

"Twenty-three species." He focused on the trees as we walked. "Not counting Tiernan's bird."

"It's a blue jay, right?" I asked.

"No, they're—"

"Wait, Steller's jays! Right? With the dark heads?" I was pretty impressed that I had remembered something from our class's nature hikes in school.

Fergus raised his eyebrows. "Some people call them that, yes. The more common name is hooded jay."

"Huh. So twenty-three, is that good?"

"Chatty one, aren't you?" he asked.

I supposed it was tricky to carry on a conversation while listening for birds.

"See anything good this morning, Fergus?" Saoirse appeared out of nowhere along the path.

I yelped. She raised an amused eyebrow.

"I saw a pair of Firecrests, just now."

"You did? Where?" I asked.

Fergus waved a hand behind us. "Back when you got the stick up your nose."

Saoirse barked with laughter, and I narrowed my eyes. She straightened her expression, but her eyes still danced with amusement.

"Have you found a golden oriole yet?" she asked Fergus. "That was what you were hoping for on this trip, right?"

"Not yet," he said. "It's a little late in the day. Maybe tomorrow."

"Well, good luck," said Saoirse. "I'll take this one off your hands for a bit."

Fergus nodded and then stopped again. He cocked his head and then wandered off the path.

"Don't you worry about losing him?" I asked.

"He knows the forest better than anyone." Saoirse glanced down at my hand, and I realized I was tapping my fingers together, nervously. She didn't comment.

"How far to the village?" I started walking again.

"We'll stop for lunch soon," she said. "At this pace, we should be there before nightfall."

Doubtless, we were going at about half speed with me along.

"Will we be sleeping indoors?" I perked up. "Surely, the villagers don't make their crown prince sleep on the ground?"

Saoirse laughed. "A village this small doesn't have an inn," she said. "And while many of them would happily give up their cottages, there's no way Tiernan would hear of it. He's not the sort of prince that would kick someone out of their home for him, just so he doesn't have to sleep on the ground."

Interesting. The Tiernan I had spent time with so far would have done exactly that, actually.

I turned at the sound of a rhythmic jingling to see Fergus jogging along the path. I sure hoped his axe was secure.

"Found one," he said happily as he passed us. "A male in breeding plumage!"

"Nice one!" called Saoirse as he ran off ahead of us.

"He's not even out of breath," I moaned.

"Don't feel bad. I make them run training exercises with rocks in their backpacks twice a week."

"I knew it," I said.

"Knew what?"

"You are evil."

Saoirse laughed again, and I marveled at how much more at ease she seemed away from Rahivea.

"So what do you do as one of Tiernan's seconds-in-command? Other than torture the fianna."

"Declan and I have been doing more and more these last few years in preparation for Tiernan's coronation. We used to only run this fianna when he was busy with his duties as a crown prince, but for the last few years, he's been training us to take over running the whole kingdom's Fianna when he becomes king."

"Why two of you?" I asked. "Is that how things are usually done?"

"You'll find that Tiernan doesn't have a lot of interest in how things are usually done. Declan and I have different strengths, and we work well together. He's better at schmoozing the nobles, which is an important part of what the *Rífhéinní* does. Without the support of the courts, we have no manpower, no funding, and no freedom to roam."

"That makes sense," I said. "What do you do, then?"

"As you pointed out, I'm good at being evil." She raised an eyebrow at me. "I'm in charge of training, patrol and mission planning, and we work together on recruitment."

"And you're not good at schmoozing?" I teased.

"Declan has always fit in better with the nobles than me."

"Weren't you raised with Tiernan? Aren't you practically a princess, too?" I still hadn't worked out how Saoirse fit in at Rahivea.

"I'm a princess, yes, in my own kingdom, but here, I'm more of a hostage." Saoirse scanned the forest as we walked. "The nobles don't like to remember that."

"What do you mean? I thought you were like Tiernan's sister?"

"I see they taught you nothing of Seelie politics at home."

So true.

"There is an ancient custom in Faerie," Saoirse said. "To preserve the peace between nations, the royal families trade younger children—never the heirs, mind you—as part of a peace agreement with another."

"Is it so you can learn more about each other's culture?" I asked what I knew was an optimistic question.

"There is that. I certainly know more about this kingdom than my birthplace. They even gave me a Seelie name." Saoirse tucked a long braid behind her ear. "But the main purpose is to prevent war."

"How does trading children prevent war?" My stomach sank a little.

"Well, you see, if you hold the child of a neighboring royal family, they would never dare to move against you. If they did, they know the child's life would be forfeit."

I blinked. "So, if your parents ever chose to invade the Seelie Kingdom?"

"The king would slit my throat," confirmed Saoirse.

"And you said it was a trade?" I stopped and wiggled my left boot. I was getting sore spots on my feet.

"Yes. Tiernan's younger brother was raised in my home in my place."

"Is this a common thing?" I asked, incredulously. Logically, it made sense. But I couldn't imagine trading a child, never mind holding an innocent hostage against their parents' good behavior.

"It once was," she said carefully. "Generations ago, when Faerie was less peaceful than it is now, it was common practice. The courts would be filled with children from other kingdoms."

"But it's not anymore?" I asked.

"It still happens. My twin brother lives in the Unseelie Kingdom. But the Seelie fae haven't engaged in a hostage exchange for three generations."

I wondered how long a fae generation lasted.

"Why do you think he did it?" I asked quietly.

"King Fiachra made some excuse about his spies having reason to distrust my parents. I don't know if that's true. I was only three years old when I last laid eyes on them." She lowered her voice. "But what I do know is that when Tiernan's mother died giving birth to his younger brother, Fiachra never looked at the child again. They say he couldn't bear the reminder of his beloved queen's death, so he sent the child as far away as he could."

"And you've never been home?" My heart broke, both for Saoirse, who grew up without her family, and for Tiernan, to have a father who could ship a kid off like that.

"Never," she said.

"Aren't there portals to your kingdom?" I asked.

"Oh yes," she said. "There are gates to the forests of the Aziza. But not for me. It's considered too risky to let hostages return home, even for a visit."

I didn't know what to say. My impulse was to hug her, but Saoirse didn't seem like the huggy sort. I was just happy she was talking to me without threats of violence.

I misjudged a step and my foot rolled, rubbing the largest of my many blisters. I tried not to whimper, with limited success.

"You doing okay?"

"Yep." The last thing I wanted was yet another reason to slow everyone down.

"You sure?" pressed Saoirse.

"So, are you looking forward to taking over for Tiernan? He seems like kind of a pain in the neck. I bet you have all sorts of changes planned for the Fianna?"

She narrowed her eyes at me, but allowed herself to be distracted, explaining that Tiernan was actually great at his job, but that she did have a few ideas.

Luckily for my feet, we stopped for lunch shortly after. I collapsed by the side of the trail, using my backpack as a backrest. I didn't even bother to undo the straps.

Tiernan crouched down beside me and handed me a flaky sausage roll and an apple. Gone was the perfectly groomed crown prince from the palace. This Tiernan had mussed hair, simple—but still well-tailored—clothes, and well-worn leather boots. He looked like the boy I had met at the revel. It was unsettling how much that appealed to me.

"Drink some water," he said.

"Oh, you're talking to me now?" That came out a little more caustically than intended. My feet really hurt. But I did drink some water.

Tiernan, ignoring my attitude, sat down in front of me and placed a small glass jar on the ground before lifting one of my feet and unlacing my boot.

"What are you doing?" I sputtered through a mouthful of water.

"Sersh said you were limping earlier." He pulled off the boot.

"Snitch," I muttered. Then I winced as he peeled off my sock, which seemed to have become attached to two or three bloody parts of my foot. "Are crown princes supposed to deal with people's stinky feet?" I moaned.

"Crown princes can do anything they like." He inspected my foot. "And a captain is charged with making sure that everyone in their fianna is taken care of. New recruits pushing themselves to keep up with veterans is not unusual. Not very smart, but not unusual."

I wanted to argue, but my bloody feet sure didn't make me look very smart.

"Eat your lunch." Tiernan began unlacing my other boot. "And don't worry about the smell."

I huffed at him, and he laughed while he tugged my second sock off.

"Because they're gonna smell a whole lot worse in a minute." He picked up one of my feet, and with surprisingly gentle fingers, smeared pungent ointment on the spots with blisters, which is to say, my entire foot.

He then hovered his hand over my goopy foot and muttered something under his breath.

My foot tingled, and the pain of the blisters faded, but the eye-watering smell remained. Tiernan was right, it did smell worse than any amount of stinky socks, but I couldn't bring myself to care. It felt so much better.

I chewed on my apple while he repeated the process with my other foot.

"Thank you." I wiggled my toes happily as the pain faded. The blisters healed over in front of my eyes.

He gingerly set my sweaty, bloody socks to the side. "Maybe we'll burn these later."

He wiped his hands clean, and then, picking up my boots, he snapped a small golden bead over each of the bottom laces.

"That should help you break them in faster." He handed me the little pot of salve. "In case you still need it tonight."

I sighed and took the jar. "I'm sorry I'm being such a pain."

"You don't have to pretend to be tough." Tiernan settled down beside me.

I munched on my sausage roll. "I know I'm slowing everyone down."

"I take it you didn't spend a lot of time in the woods growing up." Tiernan started in on his own sausage roll. Like Saoirse, he seemed much more relaxed out here than at the palace.

"When I was younger—" as in, when we lived in Vancouver "—there were no woods nearby."

"And later on?"

"My stepmother, she's not much of one for the great outdoors. I never minded too much." I shrugged. "I'd rather be inside drawing anyhow."

"Ah yes, your mysterious art. You can't draw outside?" Tiernan dug out another sausage roll from his bag.

Kiyohime popped up out of nowhere and sat on Tiernan's knee, looking mournfully at his last bite of food. The prince laughed and broke the roll in half, sharing it with the little dragon.

"I mean, yes, of course, it's possible to draw outside." I had packed my sketchbook and pencils along on this adventure, just in case. "But inside is easier. No bugs. No rain. No sun reflecting off your paper and into your eyes."

"You could wear a hat." He finished his food, and Kiyo disappeared with a pop.

"Alright, Mr. Big Ideas, don't tell me how to draw, and I won't tell you how to…whatever this is." I waved my arms around the group of fae warriors.

"Fair enough." Tiernan brushed the crumbs off his hands. "But maybe if you give it a little time, you'll discover there's beauty to be seen out here that you'd never find under a roof."

After lunch, I reluctantly put my boots back on, and we got back on the trail. This time, I hiked with Jac who was chattering away about his latest inventions as an apprentice spellcrafter.

The young, blonde fae explained it all in detail, which was both adorably nerdy and also a bit hard to keep up with. But when he told me that he had made the beads keeping my blisters at bay, I was so grateful I gave the stunned boy a giant hug.

After what felt like hours of hiking, my feet were sore again—but not bleeding—and my stomach grumbled constantly. The sun grew low overhead, and the smell of fresh-baked bread and roasted meat wafted through the trees.

"Do you smell that?" I interrupted Jac's explanation of the enchanted pulley system he was designing. Was I hallucinating? Was I that hungry?

"Glaistig village," cheered Jac. "Finally!"

CHAPTER 22

TIERNAN

A CROWD OF GLAISTIG WAITED FOR US at the edge of the village. Kids waved from atop the low village wall or on the mossy rooftops of the small stone houses.

Padraig, the chief, clopped over toward me on his goat-like legs and embraced me in a strong hug, smacking my back.

"My prince! Thanks for sending the jay with your message. You're so late, we were starting to wonder if you'd gotten lost."

"New recruit," I explained, glancing back to see if Ella and Jac had caught up with us. She stumbled into the clearing with the spellcrafter right behind her. "I hope you didn't postpone dinner for us."

Sally, Padraig's short, round wife, joined us with a little baby snoozing on her back.

"Oh, we fed the young ones," she said. "Don't you worry. You'll have to introduce us to this new recruit of yours." She raised an eyebrow and smiled slyly.

I was about to comment that it wasn't like that when I remembered it *was* supposed to be exactly like that.

"Ella. You'll love her." At least that last part was true. Somehow, lying to the villagers felt worse than lying to my father and his court.

"I hope they don't get too attached," I muttered under my breath to Saoirse as we followed the couple to the village square where the feast was laid out.

"Right, them getting too attached would be the problem." My sister rolled her eyes as she sauntered over to the head table.

Jac had already lunged for the food, but I found Ella doing her best to melt into the shadows at the edge of the square. I strode over and unbuckled her pack. She groaned a little as it slid off her shoulders.

"No hiding. Come and eat dinner."

"I didn't know it would be a whole big thing." She tapped her finger against her leg.

"Come on." I shouldered her pack alongside my own and grabbed her hand with my free one. Just for show. "Let's get you some supper."

While I introduced Ella to the villagers, we made our way toward the smell of food. The low wooden tables were heaped with carrot stew, fresh bread, and lots of greens. The glaistig really loved their salads. Lanterns made of old jars and twine with candles inside hung from the branches. Buckets of late summer flowers adorned the tables.

Fiddles and lutes were being tuned in the background. Soon, there would be dancing.

When I had gone on patrol with the previous *Rífhéinní*, there had been tithes to collect. Now, thanks to Declan's schmoozing, the nobles funded the Fianna. They could afford it, after all.

So, the tithes had been replaced by feasts. At first, I felt awkward about the level of celebration just for us, but Sersh and Declan had talked me around.

Our visit might be the excuse for the party, but the *Aos Sí* loved a good celebration. And there is no better way to build bonds with people than by sharing a meal. I would not be like my father, ruling from his palace at Rahivea, cut off from the lives of his people.

"Congratulations on your newest arrival," I said to Sally as she plopped their middle child on my lap. "This can't be Rosie." I looked down suspiciously at the toddler, who laughed and kicked her hooves. "Rosie had only little nubs of horns last time I saw her."

"They grew! See?" She tapped the top of her horns proudly. "I'm three now."

"What? Impossible!"

She laughed again and stole the bread off my plate.

I glanced across the table and caught Ella staring wide-eyed at me. I felt my cheeks warm.

"So good with the littles." Sally patted her shoulder. "As I'm sure you'll find out for yourself in time."

I choked on my mead.

"Now, if you hold this one…" She slid the baby into Ella's arms.

"But you don't even know me!" said Ella incredulously.

Sally smiled. "You'll be fine. Just for a few minutes. It's been ages since I ate without worrying about dropping food on someone's head."

"I held her just this morning so you could eat," Padraig protested.

"Since I ate *hot* food without worrying about dropping it on someone's head," amended Sally, sitting heavily onto the bench and adjusting her prosthetic hoof before ladling herself a big scoop of hot stew.

"How's the fancy gold foot treating you?" I asked. "Be sure to talk to Jac if you need any adjustments."

"It's perfect," said Sally. "That young one of yours did an excellent job."

"Good," I said. "How can we help while we're here this time?"

Padraig launched into an explanation of leaking moss roofs. I nodded along, but my eyes strayed across the table to where Ella was attempting to dip a roll into the stew and eat it without dripping on the baby's head.

Her face was soft in the lantern light. I told myself that the sight of her with a baby in her arms was only aesthetically pleasing and didn't stir anything within me.

"She's awfully pretty," whispered Rosie in agreement with my thoughts.

I tore my attention back to the business at hand.

"I have an idea," I said to Padraig. "About the roofs."

"So serious tonight!" Sally exclaimed. "You'll have all night to talk. Go dance with your sweetheart first, before someone else steals her away."

Ella straightened, adjusting her hold on the baby. "Oh, that's okay, I understand if you're busy."

But I had caught the wistful way she had looked at the dancers. The tapping of her foot under the table.

Sally plucked the baby out of Ella's arms and motioned for Rosie to follow. "Bedtime, my love."

Rosie sighed dramatically. "When I am grown up, you'll dance with me too, right?"

"I promise," I told her.

The little girl nodded seriously and then scampered after her mother.

I took Ella's hand, and we walked to the dancing green. It was getting harder and harder to pretend I wasn't looking for any excuse to touch her.

Rian and Orla were dancing already, and Jac looked dazed as he spun with a pretty glaistig girl.

I spun Ella into position with a grin, and she gave me an appraising look.

"What is it?" I laughed. "Do you still not trust me?"

"Should I?" she asked. "You're a completely different person out here. Which one is the real Tiernan?"

Should she? I certainly hadn't told her the whole truth, but I found I wanted to. She wasn't the traditionally-minded Seelie noble I had expected. Maybe she could be an ally.

"I'm not sure where to start," I confessed.

"Your father," she said.

"Not the topic that usually comes first to mind when I'm dancing with a beautiful girl. But yes, continue."

"The way you two discussed the patrol, I thought it had more to do with showing the small folk who was in charge and less about snuggling their babies." Ella glanced back at our table as we danced.

"Right, that." I pulled her farther from the musicians to make talking easier. "You're not old enough…" I started.

Ella rolled her eyes. "Yes, yes, you're very old."

"Well, I'm old enough that I already had a place in the Fianna during the *Aos Sí* uprising one hundred years ago, along with Saoirse, Declan, Leith—"

"The prince with the human fiancée."

"Yes, I suppose you saw them at Saoirse's birthday. And Brenna. She was…" I wasn't sure I wanted to discuss Brenna with Ella.

"You cared about her," Ella said softly.

"We planned to be wed." I looked off into the crowd. "I wasn't *Rífhéinní* then, just captain of our fianna." I paused. It wasn't a time I liked to remember.

"What caused the uprising?" asked Ella.

"Generations of being treated by the *Tuatha Dé Danann* as children at best and slaves at worst. They reached a breaking point. There were riots and fighting broke out. The Fianna were sent to quell them."

"And by quell them…"

"They were to go home peacefully or they were killed," I said, tightly. "Most of the fiannas gave them a chance to leave peacefully."

"That's awful," Ella whispered.

"I still have nightmares about those times," I admitted. "They didn't even have weapons. The *Aos Sí* aren't allowed any. It was trained warriors against folk half their size with shovels and pickaxes."

"What did you do?" Ella squeezed my hand, and I realized we had stopped dancing on the edge of the green.

"What we could. We saved as many as we were able to, but one fianna can't be everywhere."

"What did your father think of that?"

"Fiachra was…displeased with me."

"How displeased?"

"So displeased that he disbanded my fianna. All my members were sent to other units. Brenna was killed a month later. An accident, they told me." I tried to give Ella a reassuring smile but knew that it wasn't up to what she would call my charming standards.

"Leith's parents were openly upset about the way Fiachra handled the matter," I continued. "And other nobles were starting to join with them." I paused.

"What happened to them?" Ella asked.

"It was officially deemed a hunting accident."

"Officially?"

"I've never been able to prove the king ordered any of their deaths, but there's no mistaking that he was behind them." I remembered how devastating it had been for Leith. Between losing his parents and then the curse, I was lucky to still have my friend. "It took me decades to regain Fiachra's trust enough to become *Rífhéinní*. To get Declan and Saoirse back with me."

"So…" Ella tugged my hands and pulled me back into the dance. "He believes you're keeping the small folk cowed."

"Correct. The role of the *Rífhéinní* is to manage the Fianna and maintain the peace in the kingdom. Fiachra and I just have different ideas about how best to keep that peace."

"You're more into dancing than fighting?" she teased.

"Well, obviously. It's much less messy." I smiled down at her. "I believe if you listen to people, treat them like people, make sure they have enough to live on, that's how you make your kingdom strong."

"That seems pretty simple to me," agreed Ella. "The difference, I suppose, is who you view as people. Your father hasn't caught on to what you're doing?"

"The king suspects, but he doesn't spend time outside of Rahivea if he can help it, except to occasionally visit the other courts. He only travels by gate to avoid spending time traveling through the countryside."

"I like your way better," said Ella.

I felt myself grow taller under her praise. "And it works. The kingdom is more at peace than ever before."

"Is that why you act the way you do?" asked Ella. "At Rahivea I wouldn't have guessed that you cared about the small folk at all."

"Yes, well I was attempting to be what you expected."

"Oh, so it's my fault you were being a snob?" Ella stepped back from me.

I couldn't have that. I tugged her closer as I explained. "As a *Tuatha Dé Danann* from a traditional court, I expected you to be just the sort of bride my father would choose for me."

"Oh." She looked at me thoughtfully.

"If you hadn't been a girl who did things like thank servants and deliver tiny apprentices back to their mothers, Fiachra wouldn't have suspected you to be anything else. No one would have been attacking you in stairwells, and you wouldn't have had to come on patrol."

"Well." Ella smiled up at me. "I suppose there are worse things than spending the month with a charming prince."

My heart swelled, and I spun her out, laughing in an attempt to lighten the mood. "I'm honored you'd choose me over deadly peril. Even with the giant bugs and all."

"Wait." She stopped spinning and looked up at me in horror. "You didn't say anything about giant bugs!"

My conversation with Padraig went long into the night, as it always did. Officially, I was there to aid the villagers, but I had learned more from my years of visiting the small folk than I had ever given back to them.

Sally had put her little ones to bed, and Ella was asleep on the bench. The musicians finally quit, claiming blistered fingers and raw throats.

I said my good night to Padraig. Then I pried Jac away from a conversation with the glaistig girl before scooping a sleeping Ella from the bench, along with my cloak that I had folded under her head as a makeshift pillow.

She stirred in my arms and muttered, "You do the dishes!" before settling her head against my chest.

She was light, lighter than I would have expected. Again, my memory strayed back to the sight of her with the babe in her arms. I didn't want to put a name to the feeling I had, but it made me yearn for something I had long known was not for me.

My father had married for love, and look where it had gotten him. The effect the loss of my mother had had on our kingdom, and Saoirse's as well, had been devastating.

I would be a good king above all else, not one compromised by selfish desires or ruled by emotion.

We reached the lantern light of the camp, which the rest of the fianna had set up before nightfall. Jac climbed into his tent and collapsed, doubtless dreaming of pretty goat girls.

I allowed myself one more moment with Ella in my arms before carrying her to her tent. Her dark eyelashes were smudges against her pale cheeks in the dim, golden lantern light.

I hoped Declan would have good news for me when we met. The sooner we found a proper queen for me, a safe queen, the better.

CHAPTER 23

ELLA

I WOKE IN DARKNESS. Just once, I would love to sleep through till morning. Kiyo rumbled grumpily and tucked her warm little body more firmly against my side. I closed my eyes and thought about sleeping. Just go back to sleep.

Unfortunately, I had to pee.

You're fine, I told my bladder.

Really? my bladder said back to me. *Then maybe you shouldn't have drunk one glass of mead and six glasses of iced tea.*

I sighed. It made an excellent point. But my bed was so comfy. Much better than I would have expected in a tent. I even had a fluffy duvet rivaling mine back at the castle, if a little smaller.

I could hear Saoirse breathing steadily in the dark and tried to match my own breathing to hers. Sadly, I was fully awake now. Not only did I have to pee, but my mind raced around in circles, pointing out all the people I was lying to. Not to mention, how upset they would all be when they found out.

Did I need to think about this now? In the middle of the night? Apparently, I did. I sighed. There was no helping it. I needed to get up and pee.

I was still in my clothes. It occurred to me that I didn't actually remember getting into the tent. I found my boots beside my bed and loosely tied them, pulling my cloak around me to ward off the cold night air.

Upon exiting my warm bed, I crept to the edge of the tent. The ground under me swayed. Odd.

I opened the flap to the outside and screeched as I nearly fell to my death. Yes, that's right. The tent was hanging from a tree.

"Ella?" Saoirse murmured sleepily. "Are you alright?"

"The tent is in a tree!" I hissed back.

Saoirse yawned. "It's *Cù Sìth* territory."

"What?"

"You know. Giant green hounds? Red eyes? The twins swear that if you hear one bark three times, you'll die, but I think that's just because it'll have eaten you by then."

I squinted into the night. I didn't see any red eyes…

"They don't climb trees," she added.

"Then how am I supposed to go to the bathroom?" I whisper-yelled back at her.

"Well, the guys just open the flap and—"

"I don't need to know. What about us?"

"Hold it?"

"Sadly, not an option." I stared down at the mossy forest floor below, looking for signs of movement.

"Well, take a lantern. You'll be fine. Sally says they haven't seen one in months."

I sighed.

"Want me to come with you?" Saoirse asked in the tone of someone who clearly did not want to come with me.

"No."

"Okay, good. See you in the morning." Saoirse rolled over again. I took a deep breath and climbed down the little rope ladder. Luckily, it wasn't a long drop.

I peered at the lantern when I got to the ground, to make sure I hadn't been rattling some poor sheerie, but it was only a little glowing ball of magic.

My heart raced as I walked past the glow of lanterns strung in front of each tent and in the trees, my mind conjuring fangs and claws out of each snapped twig or thrown shadow.

I peed faster than I had ever peed before. Yanking my pants back up, I grabbed the lantern. My fingers shook around the handle when something rustled behind me.

It was not my own feet in the leaves this time.

I froze, my breath coming in gasps.

A twig snapped. I found myself too terrified to scream. My heart hammered as my ribs constricted. My mind painted such a vivid picture of the monster behind me that even when gentle fingertips grasped my arm, I whimpered, imagining the scrape of claws against my skin.

"Hey."

Tiernan. Not a monster, just an arrogant princeling.

"Ella, you're shaking. Are you okay?"

I nodded jerkily, as a reflex. I was not okay. I had thought I was managing without my meds, had told myself that my trouble sleeping was only because of an unfamiliar bed. My growing jumpiness was an understandable reaction to the stabby politics around me.

That's not all it was, though, and I knew it.

My jaw clenched as I tried to slow my breathing. I failed. I tried to come up with some flippant comment to keep Tiernan from seeing how weak I was, falling into pieces from a sound in the forest. Afraid of the dark, like a child.

Still, nothing came out. Tiernan looked at me with concern. He took my lantern and examined me quickly before taking my hand in his free one.

"Come with me," he said, firmly.

I stiffened as he led me farther away from the safety of the tents.

"Not far," he promised. And sure enough, after only a few paces, the forest opened up to a small lake. Tiernan whispered something to the lantern, which flickered and faded. Our only lifeline to safety was gone. I whimpered.

"You're safe with me."

Sand crunched under my feet as he led me to the edge of the water and eased me down to sit in front of him, my back against his chest. I felt his calm, measured breathing and knew he had slowed it for me to match. I tried to match his breaths, failed, and tried again.

My eyes adjusted to the night without the lantern. Above me, millions of stars came into focus, like someone had gathered an armload of sequins and thrown them across deep blue velvet.

"I've never seen so many stars," I said in wonder.

"They're always there, but you have to get far enough from the city lights to be able to see them."

I supposed that was true. Even though no one would call Pilot Bay a city, it was never truly dark.

"That's not why I brought you here," Tiernan said in my ear. "Look down."

I did. At first, it seemed the lake must be as full of stars as the sky, glowing in shades of blue and purple. Tiny little shapes like translucent flowers drifted in the water, each holding a little glowing spark inside.

CHAPTER 24

ELLA

THE GLOWING FLOWERS MOVED LIKE JELLYFISH BUT trailed little shimmering paths behind them that slowly faded into the dark water.

My breath finally slowed as I watched the little flower fish. I realized how pressed up against Tiernan I was. One of his hands entwined with mine, resting on my knee. The other hand gently played with the ends of my silky hair.

"I'm sorry I startled you, Ella. I don't like to carry lanterns. The bright light makes it harder to see as well in the dark on clear nights."

"I can see why." I relaxed into him a bit more, and he tucked my head under his chin. I tried not to read too much into it. I didn't want to think too hard and break the spell the lake had put over us.

"Why are you up?" I asked instead.

"I have something on my mind," he admitted. "I couldn't sleep, so I relieved Haru and took this watch. Why were you roaming around the forest in the dark?"

"I had to pee," I admitted with a sigh. "Saoirse told me to watch for *Cù Sìth.*"

"Hmm." I felt the amused rumble in his chest. "Saoirse of all people should know better."

"What do you mean?"

"You're often a bit anxious, yes?"

"Yes." I sighed. That was me, the pampered city girl.

"Do you sleep well?"

"Occasionally?"

"And your thoughts," he said. "They circle around in the dark places of your mind more than you would like?"

"Yes, yes." I held a breath and then slowly let it out. "Apparently, I have anxiety."

"Having anxiety, that's a good description for it."

"You seem to know a lot about it," I said, suspiciously. There was no way this strong and fearless leader had mental health problems.

"I do. I grew up with a sister who felt all the same things."

"Who?" I racked my brain trying to remember if Tiernan had another sister.

He laughed. "Saoirse, obviously. You have met her."

"I have, and that's why I can't believe that the strongest person I've ever met has the same weakness inside her that I do."

"Hmm. You should talk to her about it yourself. It's not my story to tell. But I must say, spending every day waging battle against fear inside you is not my idea of weakness. There's a strength in it that I will never understand."

I turned his statement over in my mind. I wasn't sure if I believed it, but it was a relief to have finally told someone. And even more so to have had him not look upon me with pity or disgust.

"Do we need to go back to the camp?" I asked reluctantly, not wanting this peace to end.

Morning light crept through the trees, but the little flower fish continued to glow in the shadow of the branches.

"Fergus is always up with the sunrise. Like the birds. He'll be on watch by now. We can sit here as long as you need."

So we did, watching the sun push back the stars one by one as it rose above the trees. The little flower fish faded, retreating to the dark depths of the water.

We said nothing more, staying in our bubble of peace until the smell of breakfast cooking finally lured us back to the real world.

Now that I wasn't fearing for my life, I had to admit the camp was pretty magical. Five white tents shaped like bells hung from massive oak trees. They were bright against the green leaves just starting to turn gold.

The only member of the fianna that I hadn't officially met yet flipped pancakes on a large stone at the edge of the fire. A copper pot nestled in the coals beside him.

"Ella, you get some breakfast from Calder. I need to check on Fergus," said Tiernan.

"Tell him to come for a plate in ten minutes. I need to make a Fergus-sized stack first." Calder flipped a pancake and added some butter to the hot stone.

Tiernan laughed and melted into the forest, golden leaves floating down behind him.

The thin, pale cook held out a tin plate stacked with golden pancakes. I reached for it eagerly and then almost dropped it when Calder smiled at me. His wide grin revealed a mouth full of needle-sharp teeth.

I gasped and stumbled back a step.

"Ah, Tiernan didn't warn you." Calder looked down and scooped fresh batter onto the sizzling rock. "My grandmother was a dearg due, but don't worry, I have no taste for blood myself."

My eyes slid to the pot of bubbling red liquid beside the fire.

"I guess you'll be wanting some wild strawberry syrup on those. I had the good fortune of finding a batch of wild strawberries on our path yesterday." He ladled out a scoop of what was surely not blood and poured it over my pancakes. "Don't forget a fork now." He nodded to the forks beside him.

"Thank you!" I squeaked out as I grabbed the fork and scampered away to sit on a stump.

The rest of the fianna began to stir, no doubt roused by the smell of what turned out to be the most delicious pancakes I had ever eaten.

I did a mental tally. I had seen them all briefly at Rahivea at the training session, and a few of them had taken turns guarding me, but after hiking with the fianna yesterday, I thought I had gotten them all sorted in my mind.

There was Tiernan, of course. Saoirse and Declan were his seconds. Declan was off finding Tiernan a hot fae princess. Fergus, the birder, and Haru, who still didn't seem to be my biggest fan. Jac the spellcrafter, Calder the cook, who wasn't going to suck my blood, and Orla and Rian, twins with pale blue eyes and white blonde hair.

"How do you tell them apart?" I whispered to Jac as he wolfed down a stack of pancakes as big as his head.

"Orla wears her hair braided around her head, Rian has the braid down her back," he said.

I eyed them suspiciously. "That's the only way you can tell them apart? Sounds like a perfect way to mess with people."

I thought I was being quiet but Orla raised an amused eyebrow at me. Or was it Rian?

The twins had been scouting ahead in the trees yesterday, quiet as ghosts. I'd hardly seen them.

"I'm sorry," I told them, awkwardly. "I know I'm slowing you guys down a lot."

"It's fine," said Rian. "Eight is an unlucky number for a fianna."

"Better to be slow than cursed," agreed Orla.

"Cursed?!" I sputtered.

"A fianna is meant to have nine members. Or multiples of nine, if needed." Rian took a drink of tea.

"Superstitious nonsense," muttered Jac.

Orla glared at him. He blanched and became very interested in his food.

"But isn't Declan meeting up with us later?"

The twins shot each other sharp looks.

"It's only for a day or two, at Port Delfare." Tiernan emerged from the forest with Fergus behind him.

The twins considered this silently, then they both nodded and resumed eating. Apparently, that was fine.

"I see you've met everyone, Ella," said Tiernan, clapping his hands together. "Let's finish breakfast and then break down the camp before we head back to the village." He grabbed a tin plate stacked with pancakes. "Calder, that smells amazing."

"How does all this gear fit in our backpacks?" I asked Jac, looking around at the tents and remembering the size of my bed inside. I wasn't a backpacking expert, but the math didn't work.

Jac launched into a rapid explanation of the research he had done in the human world on the latest backpacking technology and how he had improved it with faerie techniques and materials. Despite my interest in the strength of whatever material the tent floors were made of, I still felt relieved when Tiernan sent him off to pack up his gear.

"That one sure can talk."

"He likes you." Tiernan settled down in the spot Jac had left.

"At least someone does." I fed Kiyo another bite of berry-soaked pancake while Haru glared at me from across the fire. He still hadn't forgiven me for the tart incident.

"He'll come around, eventually," Tiernan said around a mouthful of pancake.

Had he forgotten that it didn't actually matter what Haru thought of me? There wasn't going to be an eventually. We'd be meeting up with Declan in Port Delfare, and surely, he would have found a princess for Tiernan by then. After all, how hard could it be to marry off a man who was kind, funny, and about to inherit a kingdom?

CHAPTER 25

ELLA

TWO WEEKS AFTER OUR VISIT TO THE glaistig village, I sat with my bare toes enjoying a patch of
emerald green moss by the side of a clear sparkling
river. The coolness of the smooth stone canyon wall
seeped into my back. We had been following the tumbling
river down from the icy mountain lake of the kelpies yesterday.

Before the kelpies, the fianna had visited a village of
tiny butterfly-winged piskies—their entire city was built in
a giant cedar tree—and then a den of grogachs. The
smelly, hairy, little fae had made me uncomfortable at first,
but I'd come to appreciate their mischievous sense of hu-

mor. Their snail stew, however, was never going to become a favorite of mine.

The kelpies, of course, did not wear clothing since they were water horses. And the grogachs wore nothing beyond the odd leaf.

But the piskies understood fashion. The little faeries fashioned intricately detailed clothing from flower petals, leaves, grasses, and even insect wings and iridescent beetle shells.

I had sketched quickly that night by lantern light—once Saoirse had fallen asleep—and now was slowly going back and adding more detail. This, of course, eventually led to me designing my own piskie-inspired gowns of butterfly wings and jackets of rose petals. Sadly, I wasn't small enough to wear hats made out of acorn caps.

I was so engrossed in my design that I didn't notice Tiernan until he was right next to me.

"Look," he whispered, crouching quietly beside me.

I glanced over at the rock he was pointing at and gasped. A little salamander, its body no bigger than my thumb, basked on the warm rock. Its skin was a deep red. Its back was encrusted with pink crystals sparkling in the noon sun.

"It's beautiful," I breathed.

"That one's a female. The males have spiked noses, see?" Tiernan pointed to another rock farther down the river where a green salamander snoozed. Sure enough, its aqua crystals extended between its eyes and came to a sharp point at the end of its snout.

Kiyo portaled over with a pop and a squawk, and the little red salamander jumped and scurried off the rock into hiding.

"Cousin of yours?" I asked the little dragon.

She sniffed indignantly and curled up on my open sketchbook. I tipped the little dragon off, and she vanished in midair to find a resting spot where she was more appreciated. Probably with Haru, who, I noticed, had taken to saving treats for her.

I closed my sketchbook.

"Still keeping secrets?" Tiernan settled beside me, leaning back against the canyon wall.

"It's just not very interesting." I wrapped my charcoals and tucked them into my bag. "I'm not that good."

"I find that hard to believe. Can I see?"

I hesitated.

"I mean, only if you want me to."

I did want him to, I realized. I was growing tired of keeping secrets. Maybe I could start with this one. Maybe it wouldn't hurt to let him see this part of me.

I sighed and handed him the sketchbook. Tiernan shot me a smile but not a smug one like I would have expected. He looked almost…honored. I was reading too much into this.

Tiernan turned to the first page, and I resisted the urge to grab the sketchbook back from him. Why had I agreed to this?

"That's what Orla wore to Sersh's revel," said Tiernan wonderingly. "I didn't know you met her that night."

"I didn't. You said you'd be right back and then you were off talking with her instead." I tried to keep my tone matter-of-fact.

Tiernan laughed. "She had been scouting and was giving me an update. I'm sorry I made you jealous."

"You did no such thing," I said airily, leaning over and flipping the page.

"Where are these from?"

"The Lughnasadh festival." I was relieved he was moving on.

"Oh, and I recognize that one from the banquet that night. These are incredible!" He turned the page. "Dresses again. The vest my father wore to dinner. And are these the gardener's uniforms?"

"I was interested in how they're adapted to all the different body types." I leaned closer to look with him. Then I remembered what was on the next page.

"Wait, um, skip that page!" I flipped two pages at once.

"Why should I…you're blushing." Tiernan laughed.

"It's just, not very interesting." I pointed at a sketch of one of my day dresses. "This one is much better."

Tiernan batted my hand away, going back to the previous page.

"I knew it!" he crowed. "You were drawing me during the fianna training." He smirked at me. "I thought you only drew clothing."

"It's important to work on anatomy too sometimes," I said in a rush, succeeding this time in flipping the page.

"Fine, fine. But let me know if you ever need to do any more…anatomy practice." Tiernan bumped his shoulder against mine.

I closed my eyes in mortification.

"So, these are all sketches of unfinished garments?" he asked. "From your ill-advised visit to the modiste's workroom?"

"Yes." I opened my eyes, grateful he was letting the moment pass.

He continued through my sketches, commenting on each drawing of the small folk we had visited, the occasional sketch of a leaf or flower that had caught my eye, and even a chickadee that had posed helpfully for me a few days ago. Finally, he reached the final sketch and handed the book back to me.

"These are incredible, Ella! You have such a gift. Is this why you wanted to spend time in Rahivea?"

I nodded. "I need to work on my portfolio so I can get the chance to learn from some of the best designers and…" I ducked my head and busied myself with tucking the sketchbook away. "Oh, it's nothing very important."

"Hey." Tiernan waited until I looked him in the eyes. "You love it, don't you? Drawing and designing clothes."

"I do," I confessed. "I know it's silly but it makes me really…happy. I love drawing. I love the problem-solving aspect of drafting patterns. I love making dresses that make people feel beautiful. It's not going to change the world or anything, but I do love it."

"Then it's important. And there's more than one way to change the world. Making people happy, bringing beauty into the world, that's important too."

I blinked back a sudden rush of tears.

"Did I say something wrong?" Tiernan looked at me, concerned.

"No, no. I just…" I would not cry about this. "No one's ever said it like that to me." I leaned my head against his shoulder. "Thank you."

"I meant it. If everyone shared their gifts with the world, think what that would be like."

I nodded against his shoulder.

"Wait until you see the outfits at the Samhain ball. This is why you were so insistent on attending, right?"

I nodded again.

Tiernan tucked his arm around my shoulders. "The costumes are sure to be even more over the top than usual because of…" he trailed off.

"Because you'll be choosing a bride." I sat up a little straighter. I shouldn't be snuggling against someone else's future husband.

He squeezed my shoulder and removed his arm, clasping his hands on his knees. "You'll have all the inspiration you need to finish your portfolio and follow your dreams."

I would. Why didn't that sound as enticing to me anymore?

CHAPTER 26

TIERNAN

IT WAS TIME FOR A RETURN TO civilization. After a month of traveling from village to village, we reached the squat stone arch of a crossroad gate. Its carved symbols had been worn shallow from time and weather. I waited for Ella and the rest of the fianna to gather in the gate's clearing where two dirt roads met.

"We'll be staying in Port Delfare for about a month until the middle of Gort," I told the group. "I need to sort out something with the merchant's council, and Jac has lessons with his spellcraft master. We'll drop our bags off at the townhouse and then Saoirse will meet Declan with me."

Saoirse nodded, adjusting her pack.

"Fergus, you can take Jac to pick up his books from his spellcraft master."

Jac punched the big man in the arm happily. Fergus was looking up at a treetop and jumped.

"Haru and Calder, you're on market duty. Get supplies delivered for our first week. Rian and Orla, you can show Ella around the townhouse and have first dibs on a bath," I finished.

"Yes, yes, let's hurry up and get away from the crossroads, please." Rian looked over her shoulder warily.

"Dreadfully unlucky place," agreed Orla, rubbing her hands on her arms.

I kept from smiling. The twins were the most superstitious pair of fae I had ever met, but no one could argue with their scouting abilities. Being jumpy had its uses.

One by one, the fianna members disappeared through the crossroad's gate. I went through last.

It was always a shock to the system, leaving the woods and entering Port Delfare's busy market. The mossy smell of the forest was replaced by briny fishiness. The soft chirping of birds only Fergus could identify was replaced with the yelling of merchants and buyers from across the Seelie Kingdom and beyond.

Ella stared up at Port Delfare's Market Gate. Two giant wooden merrows arched overhead, visible to the whole market. Their floating wooden hair met at the top, and their curved fish's tails sprang out of the stone platform.

"Let's get off the street." I took her hand so she didn't get lost in the press of people going in and out of the gate. Market day was always busy.

We wove through a maze of stalls that sold everything from fish to clothes to jewelry to weapons from across the realm of Faerie. Once we turned onto a narrow, cobblestoned side street, I knew I should drop Ella's hand but found myself unable to untangle my fingers from hers.

She didn't object, walking beside me as she took in the city. Port Delfare was built up the hills surrounding a wide bay. The streets wound their way down the mountainside, lined with colorful houses, bright against the cloudy sky. Some had the garden rooftops common in Rahivea but many were topped with shingles or polished metal.

Down in the bay, boats of all sizes floated, from little fishing boats to ships with multiple masts as tall as the trees in the piskie village.

"Look." I pointed at the sea beyond the bay where a scaled back breached the water. Ella gasped as a tail the size of a galleon's sail crashed against the surface while the giant sea serpent dove.

"A *cirein-cròin*!" Rian called from ahead. "Excellent omen."

"Don't they eat ships?" Jac scowled at her as he walked.

"Yes, but it has a hatchling," Orla pointed out.

Sure enough, a smaller tail—only as big as a two-story house—peeked out from the waves before sliding into the inky sea.

We all watched—Ella's free hand over her mouth in delight—as the pair surfaced one more time before disappearing under the waves. Then we continued walking until the salty air smelled less of fish and more of flowers. Every house on the row was crafted out of the same white stone and had a lush garden courtyard out front, but each one differed in height and design. Many had balconies with tumbling flowers. The sound of fountains and birds drifted through the air.

Reluctantly, I released Ella's hand and guided her ahead of me through the gate to the townhouse's courtyard, rubbing the snout of the left gargoyle for luck, just like the rest of the fianna had before me.

Haru reached the entrance first, and he pressed his hand on the gold plate next to it to unlock the heavy wooden door.

Everyone unloaded their gear into their bedrooms and then set off on their assigned errands.

Morna was waiting for me in the courtyard. She flew over and landed on my shoulder, nudging my cheek to transfer an impression of Declan in front of a window display of breads and cakes.

"He's at the bakery," I told Saoirse as she joined me outside. I handed the bird a treat. She nudged me again affectionately and then took off into the air. I knew she would stick around the townhouse until I sent her off with Declan again.

"Of course he is," said Saoirse. "It's been two months. He must have sticky bun withdrawal."

Declan's favorite bakery wasn't far from the townhouse, and we reached the small shop in a handful of minutes. Pressed in on both sides by its neighbors on a narrow street, the bakery had a little shop where you could buy treats and tea. The baker's home rested above it with a window box of herbs and berries.

The smells of yeast and sugar hit me in a warm gust as we entered the bakery. Declan lounged at a table in the corner.

My friend had a talent for lounging anywhere, even on a tiny wooden stool with steaming tea in his hand.

He straightened to wave us over, and we exchanged back-pounding hugs before we slid onto stools of our own. Saoirse sat with her back against a wall so she could keep an eye on the door more easily.

The baker's pretty daughter dropped a plate of sticky buns on the table with a wink for me. I smiled back out of habit, but I couldn't be bothered to flirt today.

She pouted as she flounced off, and Declan raised an eyebrow.

"Any prospects?" I ignored his curiosity.

He sighed and picked up a sticky bun, flicking the nuts out of the caramel.

"I visited all of the mainland Seelie courts known to be more…modern minded," he said carefully. "And did not find a good match for you."

I bristled. "No one wants to marry the crown prince of the Seelie Kingdom?"

"There, there," said Declan. "You're very handsome, don't worry."

Saoirse snorted, taking a sip of her tea.

"What's the problem? Is it the responsibility?"

"It's your father."

I exhaled in frustration. "He got to them first."

Declan nodded. "Before your little ruse with Ella started." He unwound a section of sticky bun and popped it into his mouth.

"And this doesn't prompt any of them to believe change is necessary?" asked Saoirse.

"They fear for their daughters." Declan licked his fingers. "They were reminded of what happened to Brenna."

"Fiachra threatened them." I drummed my fingers on the table. "They're sympathetic to our cause but none are willing to risk the lives of their daughters."

I ran my hands through my hair in frustration. "So, who's left?"

"Well, I have not yet been to the Isle of Mist nor the Coral Court."

"You think the merrows would interfere in land politics?" Saoirse leaned forward.

Declan shrugged. "Fiachra probably hasn't threatened them, at least. And then there is the possibility of an alliance with a foreign princess. That was, after all, the original purpose in bringing Saoirse here as a child."

"Then he shouldn't have raised us as siblings," I said. "What do you say, Sersh?"

"I'd rather marry a grogoch."

"Ouch!" I pressed a hand to my heart. "But fair. Where do you think Declan should try next? Alfheim?"

"I think you're being purposefully obtuse," my sister said.

I raised my eyebrows.

"You already have a sweetheart the *Aos Sí* adore. She rescues crying apprentice children, is not afraid of your father, and has won over your fianna. I caught Calder putting extra berries in her pancakes this morning."

"Ella is not an option," I said flatly, picking apart my roll but not eating any.

Declan looked from me to Saoirse. "Has our decoy bride been doing well, then?"

"She is sweet, courageous, and quite pretty. Just ask Tiernan."

"Tiernan?" Declan looked at me, intrigued.

I avoided his gaze, looking out the window. "Ella kindly offered to help, temporarily. I will not be trapping her here."

They both looked at me.

"Besides, there's no way the courts will accept her. She's practically a commoner."

"They accepted Isobel," pointed out Declan. "She's a commoner and a human."

I gave him a look.

"Sort of accepted her," amended Saoirse. "Most of them."

"Leith is only the Rose Prince. I will be the high king. I must marry someone who can help me hold this country together."

"Nobles aren't the only Seelie fae. And I never took you for a snob, after all," said Declan.

"You know I'm not," I gritted out.

Saoirse and Declan exchanged another look.

"Are you really so afraid?" asked Saoirse softly.

"I will not repeat my father's mistakes." I rose abruptly from the table and turned to Declan. "Find me a princess who will support our plans. I need to secure the future of our kingdom, and Ella needs to go home."

CHAPTER 27

ELLA

I PEEKED OUT THE FRONT WINDOW AND breathed a sigh of relief at Jac and Fergus's retreating backs. Most of the fianna had left on their errands, and the chaos of so many people rushing around the townhouse had subsided.

I wandered across the main room, my stocking feet sinking into the lush green carpet. Everyone had taken their boots off at the door, which had made the Japanese-Canadian in me sigh in relief. It was something that had driven me crazy in the palace where everyone wandered in and out in boots all day.

Looking closer at the carpet, I realized it was actually moss, like the corridors in the palace, with the occasional tiny white mushroom poking through.

"There are slippers in the basket by the door if you get cold feet." Orla entered the large room, her sister behind her. They both wore shearling-lined slippers.

"I'm fine." I felt more than fine. It felt good to let my toes wiggle after a month in boots.

"Suit yourself." Orla shrugged. "Tour?"

"Yes please!"

"This is the main living area." Rian waved her hand to indicate the large open room that seemed to be a seamless combination of modern human and faerie comforts.

The main feature of the living area was a sectional in caramel leather large enough to comfortably seat the whole fianna. Cozy tasseled blankets and embroidered velvet pillows were strewn on the sofas.

In classic Seelie fashion, gold lanterns and trailing plants hung from the ceiling with more plants arranged on the low bookcase in front of the tall windows. Sheer white curtains let light into the room while blocking the view from the street.

"Who waters the plants?" I ran my hand over a feathery fern.

"Tiernan keeps a small staff," Orla said. "They don't live here, but they keep everything watered and cleaned."

"And hopefully, the icebox stocked." Rian prowled past the long oak table in the middle of the space. A stone fireplace took up most of the wall in the dining area with gleaming, deadly-looking weapons displayed on the wall above it. A sparkling chandelier crawling with ivy hung overhead.

I followed the twins around a marble countertop separating the kitchen from the rest of the space to a suspiciously modern-looking mint-colored fridge.

"Is it unlucky to have an empty…icebox?"

Rian opened the fridge and pulled out an apple. "No, I'm just hungry."

Had there been appliances in the palace? I hadn't noticed any when I had dropped Isla off, only wood stoves and fireplaces with cauldrons bubbling.

This kitchen was light and bright with shelves of stacked dishes and jars of what looked like teas and spices. The farmhouse-style sink had a trickling waterfall running into it, with little ferns growing between the smooth river rocks.

"Do you want anything?" asked Orla, digging through a basket and coming up with some of those little round croissants.

I took one, still looking around. "This is all more-…human than I expected."

"Leith—" started Orla.

"She doesn't know Leith," interrupted Rian.

"Right," said Orla. "Leith was Tiernan's second back when they were young. They're still very close. Leith's fiancée redecorated it for Tiernan—with Jac's help—for Yule last year."

"She's a human," added Rian. "It's all a bit shiny, but I do like having cold apples. Come on, we'll show you the rest of the house. Have you found Saoirse's room? You'll be bunking with her."

"You all have your own rooms here? Don't you live at the palace?"

"Technically, we do, but most of us are not welcomed by the Seelie nobles. Too odd," said Rian.

"Too common." Orla tapped her chest.

"Haru is too foreign. Jac is too Unseelie." Rian started up the stairs, tapping her finger against a bedroom door.

"Fergus is too interested in birds and not interested enough in fashion or politics. Calder takes too much after his grandmother. The teeth, you know." Orla tapped another door and then climbed another set of stairs.

"Saoirse is both too fierce and too brown." Rian tapped the door to the room I was sharing with the warrior fae.

"Really, only Tiernan and Declan fit in at court." Orla pointed to the door across from ours.

"They share a room? I thought if Tiernan owned this townhouse he'd at least have his own room."

"He wanted the last bedroom for a study. I don't think he likes being alone. Had enough of it as a child, I guess." Rian took another bite out of her apple.

I was still having trouble coming to terms with this version of Tiernan, which I was beginning to see was actually the real version of Tiernan.

"And this is all of our home," said Orla. "Tiernan has given us access to the main Seelie gates and the townhouse, so that each of us may come here whenever we wish."

"But it's more fun when we're all here together." Rian walked past us and opened Saoirse's door. "You'll be in here. If you keep going up, you'll reach the rooftop."

The twins left me in Saoirse's room. A four-poster bed took up half of the room. On the other side of a stone fireplace, a cot had been set up, topped with a soft-looking comforter and pillows. I stowed my backpack under the cot and checked out the small but luxurious bathroom. It was a marble jungle with plants vining up the walls and over the clawfoot tub.

"I had a cactus once," I told Kiyohime, who had woken up and climbed up to my shoulder to investigate. "I killed it."

Kiyo chirped at me.

"You're right. If I had staff to take care of my plants, I might have a bathroom like this too. Although, there might be some fae magic involved."

I ran a bath and soaked a month of camping out of my skin and hair while Kiyo finished off the bun snagged from the kitchen, which I'd left on a stool next to the tub. The hot water felt amazing on my sore shoulders and feet, even if it did sting a bit on the multiple small scrapes from branches on my legs and arms.

I was growing drowsy as the water cooled when I heard Saoirse entering the bedroom.

"There are clean clothes on your bed, Ella. Everything will get washed while we're here," she called from the other room. "And I borrowed Orla's drying comb for you."

Drying comb? I hadn't even thought of the fact that I was going to have to put on my dirty clothes again, but I was grateful. But would any of Saoirse's clothes even fit me? She was a good foot taller than me.

By the time I pulled myself out of the tepid bath, Saoirse had left again. On my cot, I found what was probably a sleeveless tunic on her. The pale turquoise linen fell almost to my knees with golden embroidery at the neck. When I fastened my leather belt around my waist, the reflection in the mirror was pretty cute, if I did say so myself.

I ran the golden comb through my hair, and it hummed with magic as it dried my hair to silky smooth perfection.

"Do you think this would work in the human realm?" I asked Kiyo.

Hungry, said the little dragon. My stomach growled in response, and I laughed.

I followed the sound of laughter and the smell of grilling fish up the last set of steps to the townhouse's roof. A waist-high stone wall edged the roof with gargoyles looking out on the corners.

I followed a stone path from the doorway winding through the green grass covering most of the roof to the dining area.

Trees and ferns grew in the corners. Little lights danced through them. At first glance, the lights reminded me of the sheerie, but they were just more of the glowing motes of light used in the lanterns. A stream with little fish in it ran along one edge, and I wondered if it connected to the waterfall sink downstairs.

I reached the center of the roof and found a stone grill and oven and a long table with padded wicker chairs. The whole fianna had gathered up here, including Declan, who had obviously just arrived. He was hugging and back-pounding various members of the fianna.

It looked like a fianna moment, so I wandered over to visit Calder at the grill. The pointy-toothed cook had his usual knives strapped to his thighs and a great sword across his back.

"That's a lot of weapons for cooking dinner." I peeked at the veggies roasting on the grill.

"What do you mean?" he asked, moving to the wooden chopping block.

"All the pointy objects?" I said.

"Oh, you mean my cooking knives." He chopped mushrooms briskly with a small dagger. "I don't have weapons. Only pure-blooded *Tuatha Dé Danann* are allowed them, you know."

"And that sword on your back?"

"Orla!" he called. "Fish!"

Orla tossed a large fish over the campfire. While it flew through the air, Calder whipped the sword off his back, smoothly slicing the fish in the air. It fell in two neat halves on his cutting board, and with three more swipes, the fish lay headless, its bones piled neatly beside it.

"It's my fileting knife," he said.

I stared at him, my mouth open.

Tiernan wandered over and laughed at my expression.

"And the fianna practices?" I finally asked. "That's for your knife skills?"

"An essential part of any chef's training." Calder arranged the fish on the grill.

"Remind me to never make Calder angry," I whispered to Tiernan.

He laughed. "It's always wise to stay on the good side of a cook. What's for dinner, Calder?"

"Go sit down." Calder brandished one of his many "chef's knives" at Tiernan.

"Doesn't that one need flipping?" Tiernan poked one of the skewers on the grill, and Calder smacked his knuckles with the flat of his blade.

"Ella," the cook said to me. "Can you keep an eye on these fish while I check on the flatbread?"

"I can keep an eye on the fish!" Tiernan sucked his red knuckles.

"Last time you kept an eye on the fish, there were no fish left." Calder stepped around me to look in the oven. "Only charcoal in the shape of fish."

"I could help Orla with the salad," offered the prince.

"Nobody wants to reattach your pinkie finger," called Orla from the table where she sliced tomatoes. "Again, I mean."

"Fine. What can I do then?" asked Tiernan grumpily.

"You can go down to the icebox and fetch up the drinks," answered Calder.

"Are you sure?" asked Haru from the doorway. "Last time he dropped them on the stairs."

"I've got them!" Tiernan ran to the stairs before anyone could stop him.

"So." I lifted a corner of the nearest fish to check the color. "Tiernan doesn't cook?"

Calder pulled a long wooden paddle with a golden flatbread out of the oven. "You wouldn't think someone who is nearly two hundred and so skilled with a blade would be so inept in the kitchen." He slid the bread onto a wooden platter. "But here we are."

My stomach growled loudly, and Calder smiled.

"Perfect timing." He raised his voice to be heard over the general chatter. "Dinner time!"

CHAPTER 28

ELLA

SUPPER WAS A NOISY AFFAIR, BETWEEN DECLAN loudly telling stories about the various Seelie courts and the others catching him up on the affairs of the villages.

I stayed quiet, feeding bites to Kiyo and enjoying the friendly bantering and Calder's excellent cooking. It was such a far cry from dinner at Kimberly's house, where it was a rare occasion to have more than two people eating at once. Most meals were taken on the way to dance or volleyball with a pile of containers left in the kitchen when they got home.

This? This felt like family.

I barely remembered dinner when both of my own parents were alive—surely, it hadn't been nearly so loud—but somehow this reminded me of that sense of peace and belonging.

But you don't really belong here. It's temporary. Think of your plans, think of Parsons.

The bright sparkle of fashion school on the horizon had dimmed.

Tiernan laughed loudly, and the sound made me smile, even though I had missed the joke. He was so happy and open here compared to those strained dinners with his father. I was glad he had made a family for himself. I was grateful for my time with them, even if it couldn't last.

The sun hung low over the sea when we began to tidy up after dinner. Saoirse handed me a stack of plates and nodded to the stairs.

"Now, don't be upset with Tiernan," she began once we were out of everyone's earshot.

"A lovely start."

"But he told me about your anxiety."

I almost missed the step, plates shifting dangerously in my hands. I attempted to speak casually. "That wasn't his secret to share."

"That's what I told him. But, even though he is a bit dense, my brother is worried about you."

"I'm fine," I snapped.

"Hmm, not grouchy then?"

"Maybe this is just my personality," I shot back.

She laughed but continued kindly, "Is insomnia also just your personality?"

"It could be."

"And the shortness of breath, the racing thoughts, the concern over what everyone thinks of you at all times, even if they might understand? Also your personality?" Saoirse rounded the corner into the kitchen.

"Possibly." I set the dishes on the counter. When I moved to grab the dishrag, Saoirse waved me off.

"It's Declan and Fergus's turn. Ella—"

I crossed my arms.

"If you don't want to talk about it, we don't have to talk about it."

"Good."

"But," she said. "You can have some of my tea for tonight, if you want."

"Your tea?" I raised my eyebrows.

"I assume you don't have any of your own or you wouldn't be in this state," she added.

Ah, tea must have been their equivalent to meds?

"Right, my tea," I said. "I did have some."

"But you ran out."

"Yes." I wasn't ready to go into the whole, *didn't think I'd need them in Faerie* thing. Or that since Kimberly had taken me off her health care plan, I had only ever been taking the minimum dose, barely enough to keep my hands steady and my heart rate down.

"I'll take you to my herbalist tomorrow. It's always better to get your own blend. Mine should help you sleep though."

Sleep. I barely remembered what sleep was.

"That does sound nice." I sighed. "Thank you."

Saoirse nodded and headed toward the door.

"Please don't murder my brother," she shot back at me. "He means well."

"No promises."

Later that night, when the tables were cleared and the stars were out, I found Tiernan alone on the rooftop. He sat with his long legs slung over the wall, looking down on the city below. His green cloak swayed in the night air. I wrapped my own cloak closer around me against the growing autumn chill. The seasons here were getting closer to what I had left behind in Pilot Bay.

"Traitor." I swung my own legs over the wall and settled down beside the prince.

"You talked to Saoirse then?"

"She talked to me," I said.

"I know you're not happy about it…"

"Correct."

"But a good leader is concerned for the health of his people."

"I'm not sick or injured," I grumbled.

"Hmm," he said. "Bodies, minds, they all need help sometimes."

I looked out over the water, remembering the salve he had given me for my feet, when my pride would have let me walk until I fell over in my bloody boots.

"You might have a point, but I'm still not happy with you."

"I'd rather have you mad at me than scared of the world."

"Ugh, it's so hard to be mad at you when you say things like that."

"Another accusation of me being too charming?" asked Tiernan playfully.

"No," I said. "You're being…nice. I haven't seen Prince Charming since we left Rahivea."

"Well, courtly manners are less important when I'm out here."

"It's more than that though, isn't it?" I looked down at the city below, trying to think my way through it. "It's like you're comfortable being who you really are when you're with them." I pointed downstairs to where the fianna was gathered. I had left Kiyohime with Haru, who had given up trying to be aloof and just spoiled her with treats instead.

He nodded. "They're my family," he said simply.

"More than your father?"

He blew out a breath. "More than the king. More than the brother I've never met. The mother I hardly remember. Saoirse and Declan are my true siblings. As for the rest of the fianna, we've had each other's backs time and again. I trust them all with my life."

I sensed that he didn't just mean he trusted them in deadly peril, but he actually trusted them with the day-to-day reality of his life.

"Sounds nice," I said wistfully.

Tiernan rested his cool hand on mine, twining his long fingers between my own. He turned to me, and my breath caught at the intensity in his eyes.

"For as long as you're here, you're one of us."

A heartbeat passed. His gaze dropped to my lips, and I felt like I was falling. Like gravity was pulling me toward him. The coldness of the night was forgotten as heat flushed through me.

"Ella," he whispered, running a finger across my cheek. It wasn't a question but an answer.

Suddenly, the door to the stairs banged open, and we jumped apart.

"There you are." Declan strode across the roof. "We need to go over things before I leave tomorrow."

"Right." Tiernan looked at me, his eyes unreadable. The inches between us felt like miles as cold autumn air rushed between us.

I had almost kissed a man who would be engaged to someone else by the end of the month. Who I would never see again once I returned home. This was a recipe for disaster.

I needed to clear my head. I swung back off the wall and pushed myself away from the prince.

"Ella, wait," he said.

I shook my head, avoiding his eyes. "You guys have to talk. You've got a princess to find, after all."

I ran down to my room, which was mercifully empty, except for Kiyo, who had left Haru to raid the silverware drawer. Dainty silver forks and spoons lay in a heap with what appeared to be a couple of crystals from the chandelier and the remains of a chocolate cookie.

"Kiyo! No more hoarding!" I flopped down on my bed next to her treasures. What was I going to do with this little dragon?

Kiyo blinked out of the heap, and a second later, dropped an uneaten cookie in my lap.

I took a bite. "Okay, I understand wanting to hoard the cookies," I said. "But you still have to put everything else back. But first, I've a message for you to deliver."

Saoirse made me a cup of her special blend at bedtime, and while I had my doubts about tea as medication, boy did I sleep that night.

I fell asleep while Tiernan and his crew were still laughing downstairs. When I emerged the next morning—in borrowed pajamas so long I had to roll the cuffs up—breakfast was over. Saoirse sat alone at the cleared table, sipping a cup of tea and reading a novel.

"So, what's in today's tea?" I sat across from her with a yawn.

"Caffeine." Saoirse waved her free hand at a teapot on the table beside the fruit basket. "You look like you could use some."

I nodded blearily. "Why is it that when I finally get a good night's sleep, I feel even more tired than I did yesterday?"

Saoirse shrugged. "It's the same with me. My theory is that once your body remembers what sleep is, it wants more of it. Your breakfast is in the oven," she added before going back to her book.

I got up and peeked in the oven. Sure enough, inside sat a plate covered with a square of linen. Once I pulled it out, I found two large muffins smelling of plums and spices and three small blue eggs. I sat down and slathered butter on the still warm muffins.

"There was a custard too, but Calder noticed you don't eat dairy."

"I can handle butter but everything else gives me a stomachache. Oh, these are so good!" I took another bite of the muffin.

"Haru is the same. If he eats dairy, we all suffer the consequences."

"Where is everyone?"

"Jac is back with his craftmaster, and Fergus went along because the craftmaster has an excellent library with books on all sorts of topics."

"Like birds?" I asked.

"Like birds," she said. "Birds, trees, dragons, things."

"So is Jac like an apprentice to him?"

"Sort of. We found Jac five years ago. He was little more than a kid, half frozen on the Unseelie side of the *Bhanmhor Sliabhraon* range."

"So you adopted him?"

"More or less. It wasn't that simple. Not everyone was on board with an Unseelie in one of our fianna, but Tiernan insisted. He has good instincts about people. He knows who he can trust." She didn't look at me, just sipped her tea.

I peeled one of the little eggs before eating it in two bites.

"Anyway, Jac. Jac has the sight, which is rare enough. That, coupled with his knack for building and mechanics has made him a formidable spellcrafter already. We all try to make sure he gets time to study."

I bit into the second muffin, tasting molasses and cloves. "He said he spent time in the human realm, too?"

"Humans have more interest in innovation than is perhaps healthy for them, but there are certainly things we can learn. Have you ever visited their realm?"

I coughed, choking on my muffin. "My stepmother doesn't like to let me out of her sight," I said bitterly, which was not exactly a lie. I was tired of lying. Not that it was any better to tell half-truths while still letting them believe I was fae. I wanted to come clean, but I also didn't want to lose this newfound feeling of belonging.

Unseelie prodigies were one thing, but how would they feel if they knew I was a human and had been lying to them for over a month?

"Well, maybe you'll get your chance someday." Saoirse shut her book and stood. "Today's expedition will be closer to home. Get dressed. It's time to visit the herbalist."

CHAPTER 29

ELLA

KIYOHIME PORTALED BACK TO ME AS SAOIRSE led me down narrow cobbled streets toward the market district. I had lured the ryū into my bag with the promise of a leftover muffin before Saoirse had time to glance over and see the piece of paper fastened to Kiyo's ankle. Reaching one hand into my bag, I untied the note and left it there to read when I had a quiet moment.

We left the grand white townhouses behind and made our way through a more middle class neighborhood. Snug houses topped with vegetable gardens came alive as children squealed overhead and parents strung laundry between rooftops to dry.

As we got closer to the harbor, there were fewer and fewer homes and more shops. Bakeries, bookstores, enchanted houseplants…Was that a fabric store?

I peered through the wavy glass of the window trying to make out the designs on the textiles.

"No shopping. I'll bring you back some other time." Saoirse tugged me along. "Madam Singh is expecting us."

"I'll be going home soon, remember?" And home was farther than she knew.

"Probably, but I don't see any reason why you can't visit."

"Maybe." I was touched that Saoirse wanted to spend more time with me, but even if I could find my way back to Faerie in the future, the thought of seeing Tiernan and his perfect bride felt like a twist to the dagger already threatening to pierce my heart.

"Here we are." Saoirse stopped in front of a narrow storefront, its stone facade covered in green plants and creeping vines. *Madam Singh*, read the neatly painted wooden sign above the bright yellow door.

Saoirse ducked through the door, brushing a trailing vine away from her twisted knots of black hair. I followed her into a bright shop, sunshine streaming in through the front windows. More plants of all shapes and sizes crowded around the windows, and glass jars lined the remaining walls. Some were clear, some tinted in shades of blue and brown. A low wooden counter with neatly stacked bags and empty jars stood near the back.

I was examining a jar of little purple flowers that appeared to be faintly glowing when a small woman wheeled into the room. Her smooth white hair, braided into a knot at the nape of her neck, contrasted with warm brown skin a few shades lighter than Saoirse's. Graceful golden horns curled from her head. With a tap of her elegant, wrinkled fingers, the chair wheeled over to Saoirse, golden spokes shining.

"Madam Singh!" Saoirse leaned down to kiss the woman on her cheek.

"I have your usual order ready." Madam Singh patted her hand. "I added a little something to help with the dreams." She turned to me. "And who is your friend?"

Saoirse hauled me out of the corner. "This is Ella. I was hoping you'd have the time to make something up for her as well."

"Indeed." Madam Singh looked me up and down shrewdly.

I swallowed. "You can just make me the same tea as Saoirse."

"I cannot."

My heart fell, but Madam Singh added, "Every tisane is a custom blend. I'll make you your own." She waved her hand at Saoirse. "You can come back in an hour."

Saoirse nodded and then patted my shoulder. "You're in good hands, don't worry."

"If I could not worry, we wouldn't be here," I muttered.

Saoirse just laughed and exited the shop, the little bell ringing behind her.

"This way, if you please." Madam Singh wheeled ahead of me into the back room, a comfortable sitting room with low bookshelves, diagrams of various plants on the walls, and a couch draped with blankets.

A large, fluffy white cat glared at me from the middle cushion.

"Yarrow, move for our customer, if you please." The herbalist pulled out a book and then tapped her chin before choosing another.

Yarrow did not please. I sat gingerly on the couch. Yarrow's tail twitched.

Kiyo poked her head out of my bag, saw the cat, and quickly disappeared.

"Yarrow doesn't eat ryū, don't worry. He's much too lazy.ö Madam Singh parked her chair across from the couch and flipped open her notebook. "So, child, this will be a bit tricky as you're a human.ö

"I…what?" I fumbled for my earrings. Still there.

"No doubt you've been successfully hiding it from your companions, but when you get to be my age, you can tell these things." She scratched a note down and then glanced up at me. "Don't worry, I won't reveal your secret. I'm sure you have your reasons, but it will mean that I'll likely need a day or two to collect the necessary ingredients for you."

"Thank you." I reached out to pat Yarrow, needing something to do with my hands. He looked at me. I retracted my hand. "I'm sorry to be causing extra work for you."

"Nonsense, it's good to have a little variety. Keeps things interesting. Now tell me, how have you been feeling?"

I told the little woman about my anxiety, and she *hmmed* and took notes, occasionally asking a question.

"And are there any flavors you prefer? Citrus? Mint? Lavender?"

"I like cinnamon and spices," I said.

"Ah, yes. I've heard Indian chai is quite popular in the human realm these days." Madam Singh wrote down another note. "I'll have something ready for you the day after tomorrow."

"Thank you." I smiled. Something about the herbalist put me at ease.

"Ella," called Saoirse from the front room. My hour must be up.

"Coming!"

"One more thing." Madam Singh picked up the cat from the couch and settled him on her lap.

"Yes?"

"You might feel better if you tell your companions the truth." The herbalist scratched Yarrow behind his ears, and the cat began to purr. "I'm not saying that it will make your anxiety go away, but it might take it down a notch. It can't be easy keeping secrets all day."

"It won't be forever." I smiled wistfully. Only a month and a half until the Samhain ball, after all. And then I'd be going home.

"I hope so," she said. "We're not meant to live life separated from everyone, child. You need to let people in."

I nodded, but as I left, I couldn't help thinking that I had already let too many people in. First Amber, then Tiernan, now Saoirse. Leaving for New York had always felt like freedom, but more and more, it was just looking lonely.

CHAPTER 30

ELLA

THE NOTE FROM AMBER HAD SIMPLY READ: *You're right. We do need to talk*, and had given me a date and time in the human world. The following afternoon for her. Three and a half weeks for me.

Three and a half weeks of swapping folktales with Haru, learning how to bake bread with Calder, and being lectured by the twins whenever I did something new that was bad luck. Three and a half weeks of being amazed by Jac's inventions—a gold-etched cup to keep my drinks hot or cold and silverware that didn't portal to drive Kiyo crazy—watching birds from the rooftop with Fergus, begrudgingly talking about my *feelings* with Saoirse, and sketching in the evenings while Tiernan told me stories about the funny things he had seen on patrols.

Three and a half weeks of wondering how I would ever be happy without them all.

At last, the time to meet Amber came, and luckily, my special tea was running out, giving me an excuse to go out and pick up more from Madam Singh. Jac accompanied me on his way to grab more books from his spellcraft master.

"She's got this book on human cell phones," said Jac as we walked down the cobbled street. "Did you know humans can talk to each other any time they like without a mirror or anything, but they mostly just send each other videos of cats? Why do you think that is?"

"Humans are a mystery." I reached Madam Singh's bright yellow door. "This is my stop."

"How long will you be?" asked Jac.

"A bit."

He tapped his fingers against his leg, obviously antsy to go learn more about the bizarre habits of humankind.

"You go on ahead," I told the young fae. "I'll be fine."

"You're sure?" asked Jac. "I'll be back in a half hour or so."

"Totally, go ahead. I've heard they sometimes make hats for those cats, you know."

"Hats? Okay, I'll be fast!" Jac dashed off, leaving me alone for the first time in ages.

After a brief discussion about dosage and time of day to drink the gloriously spicy-smelling tea and paying with some of the money Tiernan had given me, I ducked out of the herbalist's shop and made my way to the Market Gate.

I still didn't know my way around very well, but luckily, the Market Gate was close by and very large, making it easy to spot from three streets down. When I reached the wooden mermaids, I was barreled over by my friend swathed in a red velvet cloak with gold trim. She squealed loudly enough to send ten gulls, a chickadee, and a raven flying off in all directions.

"I thought this was a magical cloak," I said. "How come I can recognize you this time?"

"Because you're expecting me. That's how the cloak works. It's a bit weird. Now…" She hooked her arm through mine. "Spill the tea, if you please. Also, is the shopping in Port Delfare as good as I've heard?"

"Let's take a walk, and you can see for yourself!"

We made our way down the street, enjoying the sunshine and the bustle of the market district. We stopped at a cart selling cinnamon sugar doughnuts in the shape of fish. One for each of us and two for Kiyo. I made the little dragon eat hers out of my hand so she wouldn't get my sketchbook sticky again.

"I almost kissed Tiernan a couple of weeks ago," I confessed.

Amber squealed. "I knew it! Wait, what do you mean *almost?*"

"We got interrupted."

"Classic excuse." Amber licked cinnamon sugar off her fingers. "So since then…"

"I've been avoiding being alone with him."

Amber rolled her eyes. "Ugh, you're hopeless. Tell me the truth. Do you like him?"

"Of course." I fed the second fish to Kiyo, who made a noise that sounded suspiciously like purring as she nibbled the sugary treat. "What's not to like?"

"Give me details, girl."

I sighed. "He's just not who I thought he was. When we were in Rahivea, he acted like this arrogant prince who didn't seem to care about anyone but himself."

"But not anymore?"

"I've gotten to know him better on this trip—the real him—and he's kind, he's funny, and when I showed him my sketchbook—"

"Wait, you showed him your sketches? That's a pretty big deal, right?"

"Very," I agreed. "He seemed interested, actually interested, in my designs. He said it was rare to meet someone with such talent and passion."

"Hot! And what else?"

"He would do anything for his kingdom. Even…" I faltered.

"Even what?"

I stroked Kiyo's fluffy mane. "Even marry someone he doesn't love," I whispered.

Amber stopped and looked at me. "This sounds like more than you just like him," she said. "You love him, don't you?"

"Yes," I whispered. I felt something release in my chest at saying it out loud.

We were almost to the herbalist now, and I saw Jac waiting outside, tapping his leg worriedly. I felt bad, but I needed more time.

Grabbing Amber, I pulled her into the nearest shop.

"Welcome to Hazel's Enchanted Houseplants!" A knee-high faerie, who appeared to be composed of mossy rocks, beamed up at us. "Can I help you find anything?"

"Um," said Amber.

"We just got a shipment of night-glowing hoyas, perfect for a child's bedroom, and shrieking succulents are half-off," said Hazel. An ear-splitting scream came from a back corner.

Kiyo clawed up my arm and huddled around my neck.

"I can't imagine why they don't sell," murmured Amber.

"I see what I want." I hauled Amber to a back corner full of tall potted shrubs.

"Let me know if you have any questions!" called Hazel.

We crowded into the corner with the fluffy purple plants.

"So, what are you going to do?" whispered Amber.

"I don't know!" I whispered back. "Nothing? He needs to marry some fae princess who all the nobles will approve of to become king and save the kingdom from his horrible father. I can't ask him to give up all that for me! Besides," I said, even more softly. "What if he doesn't feel the same way?"

"Or…ah! Stop that!" Amber smacked away a branch gently stroking the side of her face.

"Comforting shrubs are twenty-five percent off!" piped up Hazel from the other side of the store.

"Thank you!" we both called.

"What if Tiernan feels the same way, but he's worried that you don't love him?"

"Do you think so?" I perked up.

"I have no idea," said Amber. "All I know is that one of you is going to have to be brave if you're going to figure this out."

"Being brave is not my strong point."

Another branch bent over and began to stroke Kiyo's back. The little dragon chirped and leaned into the purple fronds, almost falling out of my arms.

"I need to tell him the truth first," I decided. "I should tell him who I really am."

"Excellent idea," said Amber. "Is he at the townhouse?"

"Right now?" I froze, clutching the strap of my bag.

Amber rolled her eyes. "Or you could be like Isobel and work up a ridiculous scheme to avoid having a normal conversation."

"Well, when you put it like that…"

"Exactly. My work here is done."

We extracted ourselves from the embrace of the comforting shrubs—reluctantly in Kiyo's case. Then Amber picked out a vanilla cookie-scented cactus for Lily before she headed back to the human world.

I poked my head out of Hazel's shop as Amber left. Jac wasn't in front of the herbalist's anymore. I grimaced and started toward the shop. Hopefully I hadn't gotten him into trouble. If he wasn't waiting inside Madam Singh's, I'd send Kiyo to get him.

"We might be in trouble," I told the little dragon.

"You most certainly are," said a rough voice from behind me. A large hand clamped over my mouth before I could scream, yanking me back.

Kiyo squealed and fell to the ground.

Get help! I yelled mentally at her, twisting futilely to get away.

My heart almost stopped when a raven dove down toward her, claws out, but Kiyo portalled safely away before it caught her. I could only hope she had the sense to find somebody close by.

My kidnapper dragged me toward the alley behind Miss Hazel's. I kicked at his knee but missed.

"Come along now," he grunted. "This is a nice part of town. The king won't be happy if I leave a mess."

Fiachra. It had been naïve of me to believe I was beyond his reach just because we were away from the palace. My panic grew as the guard dragged me, struggling, farther down the alley.

I managed to elbow him, but the man didn't so much as grunt.

"Ella?" Tiernan's voice called frantically from the street.

I bit down on my kidnapper's hand.

"Tier—!"

The hand clamped down on me again. "None of that, now." The man pulled me along faster.

But not fast enough. Tiernan barreled down the alley, sword drawn, Jac and Fergus on his heels. A flash of black streaked across my vision as the raven immediately took flight, but not before Tiernan spotted it.

My would-be assassin must have realized he wasn't going to be able to outrun the prince while dragging me along. He abruptly shoved me at Tiernan while turning to run.

Tiernan's sword clattered to the ground as he caught me. He dropped to his knees, holding me tightly while Fergus and Jac dashed past us in pursuit of my attacker.

"Are you okay?" Tiernan gathered me closer against his chest.

I nodded then winced at a crack and a grunt from farther down the alley.

"Don't worry; they got him." Tiernan pushed me away to arm's length. "What were you thinking?!"

I was stunned by the raw fear on his face.

"I'm sorr—" I started but was cut off by his lips crashing down on mine.

I froze, overwhelmed. For all my talk to Amber, I don't know if I had believed that he actually cared about me. His lips were hot against mine, and I knew I should be kissing him back, but he pulled back before I could get over my shock.

"Sorry." His eyes widened. "That was… I didn't mean to… I never should have agreed to this!" Tiernan ran his hands through his ginger hair, making it stick up wildly. "I never should have put you in danger like this. I know what my father is like!"

"It's okay." I smiled weakly, trying to reassure him. "I'm alright."

"And you're going to stay that way." Tiernan pulled us both back to our feet. "This has gone on long enough. We've given Declan plenty of time."

"What do you mean?" I went cold.

"You're going home."

"What?!" He was going to kiss me like that and then send me away?

"Today." He looked in the direction of the Market Gate. "Now."

CHAPTER 31

TIERNAN

I WOULD HAVE TAKEN ELLA STRAIGHT TO the gate then and there, but she insisted on checking on Kiyo first. Fergus and I had been at a weapons shop only a few blocks away when Jac had found us, worried about losing Ella. On our way back, Kiyo had found me and showed me Ella being dragged off by a thug, and that's when all reason left me. At least I had thought to send Kiyo to the townhouse with Saoirse before tearing off after Ella.

Ella.

I really hadn't meant to kiss her.

Jac and Fergus dragged the unconscious man my father had hired off to the authorities before I did something rash. Murder in the streets was my father's way of dealing with things, not mine.

But, oh, I was tempted.

As I took Ella back to the townhouse—my arm around her waist as I seemed to be incapable of letting go of her—I realized this was much worse than I had thought.

I had known I was growing to like her more and more. I had realized I was too attached. But it was more than that. The terror I had felt at the thought of losing her was impossible to shrug off.

I was in love with her.

Saoirse met us at the townhouse gate holding a distraught Kiyohime, who immediately jumped into Ella's arms, rubbing her little face against Ella's cheek.

"What happened?" Saoirse ushered us inside, her eyes wide.

"The king happened," I said, bitterly.

"Here?" Saoirse shut the door behind us.

I nodded jerkily. "He sent a thug after her. Fiachra must feel more threatened by her than I realized."

"I'm fine," Ella insisted, but both Saoirse and I noticed her hands shaking.

"Did you pick up your tea first?"

Ella nodded, rummaging through her ever-present shoulder bag and pulling out a large jar of herbs.

"Sit her down, Tiernan, and I'll make her some tea." Saoirse looked at me again. "Maybe you could use a cup as well."

I realized my hands were shaking too. I needed to calm down. It was bad enough that Ella had been attacked twice now. She didn't need to deal with my increasingly messy feelings on top of that.

What had I been thinking, kissing her like that?

I wrapped Ella up in a quilt and sat with her on the couch, keeping my arm around her shoulder. I tried to convince myself it was to keep her warm, but I knew I was just soaking up these last moments with her before she went home for good.

Saoirse came back with two cups of tea. "For your nerves," she murmured, ignoring my glare as she handed me a cup of chamomile. "And for you, Ella. This smells great!" Saoirse gave Ella a cup of strongly-spiced tea. "Call if you need anything."

Ella relaxed as she drank her tea, stroking Kiyo's fluffy mane. "Make sure you keep an eye on this one. She has half the house's spoons hidden under my pillow."

"Of course, but you can take her with you, you know. She was a gift, after all."

"She should stay with you." Ella scratched the little dragon under the chin, causing Kiyo to hum happily.

"Does your stepmother not like pets?" I guessed.

"That's one of the reasons, yes." Ella sipped her tea. "But it won't be for long. I'll see her in two weeks, after all."

"What?! Ow!" I sloshed my tea, burning my fingers.

I heard muffled laughter from the kitchen. Eavesdropper.

"When I come back for the Samhain ball," Ella said sweetly.

"Ella."

"Mm hmm?"

"Be reasonable. You can't just show up at the palace again. It's not safe."

"Your father will surely be very distracted trying to marry you off to some princess, right?"

"That's not… Listen."

"No, you listen." Ella poked me in the chest with a finger. "We had a deal. I would help you, pretend to be your girlfriend, and you would give me an invitation to the ball."

"Yes, but—"

"This," she waved her hand, "will all be a waste if I can't finish my portfolio." She smiled brightly at me.

"It means that much to you? You would risk your life to attend this ball?"

Ella looked at me steadily. "Some things are worth the risk." She took another sip of tea and looked away. "Don't tell me you'd break your promise?"

"This is a bad idea." If only I had the strength to refuse her. I shouldn't let her sway me, no matter how much I wanted to see her one last time.

"When has that stopped us before?"

I couldn't help laughing.

"Wait here." I set down my teacup and stood.

"I'm not the one trying to rush me out the door." Ella sipped her tea, pointedly.

"Are you getting what I think you're getting?" called Saoirse when I passed her on the way to the stairs.

"You're awfully nosy," I informed my sister.

"Oh, you know, it's only the fate of the kingdom!" she called up after me. "No big deal! I don't know why I'd be interested!"

"Some of us are trying to nap!" yelled Haru from his room.

"She just wants to come to the ball," I said more quietly as Saoirse followed me up the stairs. "I promised her."

"Oh, I see. The ball, for sure."

I rolled my eyes as she followed me into my study. I pulled open a drawer. Not this one.

"Bottom left."

As usual Saoirse was right. I pulled out the intricately carved wooden box.

"Five minutes ago, you're sending her home for good. Now you're giving her these? What did she do, bat her eyelashes at you?"

"I thought you liked Ella." I leaned against my desk, facing my sister.

"I do like Ella, which is why I'd like to make sure she survives her relationship with you."

"Do you think I shouldn't let her come?" I ran my hand through my hair.

"I think you should figure out what you want."

"I want to be someone who keeps my word." I waved the box at her.

"We'll talk more later," Saoirse promised, ominously.

"I look forward to it," I said. "Maybe you could actually give us some privacy now?"

"Of course. I wouldn't want to interrupt you finally kissing her."

I froze.

"Sweet Danu, you already did! We are definitely talking later."

I ignored her and went back down the stairs to Ella. She set down her tea cup, the quilt slipping off one shoulder, when I handed her the box.

"For you."

Ella opened it and gasped as she saw what lay within. Slippers made of sparkling glass, the heels and soles crafted from etched gold, nestled in a bed of blue velvet.

"These are so beautiful." She ran a finger along a golden heel.

Kiyo perked up and scampered over to peer into the box with us.

"They were my mother's." I sat down beside her.

Ella gaped at me. "I can't take these!"

"It's only a loan, don't worry."

Kiyo licked the heel of one glass slipper.

"These are not for your collection, little thief.ö Ella plucked the ryū out of the box.

"When Clíodhna crafted the Glass Gate," I said, "my father was courting my mother. He asked Clíodhna to make these for her out of the same glass and gold as the gate. With these slippers, my mother could travel through any Seelie gate, even the one locked to anyone who isn't part of the royal family."

"The Glass Gate," Ella guessed.

"He wanted my mother to be able to visit him anytime she wanted."

"That sounds very romantic. And very unlike your father."

"He wasn't always like he is now." I leaned back against the couch. "He changed when my mother died. It broke him. It was like the kindness in him died too. I've always thought that maybe it would have been better for him to never have loved anyone that much if losing her made him into such a monster. The whole kingdom would never have had to suffer if he hadn't suffered the loss of her so sharply."

"Do you still think that?" Ella covered my hand with hers.

"I don't know what I think, anymore." I stared at her hand, fighting the urge to turn mine over and lace my fingers through hers.

Kiyo chirped and Ella laughed, breaking the heaviness of the moment. The little dragon had wedged herself into a glass shoe and gotten stuck.

"Come on, Kiyo." Ella removed the dragon and closed the lid. "Let's go find you a nice shiny fork before I go home."

Watching Ella disappear through the Market Gate was even harder than I thought it would be. Almost impossibly hard.

I stood there holding Kiyohime, feeling like half my heart had stepped out of my chest and left.

Someone whistled behind me, and I turned to see Saoirse leaning against the side of a shop.

"Come on, sad boy," she said. "You can help me get supplies. We need food for breakfast in the morning and lunch on the trail."

"Sure." I schooled my face into a relaxed smile and walked over.

"Good effort." She handed me a basket. "But, that doesn't work on me."

We headed for the outdoor market, a large tented area full of butchers, bakers, and produce sellers all loudly announcing their wares.

"So, you kissed her," Saoirse said. "I thought you two were *pretending* to be sweethearts. Did you get carried away?"

"Something like that." I picked up a wheel of cheese and sniffed it.

"Well, she is very pretty." Saoirse plucked the cheese from my hand, passing me an almost identical wheel of cheese. "It could be worse."

"I don't think it could be, actually." I put the cheese in my basket. Kiyo wandered in after it and then suddenly chirped and disappeared. Probably off to find Haru and his treats.

"What do you mean?" She examined a basket of apples. "It's not like you're in love with her."

Saoirse looked up at me when I didn't reply. "Sweet Danu, you are in love with her."

I groaned. "This is a disaster."

"So dramatic." Saoirse rolled her eyes. "I'm no expert, but from what I understand, falling in love with someone while you're looking for a bride is a good thing." She looked up at the fruit vendor. "We'll take eight apples, please."

"I can't marry her."

"Now, the step-niece of a prince is not as good as a daughter, I'll give you that." Saoirse took the bag of apples. "But I think you could convince the nobles. And, there's no doubt she would help you stand up to your father when the time comes."

"Listen to me," I said through gritted teeth. "I can't marry her!"

"I thought you said you loved her?" Saoirse looked up at me.

"I can't marry her because I love her." I slammed my fist against the produce counter, causing everyone in a ten-foot radius to stop and stare at me.

Saoirse sighed. "Come on." When she dragged me to a bench in the market square, she sat me down beside her. "Explain."

"I swore I would never be like him." I stared out past the town's rooftops to the sea.

"Look at me."

I looked into her dark brown eyes.

"You are not your father," she said, slowly and clearly.

"You don't know that. You never knew him before my mother died."

"And you don't know what your father was like before he met her," she said.

"What do you mean?"

Saoirse tipped her head back, looking up to the sky. "Fiachra was the one who took away the rights of the *Aos Sí* to carry weapons."

"I thought that was my grandfather?" I squinted.

"It happened under his rule," Saoirse said. "And he was a piece of work too, obviously, but it wasn't his idea. You should hear some of the stories the villagers have told me. Fiachra did not become a monster because he lost your mother." Her voice softened. "He was just a better person while she was alive."

"Why have I never heard the stories?"

"The small folk don't like to speak badly of the king in front of you. Surely, you've noticed?"

I let this sink in for a moment. "So what do you think I should do? I thought you agreed with me that the kingdom was more important than one person's happiness."

"I do," she said. "But have you ever considered that, maybe, one person's happiness could make the entire kingdom stronger? Two people, I suppose, if Ella feels the same way."

"You truly believe I'm not capable of being like him?" I asked. "What if I lost her, Sersh?"

Kiyo reappeared and promptly curled up and fell asleep on my knee.

"You survived losing Brenna." Saoirse leaned over and scratched Kiyo's head.

"Only because I had you and Leith and Declan to pull me through."

"And you still have us. You're a good man, Tiernan. To your core. You love your people, and nothing will change that. But you need to realize that it's okay to be happy. For someone who smiles all the time, you sure are hard on yourself."

It was okay to be happy. I rolled the idea over in my mind. I imagined a life with Ella at my side.

And I smiled.

CHAPTER 32

ELLA

IT WAS EARLY MORNING IN THE WOODS, outside of Pilot Bay, and I breathed a sigh of relief when I saw the roses climbing up the aspen trees. This was my first time going through a gate on my own, and while I had pictured this spot firmly in my head, I had never seen it before in daylight.

I removed my earrings with their faerie glamour and slipped them into my shoulder bag before hiking down the mountain.

When I hit the edge of town, I considered stashing my cloak in my bag, but it was cold and my fae tunic and pants underneath didn't look any more normal.

If anyone saw me this early in the morning, maybe I could pass this off as some sort of Lord of the Rings costume.

I reached Kimberly's house, unlocking the back door and creeping as quietly as I could down the stairs to my basement bedroom.

I pulled the sheet door aside, and my heart stopped. The wooden box was out from under my bed, its lid tossed haphazardly onto the floor.

No, no, no! I dropped to my knees, my hands shaking.

My mama's kimono was gone. The pumpkin cookie jar lay in pieces with no sign of my carefully saved bus ticket money.

I fell to my knees, slicing my right finger on a pottery shard as I frantically rooted through the box to see if anything had been left.

There. My fingers brushed something under the tissue, and I pulled out Mama's hair comb. I clutched it to my chest, tears running down my face. Madison must have seen my kimono when I showed it to Amber.

Rage shot through me, and I ran up the stairs.

"Madison!" I slammed her bedroom door open.

"I don't want an enchilada," she muttered and rolled over in bed. I grabbed her by the shoulders and shook.

"Where is it?"

My stepsister cracked a bleary eye at me. "What?"

"I know you took it from under my bed, where is it?"

"Gone."

I went cold.

"The party was bring your own booze." She closed her eyes again.

"Not the money, the kimono! Wait, you spent two thousand dollars on alcohol?"

"And a limo. Best party ever." She pulled the blanket over her head. Her muffled voice said sleepily, "Hilary has it."

I took a deep breath. The money wasn't important. And I didn't have time to commit a murder this morning.

I marched across the hall into Hilary's bedroom and flipped the light switch.

A strangled moan escaped my lips. There, on the ground, lay what remained of my mama's kimono. The bottom hem had been completely ripped at the knee and the sleeves hung on by threads. The entire thing was covered in rips and what I hoped was fake blood. Although part of me wouldn't have minded if she had been attacked by wolves.

"What did you do to it?" I shrieked, gathering up the pieces. The obi looked mostly intact but the kimono itself didn't have a piece bigger than my hand without a stain or rip.

"Ugh, why are you so loud?"

I ripped the blanket off Hilary causing her to screech like she was being attacked.

"What is going on in here?" Kimberly boomed from the doorway, elegant in a silk robe.

"Your daughters stole my money and destroyed my kimono!"

My stepmother's eyes flicked to the tattered silk in my arms and then to her daughter who tried her best to cover her head with a pillow.

"Hilary, this is completely unacceptable," said Kimberly.

I looked at her in shock. Was she finally going to take my side?

"After all the money I spent on that Scarlet Witch costume you swore you needed for that Grad event, you go and root around for used clothes under a bed? It's disgraceful!"

"I wanted to be a zombie geisha," Hilary whined from under her pillow.

"Well, next time, think of these things before I special order you a costume." Kimberly turned to leave.

"You're going to let them get away with this?" I asked. "Don't you care that your daughters are thieves?"

Kimberly's eyebrows shot up. I had never given her any reason to expect a spine on me before.

"Honestly, Ella, I assure you I spent more than whatever was in that little cookie jar feeding and clothing you for the past ten years."

Cookie jar. So, she had known.

"That was your job. I was a child!" I hugged my bundle of stained silk closer to my chest.

"And you're still acting like one, I see," she said. "Go to your room. Honestly, I don't know what's come over you. Barging around at the crack of dawn and yelling at everyone. If you insist on being awake, you can start breakfast. We'll discuss this at a more reasonable hour."

For a moment, I almost obeyed her. The compulsion was so ingrained in me.

I straightened my spine. I hadn't fought off assassins, raised a baby dragon, and marched halfway across Tír na nÓg just to end up right back where I had started.

"No."

She turned back. "What did you say?"

"Make your own breakfast." I clutched the sakura comb tighter in my hand before I pushed past my stunned stepmother and down the stairs. "I just need to get a few things, and I'll go."

I was packing up my old sketchbooks and my watercolors when I heard the click of the basement door bolt locking.

I ran over and shook the door. "You can't lock me down here!"

"It's for your own good, Ella," Kimberley called through the door. "You're clearly not yourself this morning. I'll come down in a few hours when you've had a chance to calm down, and we'll talk."

I heard footsteps going up the stairs.

A few hours? I pulled out my watch. Faerie time spun past. I did not have a few hours. Not if I wanted to make it to the ball.

I needed to get out of here, fast. But how? I knew none of the windows opened and they were pretty high up to break. Like with the door that locked on the outside, Kimberly wasn't interested in fire safety when it came to me.

I ran back to my room and started going through the contents of my drawers. Maybe I had a way to take the door off its hinges?

Nothing. Just a bunch of sad clothes, a dead, ten-year-old phone, and a twix bar.

Kiyo appeared with a pop and landed in the drawer on the chocolate bar.

"Kiyo!"

The ryū chirped at me and pawed the foil wrapper.

"If you want that treat, I need your help first." Kiyo followed me to the door, and I sent her a mental image of the deadbolt sliding open. "Like that. Do you think you can do it?"

Kiyo chirped and disappeared. I prayed that she knew what I was trying to get her to do.

After a brief, muffled rattling sound, she reappeared on my side of the door. I turned the knob and the door swung open.

"Who's a good dragon?" I gave her a bite of choco-late. "You are!"

Kiyo chirped smugly, and I tucked her into my shoulder bag with the rest of the chocolate bar. I loaded up a backpack with my art supplies and a couple changes of clothes. After looking around the room, I nodded. There was nothing else I needed from here.

Kimberly spotted me at the front entrance.

"If you go out that door," she called, "you better not come back."

I paused. I knew she didn't just mean the house. By walking away, I risked it all, my job, my reputation, and a place to live. With my kimono ruined and my money gone, I didn't even have a plan anymore.

I opened the door anyway.

"You'll be homeless!" she yelled, panic creeping into her voice.

Home. I thought of the townhouse in Port Delfare. The sense of family and belonging that I had never felt in this house.

"This isn't my home," I said. "It never has been. You made that clear."

"Get back here!" She ran down the stairs after me.

"Good luck with the hand beading on Cissy's gown," I called as I slammed the door behind me.

Chapter 33

Ella

I WAS SEVEN BLOCKS AWAY WHEN MY anger faded and reality set in. Storming out had felt extremely satisfying in the moment, but it was six in the morning, and I had left my phone and my hoodie back at Kimberly's house.

I sat heavily on a bench downtown, in front of Pie in the Sky, shoving the kimono as best I could into the top of my shoulder bag. It didn't really fit.

Pilot Bay was utterly quiet, except for the occasional bird and the clacking of a solitary pair of boots on the sidewalk. Neve Burnett was out early to open the cafe, looking gorgeous as always in a bright pink wool coat.

"Are you okay?" The curvy baker peered at me over her floral scarf.

I snuffled and wiped the back of my nose with my sleeve.

"Oh! You're Ella, right? Amber's friend?" She tugged her scarf down and gave me a warm smile.

"I'm surprised you recognize me." I rarely had money for treats.

"Well, you do look like a homeless elf this morning." She winked.

"I suppose it helps that there's only like three Asian kids in this town," I said.

"It's true. We're not open yet, but do you want me to call someone?"

"It's really early," I said. "Nobody up but homeless elves and bakers."

"I'll send Amber a text. Come inside if you get cold." Neve unlocked the bakery door, the little bell jingling as she went inside.

Could I send Kiyo to get Amber? The little dragon had fallen asleep in a sugar coma, but when I peeked in the bag, she had disappeared. I groaned. I was running out of time, and there was no way I could show up to the Samhain ball like this.

Neve came back out. A vintage floral apron had replaced her coat. She gave me a white paper bag and a steaming paper cup.

"Oat Chai, right?" she said. "Amber always gets them for you. She's on her way over," she added.

"Thank you!" I inhaled the sweet, spicy smell.

"Oh, everybody needs a little help sometimes. And, besides, I can't sell day-old scones." She smiled and ducked back inside.

I felt better as I took a sip of steaming latte. The situation hadn't changed but everything felt better with chai. I walked toward Amber's house and met her halfway there. She looked bleary in a thick hoodie and joggers.

"Ella!" Amber started to hug me and then wrinkled her nose and patted my shoulder instead. "Welcome back to the boring human realm. What's the matter?"

"I left Kimberly's house, and I'm not going back."

"Good for you!" She linked her arm into mine. "What's in the bag?"

I passed it over, and we each munched a cranberry scone.

"Do you need help hiding Kimberly's body?" Amber asked.

"Not this time."

"Such restraint." She licked the icing off her fingers. "What happened?"

I caught Amber up on my dilemma. "So, it's really Hilary I want to murder right now."

"I'd offer to help, but Isobel assures me that murder's a sin."

"What if we only murdered her a little bit?" I asked.

"Oh, well, that's probably fine. But back to Tiernan. You didn't tell him how you feel? After my excellent pep talk? After he kissed you?"

I sighed. "You should have seen how freaked out he was, Amber. He was more scared than I was. He apologized for kissing me like…ten times. He needs some processing time." I took another sip of my latte. "I barely managed to convince him to let me come to the ball."

"Hmm, fine." Amber clearly thought I was a chicken. She wasn't wrong.

"The way I see it," said Amber through a mouthful of scone, "you've got three options."

"Oh, three?" I asked. "Do go on."

"The first and most reasonable option is to go back now and tell him how you feel."

"Like this minute, now?" I asked. "Without a dress?!"

"I mean, it's a dress. Is it really that important?"

"I think you underestimate the power of a good dress," I said.

"Fine, fine, fine. I see you're not gonna listen to reason. The second option…"

"Yes?"

"Is that you borrow one of my dresses and go to the ball. I know they're not as meaningful as your mom's kimono, but I have some good stuff, as you've seen."

I thought about that for a minute as we walked.

"You do have some good dresses," I said. "But I really wanted something that shows who I really am. When I met Tiernan, I was wearing one of your dresses, and it was the beginning of many, many lies."

"It's just a dress!"

"A dress of lies," I said.

"I think you're being a tad dramatic," said Amber. "But that's okay, because my third option is the best option."

I took another sip of my chai. "I'm listening."

"Okay, option number three. It's the best option. I mean, not the most reasonable option, that was option one."

"I'm not showing up before the ball."

"…but I think you'll like it best. Is there anyone at the palace who could sew you up a new dress in a short amount of time?" she asked. "You've been in Faerie for two and a half months. If I know anything about you, your sketchbook has about fifty new dress ideas. Am I wrong?"

She was not wrong.

"I won't have a lot of time," I said.

"Do you have long enough? And could you get a dress made?"

I dug the watch out of my pocket and flicked it to Faerie time. "If I leave right now, I should be able to get there with about three hours to spare."

Amber nodded. "That's what I thought, but even though they have amazing tailors at Kilinaire, they can't do anything that fast."

"Grainne might be able to." I mulled it over. "I should go right away and ask her."

We had arrived at Amber's front door.

"That's the spirit," she said.

"In a few minutes," I added.

"Ella," Amber groaned.

"I was dragged through an alley only two hours ago. I need a shower. "

"Are you sure I can't wash this cloak for you?" yelled Amber through the bathroom door as I washed my hair in record time.

"Or burn it," she added. "Along with these boots."

Hmm, my clothes were fresh this morning, but apparently my hiking gear was stinkier than I thought.

"Are you kidding me! It took me weeks to break in those boots!" I yelled back over the running water as I shaved dangerously quickly. After all, nobody wants hairy legs at a Samhain ball. Well, unless you were a glaistig, I suppose.

"And that cloak is *Dobhar-chú* felt!" I added. "It repels rain, snow, cold, and sun damage."

"But apparently not mud," she muttered through the door.

"They're not touching your washing machine. Throw them in a bag and I'll get them cleaned at the palace." I turned off the water and scrubbed myself dry with a borrowed towel before dressing in one of Amber's simpler faerie gowns.

"Do you know your way back to the Rose Gate?" asked Amber as we pelted down the stairs.

"Yeah, I'm pretty sure," I said. "Wait. Why don't you come with me to the ball?"

"Seriously?" She froze at the doorway.

"Seriously. I could use the moral support."

"Yes!" Amber squealed as she ran back up the stairs two at a time. "Finally, a proper Seelie Court revel!"

I heard a crash from the closet upstairs, and a moment later, she ran back down the stairs wearing a long pink dress. She threw a heavy golden velvet cloak at me and pulled a fur-lined blue one around her shoulders. Together, we dashed out the door toward the forest.

"Just a minute," I said, when we reached the arching red roses in the forest.

I pulled out the carved wooden shoe box from my bag.

"How much stuff do you have in there?" asked Amber.

"Too much," I admitted. The bag was getting very heavy with my sketching supplies, kimono and these shoes in there. Amber had refused to carry my hiking gear, so I had left it at her house for now.

I opened the box, revealing the sparkling glass slippers.

"Whoa!" said Amber. "Where did you get those?"

"From Tiernan." I ran a finger gingerly across one faceted shoe. "They were his mother's."

"That boy has it bad for you."

"They're the key to opening the Glass Gate," I told her. "He only lent them to me so I could get back in time for the ball."

"That still proves my point." Amber popped in her glamoured earrings while I switched out of my booties and into the glass slippers.

They had looked too small for me in the box. But somehow, when I put them on, they fit perfectly. Magic no doubt, which also explained why they were comfier than any leather insole should be able to make glass shoes feel.

"All right." I grabbed Amber's hand. "Are you ready?"

"Totally," said Amber.

"Really ready?"

"Bring it on," she said.

"Because we can…"

She grabbed my hand and yanked me forward through the gate. "Think hard about Rahivea!"

PART 4

CHAPTER 34

ELLA

I BARELY HAD TIME TO PICTURE THE Glass Gate in my mind before I tumbled through after her. The palace courtyard sat blessedly empty. I hadn't thought about what I would do if someone saw two girls appear through a gate that no one but Tiernan and the king were supposed to be able to use.

I switched my shoes again, and we dashed across the courtyard to the nearest small servant's door.

"Ow! Why is the ceiling so low?"

"Light," I said, and the lanterns in the stairwell flickered to life.

"Look at you!" Amber rubbed her head. "It took me six months to figure out how to work the lights at Kilinaire."

"That must have been awkward." I descended the narrow stairs.

"I had a lot of bruises on my shins," she admitted, following me.

"The ceilings are low because these are the servants' stairs."

"And all the servants are short?"

"Yes, actually. Haven't you noticed that at Kilinaire? Also, calling them servants is a bit of an overstatement as they don't seem to be paid."

"Seriously? If we didn't pay Ena a regular wage, I'm pretty sure she'd put dirt in our tea."

"Well, Rahivea is not Kilinaire. And from what I've seen, this is how most of the Seelie Kingdom operates."

"What about humans?" Amber ducked under an archway. "Aren't there any tall human servants?"

"Well, those would literally be slaves," I said. "And no. They only steal away humans with special talents. They have enough brownies to keep the floors polished."

We burst into Grainne's workroom, and all the faeries froze and stared at our abrupt entrance.

"Whoa," said Amber. "That's a whole lotta fabric. This must be, like, your dream world or something."

"Pretty much."

"Back to work," barked Grainne, flying over to us.

All the other faeries scrambled to continue tidying up the workspace. They must be done sewing for the ball.

"Cutting it close, aren't you?" asked Grainne. "Let's get you ready for the ball."

"It's kind of a long story, but I'm actually a human." I pulled out an earring and tucked my hair behind my rounded ear.

Grainne nodded. "You need a dress," she said. "This palace is crawling with foreign princesses, and the king's hand-picked choices for Tiernan. We need to make you stand out."

"You're not bothered that I'm a human?" I asked, putting the earring back in. "I've been lying to everyone!"

"What's a little glamour?" Grainne waved her hand. "We all remember what you did for Isla. If the prince chooses you, will you help him usurp the king and fight for the small folk?"

"Yes," I vowed, looking steadily into her eyes.

"Then you could be a pigeon for all I care. We don't have much time, and I wasn't given any notes for a dress for you."

"I know," I said. "I planned on wearing this kimono. It was my mama's."

I pulled out the pieces of my kimono and laid them out on a table.

Grainne looked at it and whistled. "Well, you obviously can't wear this to the ball."

"I know."

"Tell her your idea." Amber elbowed me in the ribs.

I pulled out my sketchbook and laid it on the table. Immediately, a crowd of little faeries swarmed around it, flipping pages.

"Oh, that one's not very good." I tried to flip the pages faster to get to the end.

A little faerie hissed at me. She turned back, and they continued to go at their own pace, murmuring over my designs.

"Look at the line of that skirt."

"Yes, I've never seen one like that before."

"What about that pleating?"

Grainne clapped her hands loudly. "We can all agree that Ella is very talented, but we are in a hurry. Let her show us the design."

A little knee-high faerie with quills instead of hair gave me a sharp look. "You will let us look at this later," she demanded.

"I will," I promised, my heart warming. The delight of the little faeries, and Grainne's approval, meant more to me than any scholarship to Parsons.

I bent over and flipped to the last page of my book. "Where are my pencils?"

Before I could reach into my bag, a piskie flew over with a pencil about the same size as herself. I made a few quick adjustments and explained the design to the little tailors.

"All right," said Grainne after she looked over the sketch. "You." She pointed at me. "Take off that tea dress and stand there." She gestured to a low stool. "You." She pointed at Amber. "If you're going to accompany Lady Ella to the ball, you can't go in that."

"What's wrong with my dress?" protested Amber, running her hands down her pink silk gown.

"It's a dinner gown," said Grainne in exasperation. "You need a ball gown. Children these days. There's a rack of spares in the corner. Talia will help you choose one."

The little hedgehog faerie scampered off with Amber trailing behind.

"Now." Grainne rubbed her hands together. "Let's work some magic, shall we?"

Tiny faeries moved around me in a blur of speed, first removing my dress, leaving me in my underwear and a fae-made bustier, which was far more comfortable than any bra I owned.

"Do you have proper shoes?" Grainne looked pointedly at my booties.

"Oh, yes!" I ran over to my bag and pulled out the glass slippers.

The little faeries oohed and aahed over the sparkling shoes as I stepped back up onto the wooden stool. Then they wrapped me in a swath of fabric from Mama's kimono and secured it with a silk cord around my waist.

"Um…" I looked down at what amounted to a strapless, knee length sheath of ragged, stained silk.

"We don't have time to sew this from scratch," Grainne informed me while directing a crew of piskies who were flying a piece of sparkling tulle over to me. "And a magic dress, constructed in such a hurry, has a time limit."

I could barely see the little faeries as they tucked and pleated the fabric, whispering words of enchantment and tapping pleats in place with motes of sparkling magic.

"We'll be able to stretch it a little longer than usual tonight. Samhain is rich with magic, so it should hold until midnight."

"What happens at midnight?" I asked.

"Everything we've added on by magical means comes undone."

"So it will all…fall off?" I watched as the faeries attached another layer of skirt.

"Essentially, yes. And any embellishments we've glamoured on will disappear. You'll be left only in the clothes put on by non-magical means. I would aim to leave the party before the last stroke of midnight," she said. "You should be able to hear the palace bell from the ballroom. Your mother's kimono silk will keep you from having to go home naked, if you cut it a little close."

I nodded. The workroom buzzed with activity. Some faeries grabbed rolls of trim, some speedily cut swaths of fabric, others appeared to be painting designs and adding tiny gems with nothing but a brush of fingertips.

I stood in the center of a sparkling wind storm as the piskies continued to magically attach layers to my gown. When they finished, a pair of draoi came over with my mama's obi, now carefully pressed. I instructed them on how to wrap and tie the long swath of painted silk.

"Mirror!" Grainne clapped her hands.

Two little leipreacháns rolled over a giant gilded mirror.

I gasped when I saw my reflection. The purple gown was more beautiful than anything I could have sketched. The bodice of layered silk wings draped perfectly before being cinched in by Mama's obi. I ran my hands down the pink silk obi and over the gold cord holding it in place. The skirt flared as I swayed. It was full with layers of tulle under a skirt made of more wings, painted in purples and pinks to mimic the patterns I had seen on the wings of the forest piskies. The entire gown shimmered, trailing motes of sparkling gold when I moved, like the flower fish I had watched with Tiernan in the lake.

Amber ran over in a scarlet velvet ball gown. "Wow," she breathed.

"I know." I smoothed my hands down the skirt. "Thank you. All of you. This is incredible."

"It was a pleasure to work with such an interesting design," said Grainne. "Chairs!" she bellowed, clapping her hands once more.

Two plush velvet stools were pushed behind Amber and me, and we sat facing the mirror. Imogen and another brownie raced up with baskets of ribbons and cosmetics.

"Imogen!" I knelt down to give her a hug.

"My lady," she said. "It's so good to have you back to Rahivea. I hear you're to be our first human queen!"

I blushed. "Well, if he'll have me. If everyone will."

"I shall do my part to make you irresistible," she promised, stepping up onto a stool behind me. The other brownie did the same, working on Amber's hair at lightning speed. Like the tailors, the brownies used a press of the fingers and a word of magic to secure our hair, instead of using pins and hairspray.

"Wait," I said when Imogen had finished my hair. I carefully unwrapped my mama's comb with its silk sakura blossoms, and she gently slid it into my elaborate updo.

Amber's hair was twirled and braided into a crown on her head with ruby hairpins sparkling throughout.

Imogen did my makeup in tones of shimmering pinks while Amber was painted with crimson lips and sparkling gold on her eyes to match her gown.

"Done," pronounced Imogen, placing the last sparkling jewel on my cheek.

I flipped open my watch. "We need to run, we're already late."

"All the better to make a proper entrance," said Amber. "One more thing first." She dug through her purse and came out with her phone. "Selfie!" She squeezed me in close to her for a photo.

"You're not going to be posting these on Instagram or something are you?" I asked.

"Don't be silly, these are just to remember the night by. Now spin for me, I need to take a video."

A group of little piskies clustered around her phone and chattered while I gave my dress a twirl.

"Now can we go?" I pleaded.

"One last thing." Grainne snapped her fingers and four little piskies flew over, each holding the corner of a mask. "It is Samhain, after all."

I felt small hands pressing the mask to my face with a whisper of magic and looked in the mirror. The mask was crafted entirely out of what appeared to be real sakura petals the same shade as mama's comb. Amber's mask was sparkling gold.

"Now you can go. I'll show you the fastest path to the ballroom." Imogen shooed us toward the door. "Be careful and duck your heads! You don't want to ruin all our hard work."

We followed her through twists and turns until we reached a part of the servants' passageways I hadn't been in before. I could hear the sound of music and laughter through the walls.

Imogen stopped. "Want a sneak peek?"

"Yes!" we both exclaimed.

The brownie slid open a small panel, and we bent down to peek through.

The ballroom had been transformed into an indoor enchanted forest. Tall trees with autumn leaves stood along the walls, their branches arching overhead. Lanterns hung from the trees. Glowing, golden leaves drifted down from overhead and swirled around the twirling dancers.

"Crap!" Amber gripped my arm. "Isobel's here! She must have taken a gate from Florida for the ball."

Sure enough, Amber's older sister sat in a back corner by a table with her tall, scarred fiancé. They were dressed for dancing—her in a glittering gold dress with a feathered mask, him in a tailored black suit—but instead they sat at the table with a plate of pastries and…

"Are they *reading*?" I gaped.

Amber rolled her eyes. "Typical. She won't let me come to Seelie balls when they're completely wasted on her."

"Well, she's the only human in the room who isn't enchanted," I pointed to the musicians. They were the same quartet I had seen at the Lughnasadh feast, and I wondered what they did when they weren't playing music. I clenched my fists. Fiachra could not remain in power for another century or two. We needed to take him down.

"Well, yes. That is unsettling. Is there a sneakier way for us to arrive?" Amber asked Imogen. "I'm afraid if Isobel sees me, I'll have to go home before I even get one dance. Although, maybe Ella should make an entrance."

"Sneaky is a good idea." I peered through the little window, searching for the king. I didn't see him, but he had to be in there somewhere. Best not to draw too much attention to myself.

"You can get in from here." Imogen slid the panel closed and then flipped a latch, opening a small doorway. Amber crouched in a poof of velvet skirts and ducked through the doorway.

I touched Mama's comb nervously, and adjusted my obi even though it sat perfectly. I needed all the strength they could give me.

I felt like a princess from one of her stories, but could I find the happy ending to this tale?

I took a deep breath and ducked into the ballroom.

CHAPTER 35

ELLA

I STRAIGHTENED FROM THE LOW DOORWAY, EMERG-
ING behind a table heaped with food and drinks and
shook glowing golden leaves off my skirt.

"This is amazing!" squealed Amber.

The ballroom teemed with Seelie nobility in their glittering gowns and jewels. They were all masked and many
wore elegant clothes hinting at animal or nature themes
without being overly costumey.

A number of the dancing fae seemed to be from other
parts of Faerie with skin tones and textiles that reminded
me of India, Scandinavia, and Morocco but with an other-
worldly air to them. I even saw a girl with milky white skin
and russet-colored hair, from which two dainty fox ears

poked. When she turned to whisper to her neighbor, I saw nine fluffy tails sprouting from the back of her kimono.

"Kitsune," I whispered. Were all the stories true?

"What?" Amber heaped elegant canapés shaped like flowers onto a plate.

"Look at all the dresses…" Normally I'd be reaching for my sketchbook already, but that wasn't why I was here tonight.

I craned my neck, searching for Tiernan and finding him at last, surrounded by beautiful girls. He was heartbreakingly handsome in a blue velvet coat embroidered with golden leaves and acorns. His freckled nose and cheeks hid under a gold half mask. His charming smile was firmly in place, and for a moment, I faltered, my nerves returning in full force. Who was I pretending to be?

My knees almost gave out, but a hand on my elbow steadied me. A silver-masked Saoirse stood at my side in loose silk pants of midnight blue and a draped silver top, her sword at her hip. Amber strolled causally away into the crowd, munching happily.

"I was starting to worry you weren't coming," Saoirse said.

"Well, I had to do my hair. You know how it is."

"Are you going to tell him how you feel?"

I looked at her sharply. She gazed steadily back at me.

"That's why you're here, right?" she said. "He needs you."

"I don't know," I said shakily. "It looks like he's doing just fine."

"What was it you always called him? Prince Charming? He's hiding behind more than a mask tonight. Come on."

"Wait," I said. "There's something I should tell you."

She patted my arm. "Tell him first."

Then Kiyo popped out of the pocket of Tiernan's coat and saw me. She ran up Tiernan's sleeve and must have shown him where I stood before disappearing because Tiernan turned and grinned at me from across the room. The warmth of his true smile washed over me. For a moment, the crowd melted away, and there was no one but him and me.

I started to walk to him and people began to part around me. After a moment, I realized it wasn't me they were making way for. I froze, leaving Tiernan to take the final steps to me. Everyone had stopped dancing to see who had captured the elusive prince's interest. A sea of silk rustled along with the whispers drifting from behind fans.

"Your Highness." I managed what I hoped was a graceful curtsy, and my dress belled around me.

"My lady." He swept what was definitely a very elegant bow and offered me his hand. "May I have this dance?"

I closed my hand around his and looked up into his twinkling eyes. I was taken back to the moment when I had first met him. Another dance on another night.

I had thought he had made my heart beat fast then, but as he laid his hand on my lower back and drew me close, I realized that I hadn't known then what my heart could do.

And then we were swirling, and even though all eyes were on us, the other dancers seemed to disappear into the background.

"You came." His warm breath stirred my hair. "I was getting worried."

"I was told that I had arrived at the perfect time to make an entrance," I teased.

He laughed. "That is certainly true. But in that dress, you would have stood out no matter when you arrived." He spun me out, the wings of my skirt flaring. Then he pulled me back in, my back against his chest for a moment.

"The tailors did do an exceptional job," I agreed as he spun me back into place.

"I'm sure they did, but I've seen enough of your sketches to recognize an Ella design when I see one."

I glowed under his attention. "I hope it's alright that I'm still wearing the glass slippers."

"It's more than alright," he murmured. "I only wish she could have met you."

The song ended, and we paused.

"I need to tell you something," I said quickly before I lost my nerve.

"Tiernan!" a voice interrupted me.

"Declan!" Tiernan happily turned from me to face his friend.

"May I present, the Princess Ailish," Declan said, gesturing to the girl on his arm.

Ailish was stunningly beautiful with rippling aqua hair falling to her waist, caught up on one side with a pearl-studded comb. Her silver dress drifted around her like water.

Tiernan bowed before the princess. "Thank you for coming. It's an honor. It has been many years since a merrow has traveled to our court."

"From what I've heard—" she tilted her head toward Declan "—you're in a bit of a pickle."

"You could say that." Tiernan turned back to me and whispered next to my ear. "I'm sorry I can't leave now, it would be terribly rude."

I nodded, trying to tamp down my jealousy.

"Meet me on the west balcony when this dance is over and then we can talk."

I turned to leave before I could analyze their interaction any further. Did he hold her hand as gently as he had held mine? Did he hold her quite as close? I then found myself stopped by a firm hand gripping my arm.

Declan hauled me through the crowd.

"I've just returned from my visit to the Isle of Mist, and I met with the Mist Prince, who you claim is your uncle. Do you know what he said about you?" he asked in a low voice.

"Good things, I hope?" I squeaked, stumbling alongside him.

His grip on my arm tightened as he pulled me behind a giant indoor tree.

"He said nothing at all of your character. In fact, he seemed surprised to learn that he had a niece from Takamagahara at all. When I described you, he claimed that no such step-niece existed. Would you care to explain yourself?"

"I was about to tell Tiernan—"

"Tell him what? That you're a spy? That you're a liar? That you tried to worm your way into his life under false pretenses?"

I winced. "Liar, yes, but not a spy." I dropped my voice to a whisper. "I'm a human."

Declan glanced sharply toward the enchanted musicians in the corner. "Like a human, human?"

I checked to make sure no one was watching and removed one gold earring. "These create my glamour and let me understand your language." I tapped the rounded top of my ear.

"Where did you get those?" Declan held out his hand.

I handed him the earring. "A friend gave them to me. I think she got them from Miss Chloe, I mean, Clíodhna."

"The Elder Fae is involved? Why?"

"She doesn't really like explaining things."

"True." Declan's face softened. He handed me back the earring. "And when were you planning on telling Tiernan this?"

"I know I should have done it sooner, but I would have done it already tonight if you hadn't interrupted." I slid the earring back in.

Movement on the other side of the tree startled me, but when I poked my head around, I didn't see anyone. Hopefully they hadn't overheard us, but I suppose it didn't matter. Soon enough, either everyone in the kingdom would know, or else it wouldn't matter.

"Please. Just give me a chance to tell him myself," I begged Declan. "I can't lose him."

Declan leaned back against the tree trunk, crossing his arms. "You really care about him? You're not trying to con him to get a crown?"

"I promise," I said. "The only thing I lied about was being fae."

"This is not something I can keep from him. He would never forgive me."

I winced, wondering once again if Tiernan would ever forgive me.

"Declan!" A shrill voice cut through the crowd.

The shaggy-haired prince blanched and pushed off from the tree. "My mother's found me, I need to run, or I'll be forced to dance with her friends' snobby daughters until dawn. Tell Tiernan by midnight, or I'm telling him myself."

"Well, that's the plan." I looked down at my watch. I only had an hour left.

Declan disappeared into the crowd, and I wandered over to a food table. It all looked delicious, but my stomach was churning too badly to let me eat.

I searched for Tiernan and found him dancing with the kitsune princess. He gave me a glance over her shoulder before he twirled her and then he looked back at the fox girl with his trademark smile.

"Little Kami."

A shiver ran down my spine, and I spun to see Lynet behind me. She gave me an icy smile and sipped her goblet of blood-red wine.

"There's a whole lot of foreign princesses here, don't you think? It's too bad he couldn't find one suitable closer to home." I smiled.

"What an…interesting dress." Lynet narrowed her eyes at me, twirling her goblet. "Are those wings?"

She leaned closer, and her goblet tilted toward me. I tried to dodge to the side but ran into the table. I couldn't believe I had come all the way to Faerie just to have another spiteful blonde pour a drink on me.

CHAPTER 36

ELLA

THE SMIRK DISAPPEARED FROM LYNET'S FACE AS a tornado of crimson silk barreled into her, sloshing the red wine back at her and down her icy blue gown.

"Oh no!" Amber put her hand to her mouth. "I'm so clumsy. I do hope you brought a spare dress."

Lynet shrieked and half the ballroom turned to stare.

"You—" she hissed at Amber "—will pay for this. And you!" She wheeled on me. "Don't think for a second that you've won. I'm not done here."

"He'll marry the merrow princess before he makes you his queen," I told her. "You're finished."

She glared at me and flounced away, remembering after a few paces to stumble and sob like a wounded sea creature about the horrible girls who had done this to her.

"Thank you." I hugged my friend.

Amber shrugged smugly, popping a mushroom tart into her mouth.

"Amber!" a loud voice called out.

Amber choked on her bite. "Isobel's seen me! You better go."

"Are you going to be in a lot of trouble?"

"I may be locked in my bedroom for the next month—possibly forever—but it was totally worth it. Now go. I think I saw your prince ducking out onto the balcony." She jerked her head in that direction. "Tell me all about it later!"

She shoved me into the crowd as her sister pushed past fae two feet taller than her. "There had better be kissing!" she whisper-yelled.

I ducked my head. Isobel didn't know me that well. I had altered a dress for her a year ago, but she didn't seem to have recognized me earlier. Seeing me with Amber would have made it click for her though, and I needed to find Tiernan before I was outed as a human.

I slipped through the crowd, the sound of sisterly scolding fading behind me. Many of the fae nobles were whispering happily to one another. After all, nothing improves a party like a little drama.

I slipped out onto the balcony but didn't see Tiernan. Maybe I had the wrong one. I carefully pulled my mask off and set it on the railing, willing my racing heart to calm.

I could do this.

"Might I be so bold as to request another dance?" Tiernan's hand covered mine, his voice low in my ear. I turned to face him, and he caught my hand in his, the other one suddenly on my waist. He had also removed his mask, and I admired the dusting of freckles I had come to love. We swayed to the music, softer outside.

"I have something—" I started.

"I need to—" he said at the same moment.

We both laughed, although mine came out like a nervous squeak.

"You go first," I offered. *Coward,* my mind whispered.

"Ella." He drew me in closer. "I know this all started as a ruse to fool the king, but in the time you've been here, you must know how much you've come to mean to me."

This was what he wanted to tell me? I laid my head against his chest as we swayed. Oh, I really should have gone first. I wanted to be swept away by him, I was halfway there already.

"I know this isn't what we had planned, and I know I can't offer you my heart without asking you to accept a crown." Tiernan stopped dancing and pulled back to look me in the eyes.

"There's a crown?" I teased, trying to lighten the mood. "Is it pretty?"

"No one has seen the queen's crown since my mother died, but we can have a new one crafted for you." Tiernan laughed. "Focus, Ella. Do you love me as I love you? Would you be my queen?" His eyes shone with hope. "Tell me I haven't misread your feelings."

Tiernan pulled me up against him, his hand on my lower back pressing me closer.

"I love you, of course I do, but—"

"Then nothing else matters."

His fingers brushed my jaw, tilting my face up to his. My eyes fluttered shut and all rational thought left me as his lips grazed mine. Softly first and then more deeply as my hands slipped up to tangle in the coolness of his hair, tugging him closer, trying to show him my heart with this kiss. Trying to make him understand how I felt before I risked ruining it all.

We finally broke apart, breathless, my hand on his chest. He leaned down to kiss me again, but I stopped him with two fingers against his mouth.

"There really is something I have to tell you."

"Whatever it is," he said. "We can handle it together."

My heart glowed. This was going to be alright.

The curtain swayed.

"Oops, I'm so sorry." Lynet swept out onto the balcony.

"This is a private moment," said Tiernan.

"Oh, I know," she said. "You and the human girl, so cute."

Tiernan froze, and I inhaled sharply.

"What did you say?" Tiernan asked in a low, dangerous voice.

"You didn't know?" Lynet covered her mouth in feigned shock and looked at me. "Have you been lying to him this whole time?"

"Tiernan," I said.

He took a step back.

"Hmm, I guess you have." The princess inspected her nails.

"How…" Tiernan stared at me as if he had never seen me before.

"It's a glamour," said Lynet helpfully. "The spell is in her earrings. Haven't you noticed that she always seems to wear the same ones? Never changes them to match her other jewelry? Now you know why."

"Ella?" Tiernan looked down at me.

Heart pounding, I pulled out one earring and then the other, tucking the loose strands of my hair behind my ears. My human ears.

He stood for a moment, staring at my rounded ears.

"Well, save a dance for me!" Lynet ran her hand down Tiernan's arm. He shook her off, stiffly, but didn't take his eyes off me.

Lynet shrugged and swept out into the ballroom.

"You're not fae," he said, tersely.

"That's what I was trying to tell you."

His jaw clenched. "You've had three months to tell me, but you waited until you were offered the crown."

"No," I said. "That's not it. Let me explain."

"What's to explain? You've been lying to me since we met." He gave me a look of such raw pain that I instinctively reached for him, but he stepped back.

"Only about being fae. Everything else was true!"

The bell began to toll. Midnight. My dress was about to fall apart.

"I know we were lying to everyone else," he said, quietly. "But I thought we had an understanding. I thought we had each other's backs."

"I do have your back!"

But he didn't turn around. "I think you should go."

"But—"

"Leave!" His hands clenched on the railing.

The clock struck again, and still, I hesitated.

"Thank you," he said softly.

I turned back, trembling.

"Thank you for reminding me what folly it is to believe in love."

"Well, I hope you can find a bride whose heart is as cold as yours," I said, shakily.

He didn't reply, just stared out at the stars.

The clock chimed a third time, and I finally fled. My dress hadn't begun to unravel, but that hardly mattered when my heart already lay in pieces.

CHAPTER 37

TIERNAN

MY HEART FELT LIKE IT HAD BEEN snapped in half as I watched Ella run out, but I steeled myself against it and strode back into the ballroom. The time had come to choose a queen. No more of this emotional nonsense. The worst part was that I had always known better.

I had nearly gotten myself engaged to a liar and a manipulator, someone with no reason to fight at my side. A human could never care about the fate of the Seelie Kingdom.

My mind flickered back to the sight of her with the glaistig baby in her arms, and I ruthlessly shoved it away.

I couldn't trust my heart. I felt cold realizing how close I had come to making the very mistake I had vowed never to make.

I scanned the ballroom. The blue hair of the merrow girl stood out sharply against the crowd. Declan had sent me a long message from the Coral Court, and he believed Ailish was my best choice. I trusted my brother more than my treacherous heart.

Ailish's eyes widened at the intensity on my face when I reached her.

"You're willing?" I asked. "To stand with me against the king?"

Something flickered in her eyes, but she nodded sharply.

"The merrows have suffered under his rule as well," she said. "Helping you is the best thing for my people."

"And that's enough for you? You won't regret marrying for the sake of your people instead of for love?"

She gave a liquid shrug. "Marrying for love was never going to be one of my options. Declan says you're honorable, at least. And Rahivea isn't too far from the sea…"

The princess looked no more excited about the prospect of marriage than I did, but it was enough. I held my hand out, and she put her pale, cold hand in it. I tried to forget the warmth of Ella's hand in mine and failed.

I led her to the raised dais where the musicians played. They stopped and bowed at a look from me. I winced.

Hopefully they would be the last humans our people would steal and keep as pets for their talents.

A hush settled over the crowd as all eyes turned to us. The Aster Princess seethed in the corner. Had she truly believed I would turn to her with Ella out of the picture?

I looked for my father. I had spent the whole evening avoiding him and the daughters of his allies, but now he was curiously absent.

Enough. I was delaying the inevitable.

"Folk of the Seelie Kingdom. As you know, I vowed to my mother, your beloved queen, to marry by my upcoming two hundredth birthday."

Whispers broke out across the ballroom.

"It is with my love for my kingdom that I chose my future bride. May I present your queen-to-be, Ailish of the Coral Court."

The assembled Seelie nobles bowed. I knew that while many of them had been secretly hoping I would choose their daughters, they would accept Ailish as queen. I caught the shocked look on Saoirse's face amongst the politely smiling nobles, but she would understand. She would have to.

Declan nodded at me from where he leaned against a nearby tree. I had thought he would be pleased, but his mouth was set in a grim line mirroring my own feelings.

The merrow princess waved with a smile that didn't reach her dark eyes. I wanted to reassure her, to squeeze her hand and tell her it would all be fine. To smile and put on a show for the crowd, but it seemed my charm had finally fled.

I was about to descend the steps with the merrow princess on my arm when a scream pierced the air, setting the hair on the back of my neck on end.

Ella.

CHAPTER 38

ELLA

I RAN FROM THE BALLROOM AND THROUGH the palace, tears streaming down my cheeks. Dimly, I heard the clock still chiming midnight.

Kiyo portaled in front of me, chittering as she dropped into my arms. She sent me an impression of confused worry, and I stroked her feathery-soft mane.

"I wish I could bring you with me, but the human realm is no place for a magical creature like you."

She chirped, tilting her head.

"I'm sorry." I wiped my nose with the back of my hand. "I was just so stupid! Why didn't I tell him from the very start?"

Kiyo looked at me quizzically as I started walking again. My hairstyle began to loosen, and I slipped the sakura comb into the top of my corset. My dark strands slid over my shoulders.

There was the courtyard ahead, moonlight glinting off the branches of the Glass Gate. A raven perched on its branches.

"I was scared," I told the dragon. "Scared of Saoirse at first and then the king. But even more scared that if Tiernan saw who I really was, if he knew I was just a normal human girl under the glamour and magical dresses, he wouldn't be interested."

"Perhaps your priorities are not completely in order," said a voice from behind me.

I screamed as rough hands grabbed me from behind.

"Kiyo, get Tiernan!" I yelled as the king hauled me into the courtyard.

The raven dove at the little dragon, but she disappeared with a pop.

"Did you really think I would allow you to marry my son? To undo the centuries of work I've put in to keep this kingdom stable for him?"

I tried to pull away, but his hands gripped me tighter.

"Are you going to kill me?" I asked, my voice steady even as my knees shook.

"If I must." He narrowed his eyes at me. "Were you leaving just now?"

"Yes." Tears welled up again.

"Will you return?"

I shook my head, still crying. "He doesn't want me." I could feel the wings making up my skirt falling around me, the intricate designs on them fading as the magic left them. They pooled on the ground, plain scraps of pale fabric.

"Well then, no need to get blood all over the court-yard." He propelled me toward the gate. "Despite what you may have heard, I'm not a monster."

"No?"

"I'm practical. I can't have you returning. I hope you don't fare too badly where I'm sending you." He sneered. "Poor little human dressed in rags."

"Wait, can't I go home?" My voice went up an octave. The gate loomed ahead, suddenly ominous.

"Sorry, I can't risk you coming back."

I tripped as he propelled me up the step to the gate, losing one of my shoes. The king glanced down at the sound of glass clinking against cobblestone.

"Where did you get those shoes?!" he thundered, loosening his grip slightly.

I wrenched my arm out of his grip and lunged for the Glass Gate. Thinking of the forest outside of Pilot Bay, I leapt through.

"You're dead if you come ba—" Fiachra's roar cut off as I tumbled into the forest outside of Pilot Bay. I ran a few steps awkwardly in my one shoe but no angry Seelie King followed me. He couldn't follow me if he didn't know where I'd gone. I collapsed heavily and pulled the other shoe off, hugging it to my chest, and then the tears came back.

I cried for the small folk. I cried for magical jellyfish stars. I cried for Grainne and Isla and Imogen. I cried for Kiyo. But most of all, I cried for Tiernan and the life we could have had together if only I hadn't started it off with a lie.

CHAPTER 39

TIERNAN

WHAT IS IT?" Ailish asked, then squeaked as Kiyo popped into the air in front of us.

The little dragon dropped to perch on my outstretched arm.

"Where is she?" I demanded.

Kiyo sent me a vision of Ella sobbing, her dress in tatters as my father propelled her across the courtyard.

I turned and ran for the doorway.

"Tiernan?"

I spun back to Ailish. "Find Declan. I have to take care of something."

She looked concerned, but I didn't wait for her answer. I was already dashing through the door.

Never mind how angry I was at her for lying to me, the thought of my father getting hold of her made my blood run cold.

I'd never run as fast as I did then, dashing through the palace. But when I burst into the courtyard, my father sat alone with his back against a glass tree trunk, one of my mother's slippers cradled in his hand.

"Where is she?" I demanded.

The king didn't look up. He just turned the shoe over in his hands.

"Gone," he said.

I froze. Visions of Brenna's broken body came back to me. "If you harmed her—" I started.

"She escaped. Ran home, I presume. Wherever that is."

I let out a sigh of relief. If he didn't know where she lived, he couldn't find her.

Neither could I. That was probably for the best.

"Despite what you might think," he said, "I take no pleasure in ordering anyone's deaths."

"Right," I said, bitterly. "It's for the good of the kingdom."

He jerked his head up and looked at me for the first time. "It's for you! Everything I've done has been for you."

"You had Brenna killed for me?" I said incredulously. "You ordered the assassination of my best friend's parents—and who knows how many others—for me?"

"And for her." He set the shoe down beside him on the step.

"For Mother? She would be horrified by what you've become."

"You're probably right." My father leaned back and looked up at the stars. "I vowed to her that I would keep this kingdom together for you. Stable. I've done my best, though you have done nothing but try to pull it down around our ears."

My father slumped, looking all of his eight hundred and sixty years.

"Change is not destruction," I said, softly. "Just because something has been done a certain way for as long as you can remember doesn't mean it can't be better."

"Well." My father pushed himself up and handed me the glass slipper. "I've done all I can. I suppose we'll see if you're right. Danu help us all. I don't suppose you'll see reason and wed the Aster Princess's daughter. Or any of the excellent choices I've brought for you tonight?"

"I'm marrying Ailish, of the Coral Court." Even saying the words hurt. Would I get used to the idea in time?

"A merrow?" Fiachra clenched a fist and then shook his head. "Better than a treacherous human, I suppose."

I hated to side with the king on any point, but my head agreed with him.

And my heart wasn't important.

CHAPTER 40

ELLA

WHEN I REACHED AMBER'S HOUSE—RED NOSED and barefoot, wearing only the rags of Mama's kimono—Isobel answered the door.

"Is Amber here?" I sniffed.

"Oh, hun." Isobel ushered me inside. She still had her hair up with rose-tipped pins in it but had changed into joggers and a t-shirt. "Amber's here. She's grounded until she graduates, but come in."

"I'm sorry that I got her into trouble." I set my glass slipper on the shoe rack.

"Amber can get into all sorts of trouble without anybody's help. Don't worry about that. She told me all about what happened, but by the look of you, I need to go smack some sense into a crown prince."

"It's my fault." I sat on the blue eighties couch in their living room. "I lied to him."

"Not the best way to start a relationship," agreed Isobel, tucking a quilt around me. She looked like she was about to say more, but then Amber ran into the room.

"Ella! Oooh, you don't look so good!" Her hair and makeup had disappeared like mine, and she was back in a hoodie and PJ pants.

Isobel raised her eyebrows at her sister.

"I mean…compared to before." Amber dropped onto the couch beside me and gave me a hug.

Isobel shrugged. "It's true, you looked like a fae princess. I didn't even recognize you. That dress was incredible. Where did it go?"

I started crying again.

"Lily!" yelled Isobel. "We need cookies, STAT!"

The oldest Watson sister poked her head into the living room. "Oh, she does need cookies. Hi! Are you one of Amber's friends?"

Amber rubbed my shoulder. "This is Ella. She's had a hard day in Faerie."

"Is Tiernan breaking hearts again?" demanded Lily.

This only made me cry harder at the reminder that I should never have trusted him in the first place.

"This is serious," said Isobel, grimly. "I think it'll require chocolate chips."

"I'll get started." Lily ducked back into the kitchen.

Isobel sat down on the other side of me, and I found myself in a hug sandwich.

Lily reappeared a moment later—an apron over her lounge clothes—with a tub of cookie dough ice cream and a spoon.

"To tide you over," she said.

"Is this what it's like to have sisters?" I said in wonder, scooping a spoonful of ice cream. Surely, I could get away with eating a little ice cream. Who could resist cookie dough?

"It's not all hugs and ice cream," sighed Amber.

Isobel gave her a look.

"But it's not completely terrible," she amended.

"You can stay here as long as you need to and find out for yourself," said Isobel. "Amber doesn't mind sharing her room."

Amber looked thoughtful.

"Right?" Isobel poked her leg.

"Oh yeah, totally. I was trying to imagine where I would put my shoes. No big deal." She gave her head a shake. "We're not sending you back to that house of horrors you grew up in."

"And maybe Tiernan will realize how dumb he is." Isobel patted my hand. "Want me to set Leith on him? I don't mind!"

"He doesn't want me." I ate another scoop of ice cream. "And I don't want him if he doesn't want me."

"Fair enough," said Isobel. "You don't have to decide anything right now."

I dug out a nugget of frozen cookie dough, and with a pop, Kiyo appeared on my lap.

"Um, you have a dragon on your lap," pointed out Isobel.

"This is Kiyohime." I offered a spoonful of ice cream to the little dragon who gingerly bit off a large chunk. "Slow down, little one. You'll give yourself a brain freeze."

"Lily!" shouted Isobel. "I think we need another spoon!"

CHAPTER 41

TIERNAN

PRINCESS AILISH DEPARTED THE DAY AFTER THE ball to prepare for the wedding. I wished her farewell with a handshake. I couldn't even bring myself to kiss her cheek.

The wedding was set for an hour before the time of my birth, two hundred years ago. Was I cutting it dangerously close? Perhaps.

Logic would have me accept my fate and get it over with. What was another month after all? But now that I had felt love, even my jaded heart balked at the thought of centuries ahead tied to someone for whom I felt nothing.

Not wishing to discuss this further with my father—or indeed with anyone—I kept to my room, throwing myself into the work of preparing the Fianna for its new leaders. I wrote long, detailed explanations that Declan and Saoirse did not need but that kept my mind distracted, if only a little.

I had my meals delivered to my rooms. Other than the brownies who came to deliver my meals, the only living creature I saw was Kiyo.

I tried to send her away—her pleading sad eyes and mental queries about Ella were too much for me—but she always came back. Finally, I gave in and made her a little nest on my desk out of a basket and a soft fur blanket, which was soon filled with cutlery, cookies, coins, and even a small silver dagger that had been displayed over my fireplace.

My self-imposed confinement went on for a week and a half until Declan and Saoirse pounded on my door.

"It's been nine days!" yelled Saoirse.

When I didn't answer, they let themselves in.

"I'm working," I muttered as my seconds took in my disheveled state.

Declan grabbed the quill from my hand.

"Hey!"

"That's enough being sad," he said.

"I'm not sad," I grumbled.

"Well, you should be. You. Idiot." Saoirse tapped my forehead with a sharp finger to punctuate each word. "Come on, I know what you need."

"I'm sorry." Declan sighed heavily. "But, really, you brought this upon yourself."

He hauled me up out of my chair.

"It's time." Saoirse rubbed her hands together. "For training exercises."

I groaned.

"Don't worry. Being sad requires thought. You're not going to have time for that with what I've got planned."

Saoirse had built a training course that Fionn mac Cumhaill himself would have been proud of. Her victims—I mean, the fianna—ranged over waterfalls, under logs, through trees and across rivers with so many traps designed by Jac's clever tinkering along the way, that she was right. I didn't have time to think about anything else.

We then sparred in pairs and groups until sweat poured down my body and the sun began to set. Finally, Saoirse let us quit for the dinner Calder had ready. Stew bubbled on the training camp's outdoor stove and fresh bread had just come out of the stone oven.

I sat on one of the benches around the fire, enjoying the chatter of my family.

"What did you think of the trap in the cedar tree?" Jac asked Fergus.

"Almost took my beard off," grumbled the burly fae.

"I know, right!" Jac crowed. "Last time you said I made them too easy, so I wanted to make these ones more fun."

"Decapitation is not fun," Rian called from across the fire.

"No one got decapitated!" squeaked Jac.

"Yet," said Orla, mildly.

"Did I catch a smile?" Saoirse sat down on the bench beside me. "Stop punishing yourself. You're never at your best when you're alone. That's why you need to get over your snit and go talk to Ella."

"I'm not in a snit."

"Sure sounds like a snit." Declan sat on my other side.

"And I'm not alone." I gestured at the fianna, who weren't even pretending not to listen in. "Anyway, little sister, why are you suddenly so adamant that I marry for love? You of all people should know I can be happy without it."

Saoirse snorted. "No, I of all people should know that *I* am happy without it. You are a miserable mess who locked yourself in your room for a week and a half. Not everyone needs the same thing." She waved her bread at me. "And while I hate to point this out, we will always be your family, but none of us will be ruling the kingdom with you."

For a breath, I let myself imagine ruling with Ella at my side, how her kind heart could make the kingdom better.

I waved my hand around the fire. "She lied to all of us! Aren't any of you upset?"

"Oh, I knew she was a human," said Fergus through a bite of bread.

"What?!" I dropped my spoon into my bowl with a clatter.

The bearded fae shrugged. "She doesn't know much about birds, but she uses their human names. They came out kind of funny though. I think she used an interpretation charm. Speaking of birds…"

"What?" asked Declan as I stared at Fergus.

"Eh, I'll tell you later."

"She said she'd never been to the human realm," piped up Jac. "But she knew what nylon parachute cord is. That was kind of weird. So I figured."

"Any of the rest of you?" I asked.

"Her blood smells human," said Calder.

"She only knows human folk tales," said Haru.

"She's noisy as a human in the forest," added Orla. Rian nodded in agreement.

"And none of you thought to tell me this?" I ground out.

"Thought you'd have known." Rian shrugged.

"You lied to us, too," said Haru. "You told us that you were in love."

"Aren't they in love?" asked Jac.

"Well, I mean, they are now, but the point is, we're forgiving Tiernan," said Haru.

"Thank you, Haru," I said.

"So he should be able to forgive Ella," said Haru. "Logically."

I sighed and looked at Declan and Saoirse. "Did you two know she was a human?"

"Not for sure," hedged Saoirse. "But it did seem odd that she didn't realize tea was medicinal."

Declan held up his hands. "I did know she wasn't from the Isle of Mist, but I only found that out the day before the ball. I confronted her, and she told me everything. She wanted to tell you herself."

"A little heads up would have been nice." I glared at my best friend.

"I would have told you by midnight, but I thought she should do it."

She had been trying to tell me something, but I had been so wrapped up in wanting to propose that I had brushed it off.

"She had three months to tell me," I grumbled. "Why wait until the last minute?"

"Ah yes," said Saoirse. "Waiting until the last minute. Why would anyone do that? How many years did you wait to pick a bride, again?"

"Could you be more annoying?" I asked her.

"Probably. If you don't go after her, I definitely will."

"You will, won't you?" asked Jac, puppy dog eyes in full force. "You'll go talk to her?"

I sighed. "I don't know."

I tossed and turned all night. Kiyo had enough and chittered at me scoldingly before disappearing to find a safer place to sleep.

Were my friends right? I winced when I remembered our interaction. The way I had treated Ella. Now that my anger had drained away, I was embarrassed that I had let Lynet stir up so much trouble between us. I should have given Ella the chance to finish explaining, but my temper and my wounded pride had led me to believe I couldn't trust her. But truly, I had been scared.

I was still scared.

Loving someone, baring my heart, left me too vulnerable. The pain and anger I felt when she wounded me made me fear that I might turn out like my father after all.

Easier to pull back. Easier to drive her away. Easier to say I had never really known her at all.

But in my heart, I knew that was a lie. She might not have told me where she was from, but I had seen her kindness when she interacted with the small folk. The longing in her heart that I understood so well for family, for purpose. Her love for beauty and creation.

Ugh. Saoirse was right. I was an idiot.

I sat up and ran my hands through my hair. How would I even find her to apologize? All I knew was that she was a human girl named Ella, somewhere in the human realm. I groaned and fell back against the bed.

Chirp?

I opened one eye. Kiyo came into focus.

"Hi," I said.

She gently rested her foot on the end of my nose and leaned in until her snout stopped not an inch away from my eyeball. She chirped again, and sent me an impression of Ella, wrapped in a quilt and eating some sort of frozen dessert out of a paper cylinder.

I tried to get a sense of her surroundings, but Kiyo's memory focused mainly on the food. I sat back up, and Kiyo scampered onto my end table.

"Where is she?" I asked.

The little dragon chirped again and sent me an image of a little cabin with a bright red door.

"Oh," I said. "Perfect. I'll just look for the red door somewhere in the human realm."

I pulled out a chocolate from the stash I kept for Kiyo in my bedside table. As she took it delicately from my hand, I noticed a piece of paper tied around her ankle. When I unrolled it, I was shocked to find my godmother, Clíodhna's, handwriting.

I knew that Leith's fiancée, Isobel, had met Clíodhna, but I hadn't seen her since I was a youth. Long enough that I had wondered if she'd forgotten about me. Evidently not.

Dearest Tiernan,

If you have quite finished sulking, I think you'll agree that an apology is due to the lovely Ella.

I know you grew up without proper parenting, and I am sorry for that. But really, dear boy, your manners are in need of some tutoring. If you're not going to behave better, then find a nice boring princess to marry, although perhaps not Ailish. She's not for you. But, if you promise not to break Ella's heart, you might wish to know your not-so-fake sweetheart is staying with Isobel.

Your loving Godmother

P.S. Give my love to Saoirse and Declan. They must be applauded for putting up with you.

I folded the note and stood. "Come on, Kiyo. We're off to the Rose Court."

CHAPTER 42

ELLA

THE NEXT MORNING, I FELT LIKE DEATH after my solid two hours of sleep. I had slept in Amber's room. Or more accurately, I had spent hours lying on a bed on the floor staring at the ceiling. Kiyo had disappeared when the ice cream did. I hoped she wouldn't visit me every time I had a sweet treat, as it would be difficult to explain in a coffee shop. But I couldn't deny it had been comforting to be visited by a little piece of my life in Faerie.

Lily made us blueberry pancakes, and Isobel fixed me a cup of tea.

"Did you get any sleep?" the future Rose Princess asked, setting the tea on the table with cream, sugar, honey, milk, and oat milk. "I wasn't sure what you like in your tea."

"I didn't sleep well, but it's nothing I'm not used to."

"Oh?" Isobel sat in a chair across from me.

"I have anxiety. I'm often up all night." I was surprised by how easily it came out. Tiernan might have broken my heart, but his and Saoirse's acceptance of my mental health issues had gone a long way toward helping me accept them too.

"Gotcha," said Isobel.

"I have anxiety too." Lily set a stack of pancakes in front of me. "And a dash of ADHD to keep things interesting."

I looked at her in surprise.

"More people deal with this stuff than you realize. That's why it's always good to talk about it. So you don't feel so alone." She poured more batter into the frying pan. "Are you taking anything for it? Seeing anybody?"

"I have this tea that's kind of amazing." I sighed. "But I guess it's gone now. I left my bag at the palace."

"Oh, this bag?" Amber wandered into the kitchen in pajama pants and a tank top. She yawned and tossed my trusty shoulder bag onto the table. "I made Isobel take me to grab it while you were sleeping on the couch after ice cream. I know how you are about your sketchbook."

"What do you draw?" asked Isobel.

"Ella is an amazing fashion designer," Amber told her.

"Really?" Lily flipped a stack of pancakes off the pan. "That's so cool!"

The urge came as always to hide my book and play down what I did.

"I am." I lifted my chin. "Would you like to see?"

"Yes!" yelled Isobel and Lily together. I passed over my sketchbook, and Lily sat down next to Isobel to flip through it.

"Did you design the dress you wore to the ball last night?" Isobel turned to Lily. "It was amazing."

"I did! Thank you!" I drizzled more syrup on my pancakes.

"She's gonna go to Parsons!" said Amber.

"Well, that's my dream, but I need a scholarship to be able to afford it."

The older girls nodded.

"I don't know anything about fashion—" started Isobel.

"So true." Amber took a bite of pancake.

Isobel smacked her lightly on the head and turned the page. "But these are amazing. You should definitely apply."

"We can do it this afternoon if you want," offered Amber. "Between this sketchbook and the photos I took of your dress, I bet they've never seen anything like you before."

I smiled automatically, but as I watched the sisters flip through my sketchbook, I realized that even though I was proud of my work and would never be happy if I stopped designing, I didn't know if it would be enough for me anymore. Not when I had gotten a glimpse of what it would be like to make a real difference.

"Maybe," I said.

Amber looked like she wanted to ask me more, but then a knock sounded on the door.

"Don't get up! I'll let myself in."

"Hi, Miss Chloe, would you like some pancakes?" called Lily.

The librarian poked her curly gray-haired head around the door. "Don't mind if I do. Thank you. I'm just taking my boots off." A moment later, she appeared in the kitchen.

"So." Miss Chloe sat down at the table, "Ella. You've had quite the long weekend."

"Weekend?"

"In human time. It's only Tuesday, dear. Thank you, Lily." Miss Chloe accepted a steaming plate of pancakes from the oldest Watson sister. "Now, I generally try not to meddle…"

Amber almost choked on her pancake.

"There, there." Miss Chloe patted her back. "I generally try not to meddle unless it's completely necessary," she amended. "But in this case, my godson has been difficult and—not to be dramatic—but the fate of the kingdom does hang in the balance. So, I hope you won't mind that I lured your little dragon friend to my house with cupcakes last night."

I shook my head, trying to keep up.

"I had Kiyo send Tiernan a note telling him where you're staying. I wanted you to have a heads up, in case he comes to his senses and decides to apologize. Pass the butter please, Isobel."

I shook my head. "You weren't there. He's not going to—"

A pop rang out as Kiyo appeared on the table, one foot on my pancakes.

"Hungry?" I asked her, then I noticed the glint of gold and sparkling pink dangling from her mouth. "Kiyohime! I told you to stop stealing shiny objects!"

The little dragon sent me an impression of Tiernan and dropped the ring in my hand.

I gasped.

That ring! Its gold band was fashioned like a branch with whorls and even a couple of little twiggy offshoots. In the center sat a sakura blossom. Each petal was a sparkling pink gem and tiny diamonds glinted at the center.

"It's so pretty!" breathed Amber.

Kiyo chirped and held out her front leg to display a carefully tied, rolled-up note.

Dear Ella,
I have a question for you, but first I have to apologize.

If you don't want to see me, I understand. But I hope you'll answer the door.

Tiernan

"The door?" muttered Amber. All four of them were reading over my shoulder.

"Good boy." Miss Chloe patted my shoulder. "Will you give him another chance?"

I turned the ring over, at a loss for words.

Then someone knocked at the back door.

CHAPTER 43

ELLA

I OPENED THE DOOR—NOT SURE IF I wanted to kiss my prince for the ring or smack him for how he had treated me earlier. Instead, I found myself struck dumb at the sight of the crown prince of the Seelie Fae wearing dark wash jeans and a black henley.

"Do I look ridiculous?" Tiernan shifted and ran his hand awkwardly through his copper hair, and I noticed his rounded ear tips. "Leith said I should borrow some clothes and a glamour in case someone saw me," he said. "I haven't been to the human realm for about ninety years so I could be dressed like a fool, and I would never know."

"No." I closed the door behind me. "You don't look like a fool."

He looked delicious, but I wasn't about to tell him that. Not yet, anyway.

"You're not going to yell at me?" he asked. "I know I deserve it."

"It's too early in the morning for yelling." I sat down on the back steps, and he sat beside me, close but not touching.

"Before I say anything else, I want to apologize. I know I don't deserve to have you hear me out, not when I didn't give you the chance, but I am sorry. My reaction had a lot more to do with me and my fear than it had to do with you."

I looked away from him, out at the forest. "I'm sorry, too," I said. "I should have told you sooner."

"Why didn't you?" he asked. "Did I give you reason to suspect that you had anything to fear from me?"

I shook my head. "At first, I pretended to be fae with Amber, just for fun. Then I was scared of your father."

"Fair enough." Tiernan sighed.

"Then Saoirse gave me such threats about lying to you. She can be terrifying."

Tiernan chuckled. "Oh, I know."

"And then…the truth is, I was scared of more than that. Scared to ruin things between us. But also scared for you to know who I really am. If you don't let people know you, they can't hurt you. You know?"

Tiernan nodded. "So tell me, if you're ready, who are you really?"

"I'm just Ella," I said. "That's the funny thing. I've shared more of myself with you than I have with anyone before. Everything I told you about my family, about my dreams to become a famous clothing designer, my anxiety…that's me. I'm one anxious, creative, orphaned mess." I held my hand out to Tiernan. "Pleased to meet you."

He shook my hand, gravely, "Nice to meet you, Ella. I'm just Tiernan, a prince who's been so focused on saving his kingdom that he didn't know he needed saving as well until a gorgeous, strong, creative girl came along and made him think that love might be possible. And I responded by hiding behind my fear instead of being brave enough to listen. Will you forgive me?"

"I forgive you."

He lifted my hand and kissed my knuckles. "Did you get my note?"

I opened my balled fist and revealed the blossom ring.

"I'm going to ask you something," he said. "And I just want you to listen."

"Okay." I nodded, feeling the weight of the seriousness in his green eyes.

"After you left…" He paused before continuing. "After I made you leave, I did something a bit rash."

My heart stuttered.

"I announced my betrothal to the merrow princess."

I made a choking noise, my heart freezing inside my chest, but he held up his hand.

"Let me finish," he said. "You know I have to marry before my 200th birthday."

"I remember."

"It's important that I marry someone who will help me change the kingdom. Ailish will do that."

And I felt my frozen heart start to crack.

"But she's not who I want." He leaned his forehead against mine. "She's not who I need," he said, softly. A finger under my chin tilted my lips up to meet his soft kiss.

"She's not who I love," he whispered against my lips.

"I'm not a noble," I whispered. "I'm not even fae."

"The courts will accept you if I do. If you're willing to forgive me. If you'll marry me and be my queen."

My mind raced.

"Don't answer yet." He closed my hand over the ring. "I know what I'm asking. I know this was never what you were looking for. If you decide to stay here and become the fashion designer you were born to be, I understand. This is a lot to ask."

Tiernan handed me a velvet-wrapped bundle.

"If you decide to marry me…" He unwrapped the bundle slowly. "To become my queen, just come to the stone circle at *Croí Clíoche*. The gate will be warded against intruders for the wedding, but you'll be able to get through with this." Tiernan handed me the lost glass slipper. "I believe you have the other one."

I nodded. "But what about the merrow princess? Will she be upset?"

Tiernan shook his head. "She's only marrying me to ensure the future of the merrows. She never wanted to marry a land fae and give up the sea."

"The wedding takes place two hundred years from my birth. Wait until just before, or my father will stop you." He raised his voice. "I believe my eavesdropping god-mother will know the time and date."

"I sure do," hollered Miss Chloe from inside.

Tiernan rose to leave. "Goodbye, Ella." He bent down and kissed me on the cheek. "I hope I'll see you soon. If not, keep the ring and remember me. I'll always treasure our time together. You've taught me that love is a gift, not a curse, and for that, I'm forever grateful."

I watched him until he disappeared into the trees. Then I went back inside, setting the glass slipper on the shoe rack next to its twin.

In the kitchen, everyone was busily eating pancakes.

"So…what did you talk about?" asked Amber, casually. "Was that Tiernan?"

"As if you weren't all listening from the other side of the door." I sat down and sliced a piece of my now-cold pancake.

"We had to hold back Amber," said Lily. "She was about to jump through the door and tackle Tiernan."

"Only if he didn't start with an apology!" protested Amber.

"In which case, we would have let her at him." Isobel winked.

"But it looks like he did apologize," said Miss Chloe with a twinkle in her eye.

"He asked me to marry him," I said dreamily, cutting my pancake into even smaller pieces.

"Success!" Amber squealed, giving Miss Chloe a high five.

"What did you say?" asked Isobel.

"He said he didn't want me to answer. He wanted me to think about it."

Isobel nodded seriously. "That's smart. You should be sure."

"Isobel thinks everyone should be, like, thirty and have a career before they get married." Amber rolled her eyes.

"That's not true," said Isobel. "I just think people should wait until they're ready. And I'm still needed here." She nodded at Amber who sighed dramatically. "Are you ready?" she asked me. "Till death do you part is a long time, especially in Faerie."

"I don't have any reason to stay here." I poked at a piece of pancake. "Not like you do."

"What about Parsons?" asked Lily.

"I'll never stop drawing and designing," I said. "But I can make a difference in so many people's lives."

"And Tiernan?" asked Amber. "Do you love him? Like, forever love him?"

"Yes," I said without any hesitation.

"He'll probably do dumb stuff again," warned Isobel.

"Everybody does dumb stuff." Me as much as him.

She nodded. "It sounds like you've made up your mind."

"I have," I said.

"Sounds like we've got a wedding to crash!" squealed Amber, jumping out of her chair. "Miss Chloe, we're gonna need a really good dress for this. Like, killer."

"No," I said, firmly. "Not this time."

"I bet we can get Grainne to quickly make you another one. Or you can borrow one of my dresses. I know they're not perfect but—"

"No," I repeated. All the ladies at the table looked at me. "No more costumes," I said. "No more armor. No more pretending to be something I'm not. If Tiernan wants to marry me." My stomach flipped over. "Then he can marry me. If the court is going to accept a human girl as a queen, they're gonna see me as a human girl."

"But—" Amber protested.

Miss Chloe laid a hand on her arm. "It's all right, dear."

"We're just gonna let her go like that!?" She waved my sleep-rumpled state.

"I mean, I'll brush my hair."

"We've done the best we can," Miss Chloe told Amber. "From here on out we've got to let things fall where they may."

Isobel gave the pair a suspicious look, but I was too busy planning to think about them.

"What are you gonna wear then?" sighed Amber. "Leggings and a hoodie?"

"I'm thinking. Give me a minute."

Lily slid another pancake onto my plate. "I think you're gonna have a busy day," she said. "Better start with a full stomach."

CHAPTER 44

ELLA

I LOOKED AT THE WATCH AS AMBER brushed my hair. According to the date Miss Chloe had given me, we had another hour or so in the human world before the wedding. I looked in the mirror, running a finger over my rounded ears. I had grown so used to seeing the pointed tips, I had almost started to believe my own story.

"We still have time to find you a dress. Just saying. You look very basic."

I was a stark contrast to Amber, who wore a purple spider silk dress with silver moths embroidered on the fitted bodice and full skirt.

"This is fine, thank you." I smoothed my hands down the simple, strapless, knee-length white dress I wore. Amber had forced me into a dress, but I had ignored all her fae-made dresses.

"You're getting married today," insisted Amber, pulling back one side of my hair into a twist and fixing it in place with a couple of hairpins.

"I know. You've got to trust me on this."

She sighed and slid my mama's comb into the twist, the pink silk flowers shining against my black hair.

I touched it gently. I wished I could see her again and tell her that all the stories she had told me were true.

"Alright then. I guess this is as good as it's gonna get." Amber threw up her hands.

"Thank you, Amber." I pulled my friend down for a hug.

"At least put on some lip gloss," she whispered into my hair.

Downstairs, Isobel and Lily waited in formal dresses of gold and green.

"We'll walk you to the Rose Gate," said Isobel. "And then we'll head over to meet Leith at Kilinaire. But don't worry, we'll be at *Croí Clíoche* for the wedding before you get there."

Leith and Isobel were, of course, invited to the ceremony—as were all Seelie nobles—and they were bringing Lily and Amber as their guests. At least I'd have four friendly faces in the crowd.

"I do wish I could go with you, my dear." Miss Chloe gave my hand a pat. "But I'll be watching everything in the mirror. Be sure to bring Tiernan for a visit. After the honeymoon, of course." She winked.

I blushed and searched for my shoes, grabbing the glass slippers to carry through the forest. The older sisters and I stepped outside, but Miss Chloe stopped Amber with a hand on her arm.

"You three run ahead," said the librarian. "Amber will meet you there. We need to have a quick chat."

Isobel hesitated, clearly not wanting to let Amber roam free in Faerie again.

"You can trust me," Amber insisted, looking her sister steadily in the eyes.

Isobel's face softened, and she nodded. "Okay, then. I'll see you there."

"How are you feeling?" asked Lily as we hiked up the path to the Rose Gate. "Butterflies in your stomach?"

"No," I said, and for the first time since my mama had died, it was the truth. "I feel at peace. Although, I will admit it's not quite how I imagined my wedding going down."

"Well, not everyone can take two human years and however much faerie time to plan a wedding," laughed Isobel. "Speaking of which, I was wondering—if you're not too busy being queen after this—I'd love for you to design my wedding dress."

I grinned at Amber's sister. "I'll never be too busy for dresses. What did you have in mind?"

"Well, I was thinking of something to do with roses."

We chatted gowns until we reached the faerie gate. The sisters gave me hugs and stepped through to Kilinaire.

I flipped open my pocket watch and watched one hour spin by in Faerie time, and then another. If I showed up early, I'd risk Fiachra stopping me. Maybe permanently.

Almost there…

I took a deep breath and timed my step through the gate.

The next moment, I stepped into *Croí Clioche*, the afternoon sun shining overhead.

The clearing looked very different from when I had last met Tiernan there, back when we didn't know anything about each other or where this would all lead.

Summer had given way to autumn, and mushrooms and scattered leaves had replaced the wildflowers in the clearing. But the biggest change, of course, was the crowd.

Over a hundred *Tuatha Dé Danann* in gorgeous finery were gathered around and between the standing stones. On the outskirts and flying overhead were the palace small folk, trying to get a peek at the wedding.

A little chickadee hovered nearby, and strangely, seemed about ready to land on my shoulder when Kiyo appeared with a pop, startling the bird away and landing on my shoulder herself.

"That wasn't very polite," I told her. She butted me with her head and sent me an urgent image of a worried-looking Tiernan and a depressed merrow princess. My prince was dressed more sedately than I had ever seen him, in a perfectly-tailored but unadorned suit of navy silk. The pair stood on either side of the *fáinne menhir*, but their hands weren't clasped through the stone's hole. Facing them stood the king—his raven perched on his shoulder, as always—and a woman in a deeply-hooded robe who must be the priestess officiating the wedding.

"Have you ever seen such a happy couple?" I asked her. The dragon did not look amused by my humor.

I began to walk toward the standing stones and one of the piskies spotted me.

"She's here!" the piskie whispered loudly. As I walked through the crowd of small folk I heard it passed in little voices around the clearing. "Lady Ella's here! Tell the others!"

The small folk parted for me, but the *Tuatha Dé Danann* were too fixed on the couple at the center of the circle to notice my approach.

The little chickadee came flying back, a large white flower in its beak. Behind it circled two more small birds, each holding a flower. Where had they gotten flowers from?

"You guys better not poop on my outfit," I muttered.

"It's Ella!" Isobel popped her head out of the crowd and waved at me. She nudged Leith and then whispered something to the couple beside her.

The blond fae man and Leith cleared a path for me through the crowd. Isobel and a beautiful princess with dark curly hair whispered to more nobles until the whole crowd buzzed with gossip and parted.

Kiyo disappeared from my arms, and reappeared in the center of the stone circle between Tiernan and Ailish, chittering as she landed on Tiernan's arm. He froze and looked over at me with a brilliant smile, erasing the worry on his face.

Everyone was looking at me.

I swallowed and lifted my chin as I walked slowly toward him. More birds flew around me, including Morna, Tiernan's jay.

Tiernan whispered something to Ailish, who looked like she might faint with relief. She then gave him a little shove in my direction. Kiyo disappeared, hopefully to find Haru and his snacks.

The priestess looked flustered. The weddings of fae rulers probably didn't usually get crashed.

"Stop!" the king said.

His son ignored him and walked toward me.

"This goes beyond politics, boy," the king hissed. "She's not even fae."

The chickadee landed on my shoulder, and I felt a tingle of magic as the bird pressed the flower against my bodice. It stayed still, held in place like the silk had when the faeries had made my ball gown for Samhain. The chickadee chirped, and I felt a sense of approval from the little bird. Before I could consider how that had happened, it flew off again.

Another bird added its flower to the first and then another. I walked toward the center of the stone circle, my eyes fixed on nothing but Tiernan's green ones as he walked toward me. I felt magic like nothing I ever had before as the birds surrounded me, weaving flowers and golden leaves into a full skirt and fitted bodice. It was more than just the magic of the dress. With every step, I felt a tingle of magic coming up from the land itself, even through the glass slippers.

The crowd gasped. The whispers rose in volume with exclamations of shock as the shimmering gown of glowing white flowers and sparkling golden leaves was completed.

The chickadee landed on my shoulder again, and I stepped through the circle of standing stones, flowers trailing behind me.

CHAPTER 45

TIERNAN

I HAD HOPED AND PRAYED ELLA WOULD show up, but nothing could have prepared me for the sight of her walking through the ring of standing stones in a dress of flowers crafted by the magic of Faerie itself.

I felt like my heart would burst when she smiled at me. Anything other than walking toward her felt as impossible as stopping myself from breathing.

"Halt!" Fiachra roared.

My step faltered as a wave of power slammed into me. The priestess beside the king fell to her knees.

I reached Ella, who had stumbled as well but stayed on her feet. She held tightly to my hand, and we turned to face the king.

"Ella is my choice, Father," I said, calmly.

"A human? I will not allow it." The king's face twisted with rage, and the bright afternoon light darkened, even though no clouds were in the sky. His raven, Cethin, puffed up and with a rustle of feathers, the dark wings of ravens unfolded themselves from the growing shadows of the standing stones.

I pulled Ella closer to me as the beating of wings surrounded us.

"You would break your vow to my mother?" I asked him.

A shadow raven swooped at us with a cry, but Morna and Ella's chickadee launched themselves in response, chasing the ravens away from us. More shadowy birds surrounded them.

"Better I be cursed from a broken vow than the Seelie Kingdom be cursed by the foolish sentiment of a silly boy."

The sky grew darker yet as the king's magic pressed against us. The ravens closed in.

I turned away from the king to face Ella, clasping both her hands in mine. Closing my eyes, I felt for my connection to the magic of Faerie—the connection that had steadily grown over the past few years as my father's had weakened—and felt it surge up from the earth.

I was startled to realize that the connection was echoed in Ella. She squeezed my hand and our magic wove together, becoming stronger than either of us could channel on our own.

In a flash of white light, the press of power broke off. I opened my eyes to see glowing jays and chickadees chase off the shadow ravens before all the birds faded, leaving just Cethin, Morna, and Ella's chickadee.

We turned back to face the king, striding toward the center of the stone circle, our hands still clasped.

The king stared in disbelief. He raised his hands, and I felt a brush of building power. I tightened my grip on Ella's hand, but the air hadn't even begun to darken again when Fiachra's raven launched from his shoulder, snatching the crown of golden branches from his head.

I held out my hands in shock, and Cethin dropped the crown into them. Then, with a cry, the raven flew away over the treetops.

"No, you can't—" The king's cry was cut short as everyone turned at the sounds of a crowd of small folk pushing past the *Tuatha Dé Danann* to reach us.

"Isla!" Ella smiled at a small draoi girl in a clean blue dress carrying a white velvet pillow with a crown resting on it.

It was a more delicate version of the crown I held in my hands, crafted of golden branches with leaves matching Ella's dress and golden flowers with diamond centers.

This was the missing queen's crown. My mother's crown. The *Aos Sí* had been keeping it safe all this time.

"This is for you." Isla offered Ella the cushion.

Ella knelt down and kissed her on the forehead. "Thank you, sweetheart," she whispered.

Isla beamed, and I slipped the sakura comb from Ella's hair and tucked it into my pocket before helping the little girl settle the crown on Ella's silky hair. Then the child scampered through the trees to join her mother in the crowd.

I helped Ella to her feet and then handed her my crown and knelt while she placed it on my head.

I rose, and we turned to face my father once more. Fiachra looked small without his raven and his crown. His face paled but he held his chin high.

"You have lost the blessing of Faerie," I told my father. "If you come quietly, you may choose exile."

Fiachra reached for the sword at his hip, and I signaled to Saoirse and Declan, who waited on either side of the stone circle.

"I don't want to kill you," I pleaded. For all that he was a monster, he was still my father. And I loved him, even if I wished I didn't.

"As if it could hurt me any more than you already have," sneered Fiachra, drawing his sword.

Saoirse and Declan lunged, and then froze, dropping to their knees under a wave of power. The priestess and the entire crowd followed them to the ground.

I squeezed Ella's hand and held tight to my connection to the land to remain upright.

The last thing I expected was for a woman to step through the stone circle. She was crowned with icicles and antlers with snow white hair falling in waves down her back. White fur trimmed her cloak, and jewels flashed as she walked toward Fiachra.

"Moriath," I whispered. What was the Unseelie Queen doing here? How had she marched straight into the heart of the Seelie Kingdom?

The Unseelie Queen shook her head as she approached Fiachra, kneeling on the ground under the force of her power, like everyone else. "Seems like you lost, after all? Ah, well, if you wish to be beheaded, by all means throw your life away." She flicked a hand toward Saoirse, who bared her teeth at the queen. "Or, you can leave with me now, and I will consider your debt paid."

Fiachra nodded, the fight seeming to go out of him. She pulled him to his feet.

"That's what I thought." Moriath nodded at Ella and me. "Boy king, human child, I'm sure we'll meet again." The queen swept back past the cowering crowd and through the gate, Fiachra stumbling after her.

The Seelie fae exhaled shakily and stood as Moriath's power disappeared with a snap behind her.

"How did Moriath open a warded gate into the heart of the Seelie Kingdom?" I demanded.

"I don't know." Saoirse rose to her feet, sword in her hand. "But perhaps we can figure that out later." She checked her pocket watch. "You're running out of time."

I nodded and turned to the crowd.

"The land and the creatures of Faerie presented Ella as queen," I called out as the chickadee landed on one of her shoulders and my jay landed on her other.

"The *Aos Sí* crowned Ella as queen." I tucked her hand into the crook of my arm.

The nobles continued to whisper amongst themselves.

"Will you accept Ella as the Seelie Queen? Yes, she is a human, but I've seen her heart and the love it holds for our people." I smiled at the gathered small folk. "For the land and—"

"And for your new king," she cut in, squeezing my hand.

"You love me?" I asked softly.

"I'm not just here for the dress." Ella smiled. "Of course, I love you."

"What about your plans? Your dream of becoming a fashion designer?" I shouldn't protest, but I could scarcely believe it was true.

"You gave me a better dream," she whispered, rising up on tiptoes to kiss me lightly.

I touched my forehead to hers, and for a moment, it was just us.

But I was king now, and there was more to be done.

I turned back to the gathered nobles. "You've witnessed all of this tonight. Will you kneel?"

Saoirse and Declan knelt first, followed by the rest of the fianna, and did I hear Jac squeal?

Leith, Isobel, and her older sister Lily knelt next—oddly, Amber didn't seem to be with them—followed by Princess Tuala and Prince Naven.

I held my breath as the other nobles eyed us and then let it out as the rest of the Seelie fae knelt in a wave. Even Princess Lynet was wrestled down by her mother, who seemed to realize they had lost this game.

"Thank you." Ella smiled at the crowd. "I won't let you down."

Ella and I faced each other in the center of the clearing.

The priestess eyed us both warily. "Shall we begin, then?"

"Wait!"

Isobel's little sister, Amber, pushed through the crowd, a hand in the air.

"No!" bellowed the priestess. We all turned to stare at her. Her calm face had turned red. "No more interruptions! This is a royal wedding, not some traveling minstrel play!"

"Um, Amber?" said Ella. "We're kind of in a hurry here!"

In the front row, Isobel covered her face with her hands. Leith patted her shoulder, and Lily closed her eyes.

"Sorry, sorry!" Amber rushed through the stone circle, stopping in front of us, panting and breathless. "But you don't have to get married."

"What?" Both Ella and I stared at her. The priestess fixed her with a severe glare.

"Miss Chloe—I mean Clíodhna—sent me to tell you, Tiernan, that the vow to your mother has been fulfilled. You don't have to get married."

The priestess threw her scroll down and stalked off.

"What are you talking about?" I frowned. "I vowed to find…" I blanched as realization dawned on me. "My queen."

Ella stared at me in her magical dress and golden crown and said, "Oh. Oh!"

"Right?" said Amber. "She's already queen. Killer dress, by the way, Ella."

"So, if we don't get married this afternoon, nothing bad will happen?" Ella asked, thoughtfully.

My heart clenched. She was considering not going through with it. I had been so sure of her, of us, but maybe she wasn't ready? She was still very young. She said she loved me, but what if she would be happier not settling down yet?

"Um, it's already past the hour he was born," Amber pointed out. "I'm a bit late, sorry. But look! He's not cursed!"

Ella tapped her chin, considering.

"We can wait, if you want to." I tried not to let disappointment seep into my voice. In my heart, I knew this was better. I wanted her to marry me, to spend our lives together. But I didn't want her to feel forced into it.

I'd been waiting two hundred years for her. I could wait a little longer if I had to.

Even if my heart was crumbling.

CHAPTER 46

ELLA

I GLANCED UP AT TIERNAN AND SAW that he was as white as a ghost under his freckles.

"Oh! No, don't worry!" I squeezed his hands. "I was only thinking that I had always dreamed I'd design my own wedding dress. But seriously, how could I ever top this one?"

A little color returned to Tiernan's face. "You're sure? I don't want you to ever feel like you didn't have a choice. Like you didn't get the wedding of your dreams."

"I'm sure." I smiled up at him. "Everyone I love is here. I've got a dress made by birds and magic. And I've got you. It's perfect."

Tiernan grinned at me. "I love you."

"I love you back."

He turned to the priestess who was leaning against a standing stone, reading a scroll. "We're ready now!"

"Are you sure?" The priestess crossed her arms. "No more switching brides? No more attacking fae rulers?" She glared at Amber. "No more interruptions?"

"Um, yes?" Tiernan smiled sheepishly.

"Fine." She looked pointedly at the birds still on our shoulders, and they flew off to wait on top of a standing stone.

The speed with which the priestess went through our ceremony was probably faster than completely appropriate, but we weren't interrupted again.

This time, when Tiernan and I held hands through the hole in the *fáinne menhir*, we vowed to love and protect each other until death. I felt the magic of Faerie hum between us, creating a bond that would tie our hearts together for the rest of our lives.

When we kissed to seal the bond in front of the cheering crowd, I could feel the happiness in my heart reflected in Tiernan's, and I knew I had found my home and my family in him.

When the wedding ceremony finished, Tiernan and I stood by the stone arch to receive our new subjects and help them through the Glass Gate to join the post-wedding revel at the palace.

Several of the nobles who'd sided with Tiernan's father had quietly slipped off during the ceremony, but more had remained than I would have expected, offering awkward but appropriate congratulations to their new rulers.

Tiernan introduced me to the fae from the Lily Court. I recognized Princess Tuala right away. She was the princess who'd watched the wedding with Isobel. Behind Tuala came her handsome blond husband and her parents. I was surprised to meet yet another human in Tuala's father, the Lily Prince. The tall black Frenchman gave me a huge bear hug and made me promise that we would come visit soon, while his wife, the Lily Princess, chased a toddler through the crowd.

"Have you ever been to Paris?" asked Tuala.

I shook my head. "I've never been anywhere, not until I came here."

"Oooh! I need to take you shopping. We'll plan something for spring. Paris spring, I mean."

"I'd love to."

"And me!" yelled Amber from farther down the line.

Tuala laughed and hugged me again before going through the gate. Maybe I'd be able to make friends with some of the Seelie nobles, after all.

"Mooch," said Isobel to her sister, wryly, walking up arm in arm with Leith.

Amber shrugged innocently from behind her.

"Your Majesty," Leith bowed.

"Oh, it's like that now, is it?" Tiernan laughed and the two gave each other one of those manly back-smacking hugs.

"I'm truly happy for you, brother." Leith clasped forearms with Tiernan before turning to me. "Ella. Thank you for all you've done for Tiernan and our kingdom."

"You're welco—oof!" I was pinned in a hug between the three sisters.

"You're still welcome at our house anytime," whispered Isobel.

"Even Seelie queens need chocolate chip cookies sometimes," added Lily.

"I mean, come if you want to, but I'm totally visiting you here," said Amber. "So often that you might as well give me my own room. Do you have anything with a balcony available?"

I laughed as her sisters swatted her.

"I'm sure we can find you something."

Next came hugs and congratulations from the fianna.

"I always wanted a sister," Saoirse whispered into my ear as she squeezed me tight.

"Thank you for saving us all from a lifetime of Tiernan moping," said Declan with a brotherly hug.

The rest of the fianna held back at first, but then all piled on us at once.

I laughed as we were smothered in affection, Kiyo bouncing around us. I hadn't just gotten a husband or a kingdom. I finally had a family.

We stepped through the Glass Gate after the last guest and found the reception party in full swing. Seelie nobles danced in the ballroom while the small folk darted around filling glasses and stocking the food tables.

I felt a tug on my skirt. I bent down to scoop Isla up.

"Are you really our queen now?" she asked, her whorled brown face serious.

"I am! And I have an important job for you." I looked at her solemnly, and she nodded. "I don't think this party has enough people."

"There are a lot of people here, Miss Ella."

"That's true, but not enough kinds of people." I could see Imogen and the rest of the palace small folk watching from the small doorway in the wall. "Find Imogen and tell her that everyone is invited to this party."

"Even Mama?"

"Especially Mama." I set the little girl down, and she scampered through the crowd to find Imogen.

"Well done," murmured Tiernan.

I already knew that word of mouth among the palace staff traveled quickly, so I wasn't surprised when only moments later we saw them starting to make their way cautiously through the ballroom.

"This reception is turning into chaos," sneered Lynet from behind me.

"Princess Lynet, how nice to see you." I hadn't seen her or her mother after the wedding. Perhaps she didn't like having her face rubbed in her failure.

She flipped her hair. "Well, we don't want to lose our court now, do we?"

Her mother elbowed her.

"I mean, we've always been loyal to the crown." The two fae ladies bowed.

Tiernan raised an eyebrow and tilted his head at me.

"We accept your fealty." I inclined my head. "And issue our first royal command."

"Your Majesty?"

"The palace staff are having the night off, and we're almost out of mead. Imogen!" The brownie ran over to me. "These two will be taking over serving duties for the night. Could you show them the way to the kitchen?"

"Of course, Your Majesty!" She smiled and turned to go.

"Oh, and Imogen! Be sure to tell the kitchen staff that these ladies will be serving for the rest of the night, so that they can join in the festivities."

"Follow me!" The brownie waved toward the waist high door in the wall.

Lynet stood gaping after her.

"Problem?" I asked, brightly.

Her mother elbowed her again.

"Of course not, Your Majesty," she said through gritted teeth, bowing stiffly.

"Perfect. We value your loyalty."

"That will be good for them," Tiernan said. "Do you think your stepfamily has learned how to work without you?"

"You know, I don't think about them at all," I said, surprised to realize it was the truth.

The revelry continued long into the night.

I thought I had seen the faeries put on a party.

I had seen them dancing to fiddles and drums in the clearing. I'd celebrated Lughnasadh with them. I'd danced with them in masks and finery. But nothing could compare to the combined excitement of a wedding, a coronation, and the dawn of a new era.

I would have danced with Tiernan all night, but Amber made me dance with her twice, telling Tiernan it was the least he could do, considering she was the one who brought us together. He laughed and tousled her hair. Amber gave me a look of long suffering that said, *See? Little sister.*

After the moon had set and we had danced on the mossy green of the ballroom until my mortal feet tired at last, we escaped.

I snuggled up against my prince—no, I suppose he was my husband now, and the king—on the padded bench on his balcony, enjoying the magical fireworks display from down in the city below. Glittering blooms in every color burst out, some erupting into fantastical shapes of couples dancing and twisting dragons.

"Thirsty?" Tiernan produced a bottle of champagne and two crystal glasses filled with strawberries from a basket. Kiyo appeared and attempted to fit her entire head into one of the wine glasses.

Tiernan laughed and extracted her, handing the dragon one of the strawberries.

I picked up the little dragon and gave her a kiss on the forehead. "I think Amber has chocolate chip cookies," I whispered conspiratorially.

Kiyo disappeared with a pop.

"Does Amber have cookies?" Tiernan poured us each a glass.

"She's a smart girl," I said. "I'm sure she can find some cookies." I took a sip of strawberry champagne. "So, what's next?"

"Well, there's a lot of work to be done here, and we'll need to organize a tour and see the courts to talk with the nobles about the changes that are coming."

I nodded. "What about before that?"

"Well, where should we go for our honeymoon? Take a week at Port Delfare? Or there's a château by Lough

Correagh, or we could even visit Takamagahara and meet Kiyo's family."

"I like all those ideas. But what about before that?" I set down my glass and turned to face him. "I'm a little worried," I whispered.

"I'm sorry—"

I stopped him with a finger to his lips. "It's this dress." I fluffed out the sparkling flowers. "It's made with much sturdier magic than my last one. I'm not actually sure how it comes off."

Tiernan laughed, that true laugh I intended to hear every day for the rest of our long lives together. Then he stood and swept me up into his arms as he kissed me soundly. My dress trailed golden sparkles behind me as we spun.

He said in his most courtly tone, "May I offer my assistance?"

"You may." I kissed him again as he carried me inside. Seelie King he might be, but he would always be my Prince Charming.

CHAPTER 47

AMBER

ANOTHER DAY, ANOTHER PILE OF BOOKS. I rolled the library cart into the cookbook section of the Pilot Bay Library and began re-shelving. Slow Cooker Soups, Sheet Pan Chicken, 101 Unicorn Cupcakes.

"Amber, there you are." Miss Chloe popped her head around the end of the stack. "I've been meaning to ask you a question."

"Is it, 'why does Harry Styles have a cookbook?'" I waved a book in the air. "He can sing. Apparently he can act, but does he know anything about pasta, or is it a publicity stunt?" I tapped my chin, thoughtfully. "I have no answers on that topic, only more questions."

Miss Chloe laughed. "I suspect most celebrity cookbooks are ghostwritten."

"Even Chris Hemsworth's?" I waggled my eyebrows at her.

"Chris Hemsworth has a—That's beside the point."

"I'll put it aside for you." I winked.

"Have you given any thought to what you want to do after you graduate next year?" asked Miss Chloe.

"Yep. I've given it a lot of thought," I said. "Lily and Isobel badger me about it on the regular."

"And?"

"And I still don't know. I've looked through applications for all the college programs in BC, and everything sounds super boring. When you have a sister who's gonna be a princess and your bestie becomes a fae queen, hairdresser or ultrasound technician doesn't have quite the same appeal."

"You could become a doctor like Lily."

"Please no."

"So, if I had a fae prince for you then?"

"Don't you dare," I said, wheeling on her. "I know you and your meddling ways."

"Speaking of meddling," she said. "You did quite a bit of that yourself this time around."

"I'm sure I don't know what you're talking about." I slid another cookbook onto the shelf.

"If it wasn't for you, I don't know how I would have gotten Ella to meet Tiernan in time."

"Well, yeah, that was good work," I admitted.

"And you helped deliver the dragon egg so that we could communicate with her," she said. "You got Ella to the ball on time, and you even convinced her to wear her own design. I think we can all agree that it was a truly magical dress."

"It really was." I smiled. "I'm so proud of my little protégé." I wiped a pretend tear from my eye.

"I'll be needing more help soon." Miss Chloe's mouth tightened. "Moriath is closer than I'd like to finding Neve."

"What does Neve have to do with anything? Has the evil Unseelie Queen developed a sudden love of cappuccino?"

"It's a long story." Miss Chloe shook her silver curls. "One I would be happy to tell you, if you would consider working with me in a more official capacity."

I dropped the books and spun to face her. "Official capacity?! Like an apprentice?"

Miss Chloe tilted her head. "Something like that."

"Being an apprentice faerie godmother would be so much cooler than being a lab tech!" I squealed.

"Well, you've shown a great aptitude for it. You'd only help part-time, of course, until you're done with school, but I need your help before then. I still can't travel to Faerie myself while Moriath is searching for me."

"And once it's safe for you to return?" I asked, praying she wouldn't leave me here in the human world.

"Well, in Faerie I'd be able to train you properly."
I fist pumped the sky.
"So, what do you say?"
"Magic, meddling, and make-overs? I was born for this."

EPILOGUE

ELLA

Five years later

THE DOOR TO THE TOWNHOUSE'S ROOFTOP GARDEN banged open. I felt Tiernan through our bond before I saw him and immediately slammed my sketchbook shut as my gorgeous husband walked over, a frosted glass in each hand.

Tiernan sat down on the wicker lounge chair next to mine and handed me a glass of iced chai goodness.

"What are you hiding?" He reached for my sketchbook, and I smacked him on the hand with it before shoving it under the cushion of my lounger.

"People with birthdays coming up shouldn't be so nosy!" I narrowed my eyes at him.

I designed dresses for everyone from piskie princesses to Kami empresses, but nothing gave me as much pleasure as designing clothes for Tiernan. He just looked so good in everything.

I slurped my frosted drink and smiled, closing my eyes and enjoying the peaceful sounds of summer at Port Delfare.

Ruling the Seelie Kingdom was hard work. The task of sorting out centuries of prejudice and entitlement sometimes put my magical anxiety-reducing tea to the test, so we escaped to the townhouse as often as we could for weekends or short holidays. Often, it was packed with our fianna family, but today, it was just the two of us.

A little pop made me open one eye.

Alright, the four of us.

Kiyo landed lightly on my lap. The little ryū was now full grown and long enough to stretch from my fingertip to my elbow.

"Where's Mizuchi?" I asked the dragon.

Last autumn, we had gone on a state visit to Takamagahara. Haru had warned us that his mother, the empress, might try to keep Kiyo in her natural homeland. We had tried to convince the little dragon to stay in Rahivea with Haru, but, as always, she went where she liked.

Instead of returning without her, we had—much to the chagrin of the empress—gained another ryū when

Kiyo had found true love with a smokey silver male from the empress's menagerie. Like Kiyo, Mizuchi went where he wanted, and where he wanted to go was anywhere my little sugar-loving dragon went.

Kiyo butted my arm excitedly, almost making me slosh my drink.

"What is it?" She jumped to the ground and scampered a few paces down the garden path before looking back at me expectantly.

"I'll be right back," I told my husband, who had already closed his eyes. "Don't touch my sketchbook. I'm serious!"

I followed the little dragon to a bush in the corner of the rooftop. Her silver mate awaited in a sunny patch of moss.

I gasped and Kiyo chirped, smugly.

"Tiernan!" I called.

"I wasn't peeking!" he protested.

"I've got some news for you."

The wicker lounger squeaked as Tiernan got up. "What's so important? I'm not going to be a father, am I?"

I didn't answer.

"That was a joke! Right?" He came up behind me. "Why are you hiding in the bushes? I thought we were past lurking in shrubbery? Oh!"

He stopped beside me, and we both crouched down to admire the little pile of silver and teal eggs tucked into a soft nest of moss.

"Does this make us grandparents?" I asked.

The two little dragons snuggled up happily beside their eggs. I sat on the side of the garden wall and Tiernan wrapped his arm around me.

I smiled as I snuggled into him, feeling his contentment seep into me and knowing for certain that the adventures around here were just getting started.

If you want to find out what happens when a batch of baby dragons hatch…during Isobel and Leith's wedding, sign up for my newsletter to receive a free short story!

HannaSandvig.com

Author's Note

THANK YOU FOR READING THE GLASS GATE! I always try to make my characters similar to me in some ways, and not like me in others. Unlike Ella, I don't have a Japanese parent, both my parents are happily alive, and tragically, no one has ever given me a baby dragon.

But, I do draw until my fingers are black, sew my own clothes, drink oat milk chai, and I have anxiety.

I've struggled with my mental health ever since I was little, but I didn't realize what it was until I hit my thirties. The chronic insomnia, the yelling at my kids, the tightness in my chest, the spiraling thoughts about the fate of the world, had a name. Anxiety.

I can't begin to explain how much it helped just to know what it was. It wasn't that I was a terrible mother or that the world was literally going to end at any moment.

My brain just needed more serotonin than it was able to produce.

I say just as though it's a small thing, but if you struggle with your mental health, you know it's a very big thing.

I take much better care of myself now. I have some supplements that help a lot (for my husband a couple rounds of meds were necessary). I take daily walks, and I prioritize my sleep. I tell that voice in my head spouting doom to just shhhhhh. And it's made a world of difference. But I'll always have anxiety. I'll always have hard days. Do you know what's helped the most?

Talking about it.

Talking to my friends and my husband when I'm having a bad anxiety day (or week). Talking to people I know—or have just met—who are struggling and letting them know that they aren't alone. A lot of us feel this way. It's nothing to be ashamed of; it's just brain chemistry.

I used to lay awake in the night and pray that God would just make it so I could sleep. That he would miraculously fix my brain. That he would just make me become more patient with my kids.

He never did. But I believe that he brought the right people into my life to help me figure it out. And I believe that if he had just miraculously fixed my brain, I wouldn't have gained the knowledge and the drive to talk about it with others. To talk about it now, with you.

I try not to be preachy in my books, but if you take away one thing from Ella's story, I hope it's this: you're not in this alone. A lot of us struggle with our mental health, and talking about it with the people you love and trust helps a lot.

So get some sunshine, drink your water, take whatever supplements or meds your brain needs, and chat with a friend today. You're going to be okay.

All the love in the world,
Hanna

Acknowledgements

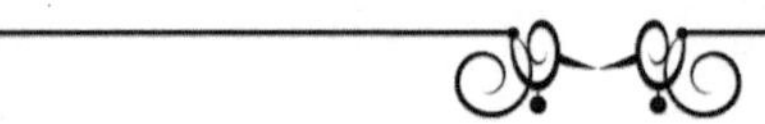

GUESS HOW MANY PEOPLE IT TAKES FOR my books to be coherent and relatively typo-free? A lot. I appreciate you guys so much. Thank you!

Thanks to my fellow Queens of the Quill. Your support of me and my stories has kept me going so many times.

Shout out to my beta readers: Valia, Tess, Kari, Maru, Laura, Stephanie, Lissa, Sara, Hannah, Esther, Pieta, and Amber. This story is so much better, cozier, and swoonier with your help!

Big thanks to my editor, Kay. I'm so glad one of us knows how commas work. And it isn't me.

Thanks to my typo-hunters: Nikki, Samii, Elizabeth, Sheala, Anne, Rachel Bryant, Nic, R.M. Munz, Rebecca, Genevieve, Gretchen, Ruth, Sarah, Anna, Katie, Constance, Rachel Hogan, Kayleigh, Emma, and Christine. You guys made this moderately dyslexic, speed-reading author's book legible.

Thanks to my mom for additional edits and, you know, giving birth to me.

Sonya, I couldn't write books without our hikes and chats. You helped me with so many parts of this book, I can't even list them all.

My girls, thank you for thinking of all the ways a little dragon could get into mischief. You guys made this book so much cuter.

Craig, thank you for supporting me in my writing adventures and inspiring me to write a fae birder.

And thanks to God for teaching me that stories are powerful and necessary. Your words have shown me that we learn with our hearts as much as our heads, and I never want to stop discovering the beauty of your stories.

About the Author

Hanna Sandvig is turning your favorite fairy tales into faerie tales with some sweet romance and enough sass to keep things interesting.

Hanna is living out her personal happily-ever-after in the mountains of BC, Canada with her husband, three daughters, and giant cat. If you drop in to visit, please bring plenty of chocolate and strong black tea.